MIDNIGHT IN BRUSSELS

Rebecca Randolph Buckley

First Printing – December 2009
ISBN: 978-0-9791701-3-3

R.J. Buckley Publishing
Queen Creek, AZ

www.rjbuckleypublishing.com

Works by Rebecca Randolph Buckley

NOVELS - Rachel O'Neill Series

Midnight at Trafalgar
Midnight at the Eiffel
Midnight in Brussels
Midnight in Moscow
Midnight in Malibu

COLLECTIONS – Short Stories and Plays

Love Has a Price Tag
Bits & Pieces of Me
My Dramedy
Shoe's on the Other Foot

DEDICATION

This book is dedicated ...

... to all women (*young and old*) who have dreams beyond their wildest imaginations of love, success, fulfillment, and promise.

My belief is we can have whatever we want; we just need to believe it will happen and have faith in ourselves and the universe, and do our homework. It is ours for the asking.

Also dedicated ...

... to the extraordinary lace makers of Belgium.

From the first moment I observed the women (young and old) at the Kantcentrum (Lace Centre) in Bruges, tossing the bobbins and creating such masterpieces, I was enthralled with the art of lace making. It was there that I first conceived Amanda's love and desire for Belgium and all it encompassed.

http://www.kantcentrum.com

ACKNOWLEDGEMENT

I wish to express my thanks to my generous hosts Robert van Nevel and Lievetje Gevaert at Carmersstraat 13 in Bruges, Belgium for wonderful accommodations and for the CD of photos and all the local information that gave me a clearer understanding of the history of the town and its citizens.

http://www.brugesbb.be

PART ONE

"If you see it in your mind, you're going to hold it in your hand."

Bob Proctor
The Secret

Rebecca Randolph Buckley

Chapter 1

The steep red rock canyon walls on one side and a deathly drop to the boulders of the creek below on the other was intimidating, but a breathless beauty to behold. The shadows of dusk made the scenic panorama even more imposing.

Arlie Jeffries glanced up one side and down the other, trying to take it all in as he drove the winding mountain road towards Globe, Arizona.

He wished circumstances were different. He wished he could start all over in a small town somewhere. One like Flagstaff or Sedona that he'd passed through earlier that morning.

Arlie missed the comfort of a small town, like where he grew up in Arkansas. And he wasn't totally convinced he was doing the right thing going to Austin, Texas - trading one woman for another. Sure he liked women, but he was thinking that maybe he wasn't cut out to live with one. He was a man's man, didn't like the responsibility of taking care of a woman, definitely didn't want kids.

"What the—" Arlie pumped the accelerator pedal as the truck sputtered and jerked to a dead stop. He swore at the top of

3

his lungs and banged his fists on the steering wheel, his temper escalating to an aneurysm high.

He should have kept the car, could've stolen license plates and switched them, that's what he should've done. He cursed himself for making one of the stupidest mistakes of his life.

Of course the stupidest mistake was placing that first bet on the craps table when he and Amanda moved to Vegas from Arkansas seven years earlier. Gambling reeled him in from the get-go, and no matter how much money he made as an electrician at the Plaza Hotel and Casino, he never had enough to cover his growing gambling debts.

Now he was running for his life. He was in to the loan sharks to the tune of fifty-two thousand. There was no way he could come up with that kind of money in the two days they'd given him. It was his last reprieve, they had told him. And they said if he didn't come through with the cash they would use him as a lesson to others who didn't pay up on time. So now he was running.

He had left home the day before, on Christmas Day, and after driving ninety-five miles had abandoned his car in an alleyway of the most rundown section of Kingman, Arizona. He stayed overnight in Kingman and early that morning had bought a used pickup truck, paid cash for it, and made it to Phoenix without mishap.

Finally, after grabbing a bite to eat at a drive-thru, he left Phoenix and drove east on Highway 60 towards Globe. His plan was to spend the night in Globe and then the next morning take Highway 70 which would take him to the I-10 west of Deming, New Mexico. There he'd dump the truck and buy another vehicle. Then it was a straight shot to Austin.

He figured switching vehicles a couple times and doing the zigzag route would cover his trail well enough so that no one could find him.

Now he found himself stranded on a mountain road in Arizona and it was getting dark. He should have left Phoenix earlier and not stopped at the Indian Casino to gamble. He sighed heavily as he dropped his head onto his hands gripping the steering wheel of the dead truck.

His thoughts shifted to his wife Amanda, wondering how she was coping with all this. He'd run out on her. Didn't tell her. He had never shirked his responsibilities to anyone in his life and now he was feeling guilty about it. She didn't deserve it. But in his fearful state of mind he believed he was protecting her, too, by fleeing the threatening fists and guns of the loan sharks.

But he had not only kept his gambling vice from Amanda, he had been having an affair with a Texan who stayed regularly at the Plaza Hotel, a business woman ten years his senior who knew more about sex and romance than Amanda would ever know.

Charmaine de la Court had captured his libido the first night they'd met in the Casino when he'd been called in to do some emergency electrical repairs near the music lounge where she had been sitting alone, drinking. The affair began that night and continued over the next two years and was still going strong, which was the reason he was on his way to Austin, Texas … to surprise her, to hide out with her. No one would ever think to look for him in Texas.

If he ever got to Texas! Now he was stuck in a broken down pickup truck in the middle of nowhere with only his feet to get him to the next town to find more wheels.

The mountain road was deserted; there hadn't been one vehicle in the past hour coming or going. According to the map, Miami, Arizona, was just ahead. He locked the truck and began walking.

A half mile further up the canyon road, just as he reached a scenic overlook near some boulders and trees perched on the

5

edge of the sheer drop to what seemed like a bottomless pit, a set of headlights came up behind him, reflecting off the canyon walls. As it got closer he could see it was a black Lincoln SUV with silhouettes of three men inside.

He gasped and his hair stood on end as the Lincoln pulled off and stopped about sixty feet behind him. Its engine was revving, only its parking lights on.

His heart stopped, and his first thought was to dart behind the boulders. But before he could act on it, the door opened and a man stepped down from the front passenger seat pointing an AK47 at Arlie.

"Oh shit!" he exclaimed aloud and froze in terror.

Chapter 2

SIX MONTHS LATER

The outdated calendar was still hanging lopsided on the end cabinet to the left of the kitchen sink. It was wider than its space and jutted a few inches into the window view of the blazing hot desert beyond.

Amanda had nailed the calendar there as a daily reminder of what had happened six months before on Christmas Day, the day her husband had disappeared. She had moved it inside so she wouldn't have to look at it all day over the big freezer chest on the screened-in back porch where she spent most of her time. They'd added the covered screened-in porch to the trailer the summer before, and now she spent her days out there lying on the not-so-new floral lemon-lime-colored swing-sofa, watching television hour after hour, waiting for Arlie to come home. Sometimes a Palm Springs local television station would come through and she'd watch older movie stars being interviewed, those who had retired and were living in Palm Springs in their grand homes. But usually only the three local Las Vegas channels were all she could get.

When she wasn't watching television or crying, she would close her eyes and dream of foreign places. She dreamed of beautiful green rolling-hills and snow-covered peaks, European villages with cobble-stoned streets, quaint shops, and romantic sidewalk cafes just like the ones she saw in the travel magazines. She'd never been to any of them. The only places she'd been outside of Mountain Home, Arkansas, were Little Rock and now Las Vegas.

Nevertheless, she loved reading about the famous tourist places in the stacks of second-hand magazines the receptionist at the doctor's office had given her. The receptionist had taken pity on Amanda, knew she couldn't afford to buy magazines like the plentiful publications the doctor would place on the tables and racks at his office. For several years Amanda had been bringing home a steady stream of magazines, had read them cover to cover, over and over. It was her favorite pastime besides watching television; both were her only touch with the outside world.

In one magazine a Belgian village stood out over the rest: Bruges - a medieval town with waterways weaving throughout, streets and lanes chock full of shops whose wares were of handmade lace, tapestry, and homemade chocolates. Amanda fantasized living in Bruges and having her own shop of lace and tapestry. She could close her eyes and visualize it. Sometimes she'd live in her dreams for hours at a time, would see herself in the shop sewing and talking to customers.

But the reality of it was she had been abandoned on a desolate cactus- and sagebrush-filled Nevada desert, twenty miles east of Vegas, in a trailer park, all alone and penniless. Each day was a long, hot duplicate of the day before.

The only time she left the trailer park was to take a bus to town to the doctor's office which was super difficult for her since she was shy and afraid of people. Or she'd walk down the dirt road to the local grocery store which was little more than a country convenience store with a better assortment of foods than what one would usually find in such convenience stores. This one had meats, fruits and vegetables, and a post office inside – since it was the only store available to the community of mobile homes and trailers miles from civilization.

When Arlie and Amanda first moved to Nevada from Arkansas and settled in, they did take one side trip, though. Amanda had convinced Arlie to drive them to the edge of the Grand Canyon which was just a few miles further east.

She remembered how Arlie hadn't been impressed.

He'd said "It ain't nothing but a big damn ditch! Who'd pay to come see something like this?"

Amanda had commented, "But it sure is the deepest, widest and longest ditch you've ever seen, ain't it?"

She would sometimes step outside of their trailer and watch the helicopters fly overhead on the way to the Grand Canyon site where they'd land and furnish lunch and champagne for their tourist passengers. She'd read about the tours in the Plaza Hotel magazine that Arlie would bring home every month and wondered how anybody could afford paying those expensive fares.

Amanda snapped from her reverie and glanced over at Arlie's bicycle that had been leaning against the nearly empty freezer for the past six months. Tears came to her eyes as she saw the cobwebs crisscrossing the handle bars to the seat, weaving in and out of the spokes. Arlie's driver's license had been suspended because of drunk driving and he had used the bicycle to get to the country bus stop when he couldn't hitch a ride into Las Vegas to work.

Everything on the back porch appeared to have been untouched for a long time. A thick layer of dust covered every surface. Amanda didn't care. Just as she didn't care if the calendar was hanging lopsided in the kitchen and she hadn't replaced it with a new one since December when Arlie left. Now it was June.

She wiped her red-rimmed eyes with the hem of her threadbare cotton sundress and reached for the remote that was on the worn, wicker coffee table: a table she'd found in the same thrift store where they'd found the rest of their furniture when they moved there.

She preferred to watch television out on the porch rather than inside the trailer. It was one of the first vintage TV sets that had a remote control. When the weather was bad, she'd cart the set into the trailer. It was small and easy to move, had a handle. Arlie had wired two illegal connections - one inside, one on the porch - making it handy to move the box back and forth. She'd also carry the electric box-fan with her to keep her cool. No air-conditioning. All she had to do was pour water into the fan's water receptacle occasionally and it served its purpose, especially during the hot summer months.

Amanda sat up and surfed all three channels. Nothing of any interest and she couldn't tune in Palm Springs, either, so she sighed and stretched out on the sofa-swing again; resting the back of her head on its hard wooden arm. With her hand resting on her forehead, she closed her eyes and took in a long deep breath of the dampness that was generating from the water fan.

Why did he do this to me? A small whimper escaped her lips and she covered her face with both hands. Soon the whimper became sobs and she turned, drew up in a fetal position and buried her face in the faded seat cushion, hoping she'd smother the hurt away.

On Christmas Day, their seventh wedding anniversary, Arlie took off in the car to go buy cigarettes. He didn't come back. The missing person's investigation came to a dead end when nothing turned up indicating there had been foul play. But part of Amanda couldn't believe that he would just run away. Deep inside she felt something terrible had happened to him and the first few months she repeatedly conveyed that feeling to the authorities.

Now six months later she was still swaying back and forth between believing he ran out on her and feeling he was either injured or, worse yet, dead.

On the days she felt he'd left on purpose, she berated herself. She should have known something was up that morning because he hadn't been driving the car; he didn't have a driver's license. She'd heard of the seven-year itch, but this was by far, by God, the worst case of it on record. How could he leave her on Christmas Day, of all days, and it being their wedding anniversary to boot? How could he do such a mean thing?

The confusing part of it all was he'd never acted as if he was unhappy, and although their life was pretty humdrum and boring at times, he'd never said he was unhappy. Of course he never said much about anything. If anyone should have had complaints, she would be the one. Arlie would be away at work hours upon hours while she stayed at home by herself, sometimes up to forty-eight hours at a time. It seemed as if he was always working. Then when he came home, he'd sleep. They hardly ever went anywhere or had much of a relationship, hardly had any conversation.

She wondered if maybe she hadn't been sexual enough for him. She'd read in the women's magazines how men needed it more than women. It did seem that way, but she didn't know much about things like that. No one ever told her about sex back when she was growing up, neither her mother nor her grandmother talked about it.

She'd always tried to give Arlie what he wanted when he wanted it, but sometimes she just couldn't do it. Sometimes she just didn't want to have to get up afterwards and bathe and change her nightgown because he'd gotten his sticky stuff all over it. She hated that, especially if she was tired and sleepy. So, when she refused to let him have her, he would turn away in anger and be snoring within five minutes.

Sexual desire wasn't what motivated her, it wasn't foremost on her mind, ever. She didn't see any sense to it at all. All Arlie did was work up to a point of excitement (at least she thought that was what it was) then he'd get on top of her and stick it in her and grunt and howl. Then he'd roll off and go to sleep and she was left with the mess to clean up.

Nope, she didn't see any point to it. She asked herself many times why was it the wife's duty to allow a husband do that to her? But she let him do it most times, anyway, because that's what married people were supposed to do.

Even still, she couldn't believe he would have left her because he didn't get enough sex from her. Surely he wouldn't leave because of that. Regardless, she'd been thinking that maybe if she had had more experience in that department she could have been better for him. She would never think of cheating on him to learn more, but there were times she had wondered what it would be like to do it with someone else. The romance novels she read made it seem so romantic and beautiful.

And sure, he wasn't very loving on the nights he came home drugged with booze. There at the last, the drunken nights had been increasing. But he wasn't abusive; he was just a sloppy, slovenly, slobbering drunk on those nights. Fell into furniture, knocked things over unintentionally, broke things accidentally. Because of his immense size she couldn't budge him if he passed out on the floor. Even though she was 5' 9", she was a thin 130 pounds. So she'd throw a blanket or sheet over him wherever he fell and would step over him as she went from one end of the trailer to the other. It seemed he never passed out on the bed; always on the floor.

It had been suggested that his disappearance might have had something to do with gambling, since he worked in the casino and spent so much time there. Amanda didn't know if he gambled or not, but she agreed he could have without her knowing.

Sad to say, all information was pointing to him just running out on her. It humiliated her to the point that she felt like everyone in the desert trailer park community was laughing and talking about her. She could just imagine them saying, 'Wonder what she did to make him want to run off like that?' She could read it in their eyes and kept more and more to herself so she wouldn't have to face their snickering stares.

The phone rang.

She raised her face from the pillow and gulped for air.

Okay. No suicide today.

Her first thought was that it might be Arlie, so she jumped up and raced to the phone in the kitchen. Pushing her long, straight, blond hair back over her ear, she lifted the receiver, hesitated, wondering if she should say anything or not. Arlie's creditors were on her like crazy. This was probably just another harassing bill collector.

Since Arlie had left, the money had stopped coming in, except for the State assistance checks that had just begun and the money her sister had been sending her each month. She didn't have the energy or the self-confidence to look for a job and she didn't know how to drive anyway, didn't have a driver's license, didn't have a car, so what difference did it make. And to top it all off, she'd never worked a day in her life, had no skills, no experience. Nothing.

Amanda was wishing she had an answering machine like everybody else so she could listen to who might be calling, before she answered.

She took a deep breath and listened for office noises on the phone. It was easy to tell if it was a telemarketing or creditor call because there would be a dead silence, then all of a sudden the office noises began. If it was one of those calls, she would hang up before the person on the other end had a chance to speak.

"Amanda?"

"Oh Paula! I'm so glad it's you." She let out her breath in a sigh of relief and leaned back against the counter.

"You all right, hon?"

"No, I ain't all right," she started crying. "I don't know what I'm gonna do, Paula. Arlie ain't comin' back. I just know it. He must be dead."

"You don't know that for sure. They haven't found his dad-gummed body yet. I'm sorry, hon, I don't mean to be blunt, but you know how I am. I say what I think without thinking. Wait a minute, that didn't sound right. Oh well, you know what I mean. Listen, honey, I wancha to come stay with us. That's why I'm calling. Our house is all done now, and boy is it a whopper! It's alongside a river and we have us a great big swimming pool. We've got plenty of room and you'll love it. You can have your own bathroom and even your own sittin' room if you want, and you can help with the baby when he pops out. What do you say? We can find you a job."

"But I don't know how to do anything, Paula. I'm of no use to anybody, not even to myself." Amanda reached for the roll of toilet paper on the nearby counter to blow her nose.

"You can waitress, honey. Anybody can waitress. I know just the place for you. Now you just pack your stuff and Drake

14

and I will be out there on Saturday. You know how he feels about his gambling. The man is addicted, he's needin' his Vegas fix. So we're coming to get you, baby. Besides, Drake's always driving truck somewhere else and he's never home. I'd love to have your company. We Conroy sisters have got to stick together, you know."

"But what if Arlie comes back and I'm not here?"

"Leave him a fuckin' note, Amanda! That's more than he did for you. Now you just get yourself together and I'll take care of everything. You'll have a job waitin' for you. You just mark my words!"

Amanda felt a slight twinge of hope. Maybe she could waitress, and then maybe she could save her money and buy a car. And maybe she'd take some classes and get a GED. And maybe she could learn to take care of herself and not have to depend on anybody else. And then maybe she could save enough money and go to one of those places she saw in the magazines.

The last thought was what tipped the scales.

"All right!" she exclaimed. She straightened up and felt better than she had in months. "I'll do it! I'll stay with y'all until I can get my own place."

"That's great, hon. You're gonna love Bakersfield. It's just a couple hours from everything - L.A. is south, the Pacific Ocean is west and San Francisco's up north. You can bet we'll have us a ball. We can close up that dad-gummed trailer and you can bring all your stuff with you. We'll be driving the pickup so you can bring it all."

"I don't have much that I'd want to bring," Amanda said as she looked around the trailer and thought about how Arlie never let her spend money on clothes and pretty things for their small hovel. She'd asked him when they'd see something in a window in one of the stores in town, but he would always say no. Said they didn't need it. He only gave her enough money to buy

15

groceries at the convenience store and some extra to spend at Goodwill when they were in town. She had wondered what he did with all his money. She'd heard that electricians in the casinos made good wages, but she'd never seen any of it, except what he gave her.

"Okay, baby, we'll be there on Saturday. I'll help you pack your stuff while Drake is off gambling. You okay about this now? You aren't going to back out at the last minute?"

"I'll be packed before you get here."

"Okay, hon. Bye-bye."

"Bye, Paula. I love you." She hung up the phone and immediately felt a surge of energy and a return to the living. She poured water in the air conditioner to stay cool while she began gathering up her meager belongings and crammed them into plastic grocery bags—her luggage. It took her two hours to pack everything she was going to take. Saturday was six long days away.

Chapter 3

It had been seven months since Arlie had been blasted off the cliff just west of Miami, Arizona. Only one of the shooter's shots caught him in the left shoulder but it was enough to knock him off the cliff. The other shots glanced him as he spun and fell, tumbling backwards head-over-heels down the long, steep slope to the rocky canyon below.

There was no way anyone could survive that fall, and no way anyone could climb down to check and see if he was dead or alive. But from the way he landed, the stalkers were convinced he couldn't be alive, even if the bullets hadn't killed him, the fall would. So they were satisfied with the hit and drove back to Las Vegas.

When Arlie gained consciousness two days later, he didn't know where he was, how long he'd lain there, or why he had a gunshot wound through his shoulder. The bleeding had miraculously stopped by itself, leaving a gaping hole caked with dark, dried blood where the wounding bullet had entered in the front and exited out the back.

Signs of infection had set in all over his body's multiple scrapes and gashes. He knew his left arm was broken in several places. The pain was almost unbearable. And he couldn't move or feel anything from the waist down. With a bit of awkward effort, still lying on the ground, he was able to one-handedly pull his t-shirt up and over his right shoulder and use it as a sling for his left arm, inserting a stick between his body and the arm, wrapping it with the shirt.

The sound of running water was encouraging; a creek or river meant at least he wouldn't die of thirst, and he could attempt to sooth his wounds with the coolness of the water.

Next he tried to rise to a sitting position. Agonizing pains shot up his spine into his head, halting movement right off the bat. After a few minutes more, he reached with his right hand and tried to straighten out his legs that were both bent at awkward angles. The legs were definitely broken, but he still couldn't feel them. He figured his back might be broken also, maybe in the lower extremities, which was why the pain shot through him when he tried to sit up, and why he couldn't feel his legs. If he kept his head even with his body, it didn't hurt as much.

He figured he must have fallen from the cliff above, and if so, it was a miracle his head hadn't been smashed open from the fall, although blood from head scrapes and cuts had run down his face and had dried, too. The gunshot wound through his shoulder was the real puzzler.

Using his right hand and arm, he managed to drag himself between the boulders and rocks down to the water's edge. It was a slow process, taking more than a couple of hours with rest stops to let the pain subside. He could imagine the damage he was causing to his lower body, but at least he couldn't feel it. Regardless, he figured he had to do something to try and save himself; he couldn't just lie where he'd fallen and die.

Arlie finally reached the shallow water's edge and rolled into the clear, cool water, drenching his wounds and quenching his thirst.

He didn't know how long he'd been lying in the water; he must've fallen asleep, when sounds of voices roused him.

"Watch out, you nincompoop! You're going to hit that boulder. Jesus Christ, Jimmy! When will you ever learn how to turn a damn canoe? Drag the right oar! Lift the left!"

"All right, all right. I'm doin' it. It's over there, Scott. That's where I caught that big one, remember?"

Arlie screamed, "Help! Help me! I'm over here. Somebody, please! Help me! Over here. Help!"

The two men instantly responded and paddled towards Arlie's screams.

Chapter 4

Amanda acclimated swiftly with her sister Paula and brother-in-law Drake in their sprawling home on the banks of the Kern River just outside of Bakersfield in the San Joaquin Valley of California. Life in Nevada seemed far behind her now. But the weather was pretty much the same as it was in the Silver State: hot in the summer, freezing in the winter. And since the San Joaquin Valley was the agricultural center of California there was always the invisible cloud of crop sprays that lingered in the air. Some said it was the cause of lung cancer and other diseases that seemed to permeate the valley in high numbers, but not all were in agreement about that.

The Central Valley, as it is called, is also blessed with the Tule fog season that will often shut down businesses and schools a day or two at a time, because it is impossible to see or drive through it. Auto pile-ups are the norm between November and March when the fog rises up from the Tule grass wetlands. It's a radiation fog as a result of high humidity after a rain and rapid cooling during the night.

But Amanda had yet to experience the Tule fog. It was still a three-digit degree summertime in the valley.

Her sister Paula lined up a job interview for her at KC's Steakhouse on her first Friday in California. KC's was a lunch and dinner house with nightly music entertainment owned and managed by Frenchie - a petite, exotic dynamo who ran her busy restaurant with an iron hand and ran it profitably. KC's was also a popular watering hole. So Frenchie capitalized on both food and beverage sales. (KC being the acronym for Kansas City in reference to the famous KC steaks.)

Drake spent a lot of time and money entertaining business associates at KC's Steakhouse, and he and Paula socialized there at least twice a week during the happy hour and dinner hour. The restaurant was known for its attractive female wait-staff and Amanda fit the bill in the looks department - slim, blond, blue-eyed and pretty. Frenchie was immediately impressed with Amanda's looks and demeanor, and her story, so experience or no experience, she was hired. It was also a special favor to Paula and Drake, her longtime friends.

The shy and timid girl from Arkansas caught on to the way of doing things quicker than most and soon became the highest tipped and showed promise of becoming the best waitress in the place.

When Frenchie handed her the first paycheck, Amanda cried. Frenchie put her arm around Amanda's waist and thanked her for working so hard; she told Amanda she hoped she'd be happy at KC's and she was grateful to Paula and Drake for recommending her.

After the display of affection from Frenchie, Amanda felt the need and desire to excel even more at her first job. She worked overtime whenever asked without complaining and became a true loyal employee, feeling appreciated more than at any other time in her young life.

It was near to closing at KC's, and five months had gone by since she began her career as a waitress. Earlier that morning the sheriff's department in Clark County of Nevada notified her that they'd found Arlie's car in Kingman, Arizona, but that was where the trail ended. They assumed he was still alive, not dead. They assumed he left of his own accord, that it wasn't a criminal matter.

Two months before, Amanda had called Johnny Mace, one of Arlie's co-workers, to let him know where she could be reached if Arlie showed up. Johnny told her he'd like to buy the trailer; said he'd been living with two other guys and wanted a place to live with his new girlfriend. At first she was reluctant to sell, but she wanted the money. On one hand she felt guilty about selling out from under Arlie, but on the other hand she decided it was his fault for abandoning her. Johnny sent her $1,000 up front and promised to pay the rest in a couple of months. Now that the sheriff had informed her they'd found the car, she didn't feel guilty about selling the trailer.

She looked at her watch and then took what appeared to be the last dinner order of the night. It had been a busy week and a busy Saturday night, she was looking forward to the following two days off, two whole days of doing nothing - although it was hard to do nothing around Drake and Paula. They were party animals.

Every Sunday if they weren't having a barbecue and pool party for all their friends, it was someone else giving one. And of course, they insisted that Amanda party with them. Just one weekend she'd like to have all to herself. Just one. As sad and dreary as she had felt those long six months alone in the Nevada desert, she found herself longing for the peace and quiet once again. She wanted to move into her own place in the worst way. If only the rest of the money would come from Johnny.

"I'll have a New York steak, rare. Baked potato with sour cream and chives, green salad with ranch dressing, please."

"Would y'all like some cheese bread to go with it?" Amanda said as she sneaked a look at the man who was still studying the menu.

His hair was graying at the temples, but blond everywhere else. He was tan and was wearing a light blue long-sleeved chambray shirt and faded blue jeans. He'd hung his jacket on the coat rack by the front door, she'd noticed, when he came in. A handsome man, she observed through her long lashes and then quickly averted his glance by looking back down at the order pad.

"Yes, I believe I would. Thank you." He handed her the menu, cocked his head and grinned up at her. "You're new here, aren't you?"

"No, I've been working here going on six months now," she took the menu and began to walk away without another glance at him.

He called out to her, "A double Scotch, please!"

With her back to him, she raised her hand in acknowledgement of his request, placed the drink order, and then took the dinner order to the kitchen – all in one graceful, fluid motion.

The piano bar crowd was filling the dance and bar area in the upper half of the room. The dining area was a stair-step down, but it all melded into one big cozy, dark, romantic atmosphere, conducive to special romantic occasions and secret liaisons. More than once Amanda had become tearful while lovers demonstrated their feelings on the dance floor or at a table toasting each other, or kissing.

At times she longed for a man's touch, even though she didn't like sex, she did like a display of affection. She and Arlie had been married for seven years; he'd been her only boyfriend

23

as they grew up together in Arkansas. She'd never been kissed by anybody else. He'd been the only man in her life, so it was painful to watch couples hug and kiss at KC's Steakhouse.

The atmosphere at KC's was conducive to canoodling: lighting was dim, gold-flecked mirrors extended up to the low ceiling from the paneled wainscoting around the perimeter of the restaurant; green foliage was hanging in pots, and planters were placed throughout the space. Tubes of mini-lights gave the area a romantic atmosphere year-round. There was a lower bar and an upper bar: the lower bordered one side of the dining room and was chair-height; the upper bordered the dance floor and was bar stool-height, the bartenders at one level serviced both.

Amanda returned from the kitchen and picked up the double Scotch from the lower bar, placed it on the tray with a salad and delivered it to her good-looking customer.

"Here you go. Your Scotch and your salad." She smiled at him.

"Thank you." He grinned up at her. "Uh, tell me, pretty lady, are Saturday nights on your regular schedule?" he asked as he took a sip of his drink.

"Yes. Why?"

"Oh, I was just wondering. I don't get to Bakersfield often, and I usually eat here or at the Woolgrowers, mostly the Woolgrowers, so I just wondered what nights you work."

"I work Tuesday through Saturday. Every night 'cept Sunday and Monday."

"Then I'll make sure I'm here on one of your nights when I come to town next time. I almost didn't make it down this trip because of the Tule fog. You hear about the pileup on 99?"

"I sure did. Everybody's talking about it around here." She thought she should at least be cordial in order to get a fat tip. "So where are you from?"

"Cupertino."

"Is that up north? I don't know much about California."

"Yes, up north, close to San Jose. Where do you hail from, honey?"

"Arkansas. But I lived in Nevada for a few years before comin' out here. So what's your name?"

"My name's Richard, Amanda. Richard Miller."

She wore a name tag so he had the advantage of knowing her name before she knew his.

"Nice to meet you, Mr. Miller."

"Call me Richard."

"Okay, I will. Well, I got to go now. Got to set up them tables over there for tomorrow's lunch. Your dinner should be ready in a minute." She walked away feeling she'd done her friendly part, but she was uneasy because she felt him watching her while she worked.

Frenchie followed her into the kitchen. "Richard's a wealthy cattle rancher from up north, Amanda, a really nice guy. I think he likes you, sweetie. Be good to him."

"I am being good to him, Frenchie. But I hope he's not coming on to me, because if he is, I'll have to tell him to mind his own dang business. I ain't into hooking up with some ol' man. No man, as a matter of fact. I'm still married."

Frenchie chuckled. She was always amused at Amanda's manner of speech. Both she and her sister Paula had a unique way of putting things - a far cry from her own French manner. "But, you must have an open mind, ma chère."

"My mind's open alright, it's just that I don't particularly want another man in it taking up all the space." Amanda turned to add garnish to the plate as she gave a moment's thought about the eligible rancher sitting at one of her tables with a shit-eatin' grin that made her nervous.

As handsome as he was and as much as she was wondering if his pecker looked like Arlie's, she shut him out of

25

her mind as she picked up the steak plate and grabbed the bread and left the kitchen.

Chapter 5

On Monday Amanda walked down the long driveway to the mailbox as usual. Paula and Drake Livingston had built on ten acres along the Kern River outside of town. But then Bakersfield is more of a city than a town with its population of 340,000. A city that is surrounded by oil fields, ranches and farms, a city made up of blue and white collar workers, medical professionals, college faculties and students, a growing corporate element, migrant farm workers, and sad to say ... the homeless and unemployed.

The Livingstons were proud of their 7,000 square-foot home with barns, garages and sheds to accommodate Drake's trucking business - a fabulous spread. It was a far cry from the log cabins of their youth in Arkansas.

But for Amanda there was far too much activity there. She had become accustomed to being a recluse while living in the Nevada desert, and then again, maybe she'd been one all along, maybe even in Arkansas while growing up.

She had spent many hours alone at her grandmother's cabin in the woods outside Mountain Home where she was born and raised. Her sister Paula was older and had her own friends and habits, so she wasn't there most of the time. Maybe Amanda subconsciously preferred to be alone. She remembered reading somewhere, "You are where or what you're supposed to be, otherwise you'd be somewhere or somebody else." Maybe she was supposed to have lived her first twenty-three years as a hermit.

Arlie and Amanda had gone to school together in the small Arkansas town and had been girlfriend and boyfriend by the time they were both thirteen, and they quit school and got married when they were sixteen. Amanda had never worked because Arlie didn't want her to work. She'd learned how to make her own clothes from her mother who had been a seamstress, so that helped pass the time. She'd buy used clothing from Goodwill or the Salvation Army, and there were always the castoffs from the people in the trailer park in the bins by the convenience store. She used some of the recycled clothing to recreate and design garments for herself – sundresses, aprons, skirts and blouses, and sometimes shirts for Arlie.

She had always thought she could take in sewing or do ironing if she had to, but going for a job outside the home wasn't a choice for her. Arlie said he'd always take care of her and he did 'til he fell off the face of the earth in spite of his promise. In that first six months after he'd disappeared, daily she swayed back and forth from feeling totally distraught and depressed to feeling spitfire angry at him for leaving her in such a predicament. But now things were different, that was all behind her.

She opened the oversized mailbox that her brother-in-law Drake had set in a square river-rock column that he had built. The box was full and she lifted out the stack of mail, clumps at a time to sift through, hoping the check from Johnny would be there.

"It came! It's here!" She screamed with glee, and ran towards the house with her arms full, dropping mail, stooping to pick it up, dropping more mail, stooping again, and then running.

Now she would find an apartment of her own in town near KC's. That's what she wanted more than anything. She'd thought of nothing else in the past few weeks. It was time for her to be on her own, to be alone again. Only this time she was looking forward to it, she needed it.

Maybe she could buy a car now, too, if she could find a cheap one. She'd been putting money into a savings account, but didn't want to touch that. Her sister told her if she started withdrawing from a savings account it would become too easy and she'd most likely end up drawing it all out before she knew it. So she was very strict with herself. That was money for Europe, and now she had more to add to it because there would be a lot left over even after finding an apartment and buying a car, she figured.

The cashier's check was for $9,000. She'd never seen that much money in her entire life. It was in her pocket and it was all hers! She wondered where Johnny had gotten that much. Then her thoughts went to Arlie and the rumors of his gambling. She didn't want to think about it, but maybe Arlie had been a gambler after all, and maybe Johnny gambled. They were close friends, so they probably did it together. She shook the thoughts of Arlie and Johnny from her mind. All she cared about was the money and what she was going to do with it. Arlie was hardly a wisp of a thought now.

"Paula, Paula! It's here! The money's here!" The screen door slammed behind her as she ran into the family room where Paula was watching Oprah. "All of it! Nine thousand dollars! Let's go find me a place to live, okay?"

29

Chapter 6

A week later Amanda spent the first night in her own place and it felt like heaven - a one-bedroom apartment in a courtyard surrounded by eight other units, the shingled exteriors resembling English cottages set around a lawn and flower garden. She fell in love with it the moment she saw the *For Rent* sign, and it was within walking distance of KC's. Perfect.

The foundation of her particular unit was a bit off-kilter, though. It leaned a tad to the left. She dropped a spool of thread and it rolled down to the northwest corner of the living room, which she found amusing, and it was barely noticeable.

She furnished the cottage with pieces she had found at thrift stores and used furniture stores and had put up lace curtains she bought at Kmart to cover the paper roller-shades that came with the place. She was as happy as she could be. Finally a home of her own to decorate as she wished and no one to tell her she couldn't.

Paula had wanted to buy new furniture for her, but Amanda wouldn't have it. Paula did insist on buying her a new queen-sized bed, though. Wouldn't take no for an answer, told her it was an early birthday present, and had it delivered the first day she moved in.

One evening on her day off from work, Amanda sat on one of the two matching bar stools at her high, white, wrought-iron café table that doubled as a cutting-board island in her kitchen. She'd found a new round cutting board that exactly fit the top of the table. As she sat in her cozy kitchen, she gazed into her charming living room. She sipped on a glass of wine and felt as if she was in another world, her very own cozy cocoon - all safe and happy.

She loved her beautiful furnishings - the overstuffed yellow-floral-blue-striped love seat, the bamboo cocktail table in front of it, the rattan chair with a lavender seat cushion, oriental framed prints on the wall next to the gold-framed mirror over the fireplace. Although they weren't exactly new and were slightly worn, they were new to her.

She had a knack for decorating that could make meager and inexpensive décor look expensive and appealing. At one time she'd even thought of going to school to become an interior decorator. That was back in Arkansas before she quit high school and married Arlie. She'd flipped through an Architectural Digest at the drug store and couldn't believe how some people lived - the extravagant furniture and artwork they had in their homes. She read the stories about the designers and their lifestyles. It had overwhelmed her and made her wish for her own palatial home. She hadn't thought about those times until lately, when she and Paula were going from store to store, shopping for furnishings for Paula's new house, and now for her own little home.

"I love my cottage!" she exclaimed aloud and began laughing. "I do love my little cottage, I do." She poured another glass of wine for herself and then began eating her salad. "I love my cottage."

Chapter 7

A month had passed since Amanda had moved into her quaint cottage—as she continually referred to it. The exterior walls were covered with gray, weathered redwood shingles from the foundation to the roofline, and the steep roof was covered with slate shingles - just like she'd seen in one of the travel magazines.

Her landlord had given her permission to plant climbing pink and yellow roses around the lattice work on the front stoop, and ivy along the street side of the building. Although it was co-joined to two other cottages to the right of it, it felt like a detached unit to Amanda. She had a front and back door with shingled porch covers and stoops, a lawn, and windows on three sides. The west side of her place bordered the sidewalk that ran along the street, the front faced north onto the courtyard, across from the units looking back at her.

She'd added bargain accessories in her three cozy rooms that she'd found at vintage, used, and antique stores in Bakersfield. She spent hours browsing and finding decor she wanted that appeared to cost more than what they did.

Paula couldn't believe how dazzling the small one-bedroom haven had become. "It's incredible, what you've done here," she said as she came through the door held open by Amanda. "Oh, look at that!" She went over to the mantle and touched a lacquered porcelain orange and white Chinese dog. "Where the hell did you find this?"

"At that place over there on Eighteenth Street. You know, where we got the love seat. Are y'all hungry yet? I've made us some sandwiches."

"You know me, I'm always hungry. This baby eats as much as I do."

"Okay, I've set it all up for us." She walked towards the tiny kitchen as Paula waddled behind her.

"You sit over there."

"Oh, hon! This is so pretty. Flowers in a vase. And look at these plates. They're new, ain't they?"

"Look on the back; they're genuine bone China from England. Found them at the Ross store."

"I just can't get over the change in you in just this short time." Paula picked up half a sandwich from her plate. "I mean, you have a job, and Frenchie says you're really good at it. She loves you, too, you know. Says you remind her of herself when she was young and stupid about men. Ain't that funny? I don't see Frenchie as ever being stupid about anything. I wish I had one-tenth of her clothes and jewelry, she's a dang fashion plate, ain't she?"

Amanda's face brightened. "One of these days I'm going to make her a pretty dress."

"Now that would be downright nice of you to do, Amanda. Anyway, like I was sayin', here you've got this place to live in with all these pretty things. It just blows my mind how you've adjusted." She bit into the sandwich and kept talking as she chewed. "I don't think I could pick up and start all over again like you did if something happened to Drake and I lost everything. I couldn't do it. I'd just die. I know I would." She reached for her wine glass. "Let's make a toast to your new life."

Amanda happily reached for her glass.

"To women all over the world: may they be as happy and as lucky as we two Conroy sisters are, Amanda."

"Well—"

"No, I mean it. What more could you want, Amanda? You've got everything you need. Well, maybe a car would be nice, but that'll come next."

"I was just going to say, I've been looking at cars."

"Now, hon ... I wasn't supposed to tell you this, but Drake is going to give you a car for your birthday. So don't y'all go out and get into any debt. Just wait till your birthday."

"I don't want Drake to buy me a car, Paula. I'll buy my own. I've been saving my money. It won't take me much longer to get the money with what I got for the trailer and all. I make pretty good tips."

"Now, you know how Drake is when he sets his mind to something, there ain't nobody gonna change it. And you know we got tons of money, what are sisters for if not to help each other when we can? So you just put that money in your travel fund. How much have you saved up for that trip you want to take?"

"Well, with the money that's left from the sale of the trailer and what I've saved from paychecks and tips, I've got a little over $6000 for the trip and $600 in my car fund."

"Well I'll be damned! That's nearly $7000, girl! How much do you figure you're gonna need for that trip anyway?"

"I'm figuring on about $10,000."

"Whew! That's a lot of money, girl! I don't how you do it. Figuring out all that stuff. But then you've always been good with numbers." Paula continued with a mouthful of sandwich. "I sure couldn't do all that figuring."

Amanda placed another half sandwich on Paula's plate. "Well, I figure if I take that much, I can stay longer if I want. I've been reading up on Belgium at the library, the costs and everything. And I got on the computer last time I was there and found the Bruges website. There's a lace-making school there, Paula. They give classes that last a week for beginners."

"You're thinking about taking a lace-making class?"

"Yes, I am. It's fascinatin' how they make those intricate designs. Here, let me show you some pictures."

Amanda went to a book case and pulled out a book on lace making. "I got this here book at Goodwill, it has everything in it. I figure I can just take a basic class and see if I like it or not first, or if I can even do it. There aren't many lace-makers out there anymore." She handed the book to Paula. "They're even offering free classes to school children so the art won't die. Bruges was one of the first originators of lace."

She went back into the living room and picked up a throw pillow from the sofa. "I'd like to learn how to do tapestry, too. Look at this here."

Paula took the pillow and felt it, unzipped the cover and looked on the back side of the tapestry. "I would imagine you wouldn't have to go all the way to Belgium to learn how to make lace and weave tapestry, if that's all you want."

"But it's not all I want. Here, let me show you this magazine I bought yesterday. It's all about Belgium, a travel magazine." She went to the table in front of the love seat and picked up one of the travel issues that were stacked high on it. "Look at this." She opened to a pictorial spread of Bruges.

"Oh, my goodness!" Paula exclaimed. "Will you look at them waterways right up against the buildings? These pictures look like paintings, don't they? Something you'd see in a museum."

"That's the main reason I'm going. It looks so beautiful and peaceful. And all the streets are cobbled - you know, made of stones, like in medieval times. Did you know that's what cobbled meant?"

Paula frowned. "No I didn't. You're sure learnin' a bunch of stuff these days."

"Well, I don't know about that." She giggled. "Actually most of the architecture there is medieval. It says that right here. I looked up 'medieval' and found out what it means. It means the same as the Middle Ages. Did you know that?"

"No, I didn't. I thought middle ages was when people get to their fifties and sixties. I sure didn't think it had anything to do with that ... that medieval stuff." Paula gulped some water.

"Well, it says it was a period of time way back between the fifth and the fifteenth centuries. Can you believe that? Here we're living in the twenty-first century and a century is made up of a hundred years."

"You are so smart, Amanda. I had no idea you knew so much about the big ol' world out there."

Amanda shrugged. "I do a lot of reading about it in my spare time. Makin' up for lost time, I guess. Quittin' school early probably wasn't the best thing for me to do. I'm teachin' myself better English, too. " She picked up a sandwich. But anyway, so that means medieval times began sixteen centuries ago. That's sixteen hundred years! Can you imagine that? It just boggles my mind" She took a bite. "And Bruges has buildings and streets that go back all the way to that time. You know, sometimes I feel like I've already been there, it seems so familiar to me; I'm drawn to it. Have you read anything about past lives, Paula? I'm reading all about that, too."

Paula stared at her younger sister in wonderment.

Chapter 8

It was nearly ten p.m. Saturday night before the Christmas holiday. KC's Steakhouse was all decked out with colorful decorations and the waitresses were wearing blinking Christmas pins and wore holly and mistletoe in their hair. Amanda had made a circular crown of holly and was wearing it. No mistletoe. Her hair was curled and pulled up to make a nest for the holly on top of her head.

The room was still crowded with partygoers and regular patrons, all the tables were taken and both bars were full of merrymakers. Amanda had four tables to take care of, one of which was occupied by Richard Miller and a few of his business associates.

"Amanda, may I please have another double Scotch?" Richard called out to her as she was heading towards the lower bar.

She nodded and sighed. That meant they were going to be sticking around for awhile. It wasn't like she didn't know it would be busy tonight, but she was tired and wanted to go home. Not only was it busy because it was Saturday, but because it was the Saturday before Christmas. Everybody and their brother would be out tonight, one last fling before the family holiday. Starting tomorrow she had four days off in a row - first time in the six months she'd been working at KC's.

She couldn't believe it'd been only a year since Arlie had disappeared. It seemed much longer. She'd been thinking about him off and on all day and wondered how she'd feel if one day he would walk in and want to take her back to Nevada. After all, they were still married. The thought frightened her, mainly because she loved her new life, and she secretly hoped he wouldn't come back until she'd at least gone to Bruges and done everything else she wanted to do.

Besides, there was Richard to think about now, although she felt guilty looking forward to seeing him every other week at KC's. He'd become a regular and always made it a point to sit at one of her tables.

But nothing was going to stop her from going to Belgium. Nothing and nobody.

The previous Monday she'd gone to the courthouse and applied for a passport and had her picture taken for it. It excited her so much, she went out and bought a new outfit and treated herself to dinner that night at a new Italian restaurant that had opened downtown. She felt as if she was in another world already, a far cry from the rundown trailer house out in the middle of the desert in Nevada, never going anywhere, never dining out, and especially never having a new outfit to wear. She was proud of herself for being able to do it all on her own.

Since she'd been in California, she'd dined in some fine restaurants. Drake and Paula had made it a point to take her to all the best ones in town. But she knew the bubble would burst one day when Arlie came back, if he wasn't dead. She felt guilty about wishing he were dead, for she definitely couldn't see him living in her cozy cottage with all her pretty things. She knew he wouldn't fit into the delicate, feminine world she had created for herself. Again, it made her feel guilty to wish he were dead or that he wouldn't come back until she went to Bruges, but she couldn't help it. She wanted to see how other people lived in other parts of the world, and she knew she wouldn't get to do that if she were with Arlie.

Amanda and Paula's mother, Inez Conroy, had never been anywhere to speak of, either. Born in the Ozarks, died in the Ozarks. She'd died of leukemia before her two daughters had reached their teens, although many felt it was heartbreak more than the leukemia that took her. Inez's husband, the girls' father, had disappeared right after Amanda was born. So after their mother had died, the girls were raised by their grandmother till she passed when Amanda was twelve and Paula was fifteen. After their grandmother died they lived on their own, taking care of themselves in their grandmother's house. When Paula turned sixteen she and Drake got married, but they stayed with Amanda until she married Arlie when she turned sixteen. Then they all moved west. Amanda and Arlie to Nevada, Paula and Drake to California. Both girls had wished their mother had been alive to go with them.

So Amanda felt like she was going to Bruges for her mother, too. She thought about the elaborate embroidery her mother used to do. She'd mend and sew clothes for people to put food on the table, had taught Amanda how to sew and embroider. Inez did housekeeping for the more fortunate people who lived in Mountain Home, and she cleaned the doctor's office on Sundays. She never had a day off to spend with her two daughters.

At night, after a long day of laborious work, she'd lie down, exhausted, and would fall asleep till morning and then start the same thing all over again – seven days a week. Amanda remembered sitting and watching her sleep at night. She'd touch her mama's pulse, wondering if she was still alive because she slept so quiet and sound, and that was before she had leukemia.

"Here you go, Mr. Miller. A double Scotch."

"Thank you. It's Richard, remember?"

"Oh, right. Okay. Richard." She gave him a broad smile and batted her eyelashes. *There you go, that should keep you and Frenchie happy.*

"How about going to lunch with me tomorrow, Amanda? There's an early Christmas Eve party at the Pyrenees, a late lunch, and I'd like to take you." His smiling, blue, sparkling eyes locked onto hers.

"Uh, well, I don't think—" she blushed and stepped back, suddenly panicking. Was he asking her out on a date?

"Go with me. I'm a good guy. You don't have to worry. I'll pick you up at noon."

"I don't know. I—I'll have to think about it." She hurried off to the kitchen.

In a quick movement, Frenchie followed Amanda. "Amanda, you should go with him. He told me he was interested in you, and he's not married."

"But I'm married!"

"I know, ma chère, but you must think about your future. What will it hurt to go to lunch with him? Let him grow on you. Lance and I are going to be at the Pyrenees, too. And so are some of the other customers that come in here, so you'll know a lot of the people. Hasn't Paula mentioned it to you? I think she and Drake are going."

"I haven't talked to Paula in over a week."

"Well, you must go with him, ma petite. Tell him you will." She reached up and gently patted Amanda's cheek. "He won't bite. Give him a chance, yes?"

Amanda had mixed emotions. Her brow furrowed as she thought about the possibility. Yes, he was a very attractive man, someone she would have never in her whole life had dreamed she could ever be with. He was so out of her class. He seemed kind and gentle, polite, attentive, successful, sexy … older and wiser … sexy …

Chapter 9

There was a knock at her door. Amanda stood still, wondering if she was doing the right thing. It bothered her that technically she was still married, even though it had been a year since Arlie had disappeared, and here she was going on a date with an older man she didn't know from beans.

He knocked again, louder.

She grabbed her fleece-lined denim jacket and purse and opened the door. "Hi, I'm ready."

"Good, shall we?" Richard held out his hand and took hers as she stepped out the door and down the steps.

His touch sent a thrill through her.

"This is a lovely little house, reminds me of the cottages in England," he remarked.

"You've been to England?"

"Yes, I have." He placed his hand in the small of her back as they walked to the curb and to his navy blue Cadillac.

"I'm going to Bruges."

"Bruges?"

"Yes, it's in Belgium." She stepped into the car, relieved that he wasn't touching her anymore. He closed the door behind her.

"So, you're going to Belgium?" he asked with a grin as he slid into the seat next to her and started up the engine, pulling away from the curb.

"I'm saving my money to go. I just about have it all now."

"That's one place I've never been. But I hear Bruges is a very romantic city. It's Belgium's Venice because of all the waterways."

"I know."

"What about the real Venice? Have you thought about going there?"

"No. I've read about it and all, but I'm drawn to Bruges. So that's where I'm going. Nothin's gonna change my mind about that either." She said it with such finality, the dialogue stopped.

They rode along in awkward silence. Richard was in deep thought about the beautiful young woman sitting next to him. Not only was she perfect on the outside, he suspected she was perfect on the inside. She was too young to have been tainted by the wiles and whims of men, too young to have been subjected to the deceiving, clever workings of the world. At least he hadn't seen the familiar signs of callousness and cynicism that he usually found in most of the women he came into contact with on a daily basis.

A great big plus was she hadn't come onto him like other women when they found out he had money. He figured Frenchie must have told her about his financial status. He'd even asked Frenchie out on a date when they'd first met five years earlier. He'd been instantly attracted to her wide smile; her short, stylish, black hair; her big dark eyes and sun-tanned skin; and her adorable Frenchness. She turned him down, though. Said she was too busy to be dating, and she meant it. He'd been disappointed at the time. But now, he felt he'd stumbled upon a treasure in Amanda, and he truly wanted her.

Amanda's long legs were shapely in a pair of designer blue jeans. Of course he didn't know she'd purchased them at the thrift store for only two dollars.

She also wore a yellow cashmere turtleneck sweater she'd borrowed from Paula. He noticed it fit her loosely, not the usual skin-tight sweater that most young women would squeeze into for effect.

"What is the perfume you're wearing? It smells delicious."

"Avon's Honeysuckle."

He was impressed that she was wearing Avon and proud of it in a time when women were flaunting designer perfumes. "You not only smell good, you look good, Amanda. Yellow suits you."

She blushed and looked away from him out of the passenger window. "It's one of my favorite colors. I like purple, too."

"It was like we planned it, we match," he added.

"I know. How weird is that?" She laughed as she took a closer look at his pale yellow sweater vest and blue plaid western shirt neatly tucked into his belted blue jeans.

He grinned as their gaze met. "Blonds must like yellow and blue, I guess."

"Yep, I guess so."

Chapter 10

The Basque bars and restaurants in Bakersfield were well known and always packed with patrons coming from all over the valley. Usually dinner was the only meal that was served at the Pyrenees in east Bakersfield, with two seatings – early and late, the exception being on Christmas Eve when the late lunch was added. The food was excellent and it was indeed like a huge family party, whether or not you knew the people sitting next to you.

The Woolgrowers, another popular Basque restaurant and bar that Richard frequented, normally served lunch as well as dinner, but it didn't have the same setup as the Pyrenees. Dinner at Woolgrowers was served at separate tables like any restaurant, at any hour, not just two seatings. But it still served family-style in tureens, bowls, and on platters.

Richard held Amanda's hand as they entered the Pyrenees bar. He commented as his eyes adjusted to the darkness, "Bakersfield is known as the Basque gourmet capital of the U.S., Amanda. Just a little tidbit of information for you, in case you didn't know."

"I didn't know, but then how would I? I know nothing about the Basque people or Bakersfield." She smiled at him.

He returned the smile and added, "Well, the Basque emigrated from the Pyrenees region near the Bay of Biscayne of Southern France and Northern Spain. They settled here in the San Joaquin Valley as sheepherders and ranch hands, and it didn't take them long to open up traditional Basque restaurants like this one. California has the highest population of Basques than any other state, as a matter of fact, and it has a major wool-growing industry because of the Basque people."

The daughter of the proprietor came from around the crowded bar to greet them. "So good to see you, Richard. Just two, this afternoon?"

"That's right. Did we make it in time for the Christmas lunch?"

"You just made it. Another five minutes and we would have had to turn you away." She grinned and motioned him to follow her.

He knew she was teasing him.

They followed her across the dark bar's worn wooden-planked floor past the ornately carved bar through a single doorway leading into the backroom which was as large as the bar room. Curtained windows were on the two outside perimeter walls; the kitchen and the bar butted up against the two inside walls.

There were two long rows of wooden picnic-style tables lined up, end to end, from the front to the far back window wall. Chairs full of diners were already seated at the tables that were covered with white tablecloths. Platters and tureens of food were being placed for the diners to pass from one person to another. Open bottles of wine were plentiful, spaced for the patrons to pour into small glass tumblers, not typical wine glasses - true Basque style.

This particular meal on every Christmas Eve was a special time, a celebratory annual event. Later on in the evening, Christmas tamales would be served in the bar to the drinking patrons. So it was an event for all at the Pyrenees.

Normally, meals at the Pyrenees and other Basque restaurants included soup, salad, beans, French fries, wine, and coffee, plus several entrees and side dishes. Entrees offered might include steak, lamb, pork, chicken and seafood dishes. Side dishes would feature sweetbreads, tongue stew, lamb stew, paella, oxtail stew, and many family-owned recipes handed down through the ages. Dessert was usually limited to ice cream, fruit and hard cheese, Gastaeu Basque (a rolled cake with luscious filling) was a favorite, and of course, there would be flan.

Amanda had never experienced such a friendly dining atmosphere. She was stunned by the camaraderie between people who had never met before and were sitting next to or across from each other and acting as if they were old friends. She waved at Frenchie who blew her a kiss from where she was sitting at the end of the other row of tables. Paula and Drake weren't there. They'd stayed at home since Paula wasn't feeling well.

Richard grinned as he watched Amanda's reaction to the Basque feeding process. He was sitting across from her, sipping his red wine from the short glass.

"This is so different, ain't it?" she asked in a quiet voice as she leaned toward him across the table.

"You mean the number of people all dining together?"

"Yes. I ain't—I mean, I haven't seen anything like this before. And the food, there's so much of it."

"There's another Basque house a block down the street called Noriega's. We'll go down there and have a drink afterwards so you can see it, too."

"Is it the same as this one?"

"Pretty much. Only it has a handball court out back."

47

"You're kidding me."

"No, I'm not. Anyone can play on it and when the Swiss Olympic team was touring they dropped by and played. It was quite an event for the regulars. There are a lot of Italian-Swiss residents in Bakersfield, too, who come to these places."

"I'd like to go to Italy and Switzerland some day. Have you been there?"

"Yes, I have. Both are incredible. I prefer Switzerland, though … it has the Jung Frau which contains the highest peak in Europe. And then there's Zurich, the lakes, the train rides up the mountains, cog trains—"

"What's a cog train?"

A short, older man wearing a Christmas tie and white shirt and a white apron reached over Amanda's shoulder. "Here you are, my friend. Your lamb chops, just as you like. Bon appetit!"

"Joe, those look perfect! Thank you." Richard reached for the platter and forked two of them onto Amanda's plate. "Joe cooks these for me. They're not on the regular menu, but I have to have them every time I come here. He makes a special garlic butter paste and smears it on them. Wait till you taste these, you won't believe it."

"But I've had so much food already, and I don't think I could eat lamb, really. They're so cuddly."

Richard's eyes were gleaming as he reached across and touched her hand that was resting on the table cloth by her wine glass. "Just try it. One bite. You don't have to eat more of it if you don't want to."

Richard decided at that very moment that he wanted to give Amanda every pleasure she could imagine. He wanted to show her the world. His feelings for her were overwhelming; he had never felt this way before. His heart felt as if it would burst, the love for her was exploding inside him, almost impossible to hide. What a pleasure it would be to introduce her to a life she'd never had.

On top of it all, he was physically attracted to her. She was an untarnished, unbiased, unassuming, untouched, intelligent beauty. He wanted her more than anything.

Chapter 11

It was nearly dark when Richard parked the car on the street by Amanda's cottage. He hurried around and opened the car door and reached for her hand as she stepped out of the Caddy onto the curb.

"I've had a real good time, Richard. Thank you. I'm glad I went with y'all."

He reached across her back and gripped her shoulder as they began walking toward her front door. "I knew you would enjoy yourself, and as I promised you, you're home before the witching hour."

She laughed. "I thank you for that, too. Although I was having so much fun at Noriega's talking to the old-timers, I hadn't noticed how the time had flown. Thank you for getting me out of there." She reached in her purse for the house key. With key in hand, she turned to face Richard on the first step. "This has been the most fun I've had in a long time."

He couldn't help but notice the tears welling up in her eyes and couldn't contain what was welling up inside of him.

"Amanda, please understand me when I say this … I want to give you all the fun you can handle. Will you let me do that for you? Will you trust me and let me show you things and places you've never seen?"

She hesitated. "How old are you, Richard?"

He laughed. "Well, I'm nearly twice your age, I'm sure. I'm forty-five, but I feel like I'm twenty-five. Why?"

"I don't mean to be nosy, really I don't. I was just wondering, and I was hoping you weren't fifty or sixty. Forty-five don't seem all that old." Her heart was melting as she gazed into his handsome face and blue eyes, and feeling his strong hands gripping her arms.

"Even if I were fifty or sixty, I'd still feel young with you."

Amanda suddenly felt nervous. "Well, maybe so. Anyway, I got to go inside; got some things I still have to do before I go to bed."

"May I have a goodnight kiss? A little one?" He moved closer to her. He could feel her body heat emanating between them. "Just one?"

She was mesmerized by his half closed eyes inviting her lips to his, and the mellow hypnotic sound of his voice.

He kissed her and they both lingered for a moment, their bodies touching in all the right places.

Amanda panicked. "I have to go in." She pulled away and ran up the steps, hurriedly unlocking the door. "Thank you for lunch and all," she said a little too loud.

"When can I see you again?" he asked with a longing, pleading look.

"Next time you're at KC's, I guess. Good night. Thanks, again." She closed the door.

Once inside she took a deep breath and dropped her purse on the cocktail table near the stack of magazines. She plopped down on the small sofa and stared across the room towards the fireplace, thinking about Richard, about the kiss, and how her heart was racing. She mustn't give in to him, she mustn't. She couldn't help but feel that Arlie had run off because of how she was in bed. She must have been awful for him to do that. And she was afraid Richard would drop her if he knew how bad she was at making love.

Besides, she couldn't let Richard interfere with her plans. She figured within six months, no later than June, she would be on her way to Belgium, anyway. She would spend at least a couple of months there, maybe more if she could swing it. She might even stay forever. So Richard couldn't be a part of her life.

Besides, she definitely didn't want another man telling her how to live and what to do. She didn't want another man restricting her comings and goings. She wanted a life of her own, without sex and all the other things a man wants from a woman.

Nope. She didn't want a relationship with anybody. Anybody!

Chapter 12

It was a stormy day in February.

Amanda decided to call in sick. She had never missed a scheduled day of work at KC's and had always been on call for extra work when Frenchie needed her. But today she had the worst case of the flu she'd ever had. If she wasn't sitting on the toilet, her face was in it. And to top it off, it was raining hailstones. She could hear the heavy ice rocks hit the roof and occasionally hit a window. The garden was covered with a white knobby blanket of it. If she weren't so sick she'd be sitting at a window enjoying the view, sipping hot chocolate with a fire blazing in the fireplace. She loved storms.

She grasped the sink as she rose to her feet from the toilet after another round of dry heaves. There was nothing left in her stomach or intestines. There couldn't be. She wondered why the convulsing and cramps still went on after the body was empty of all matter and fluids. Didn't it know it'd expelled it all?

Feeling too weak to stand, she crawled to the doorway over the wooden floor and leaned back against the doorjamb. She could see through the living room and out the windows and marveled at the beauty of the storm. How she wished she were out in it gathering hailstones. When she was a girl in Arkansas she and her sister would fill buckets with giant hailstones and put them in the ice box in their grandmother's house. They didn't have a refrigerator, so a hail storm was a blessing.

The phone rang.

Amanda crawled to the table next to the loveseat and reached for the phone.

"Hello? Oh Paula. I'm so sick. Sicker than a dog. I've been up all night puking my guts out and I have a bad case of diarrhea. No. I don't have any of that. I've got some Alka Seltzer Cold & Flu capsules, been waiting till I quit vomiting long enough to take them. No. It's just the flu. I'll get over it. Okay, but wait till after the hail stops. Don't come out in this storm. Okay. Love you, too."

Twenty minutes later Paula was at the door, knocking.

"Just a minute!" Amanda called out while she raised herself from the loveseat where she'd just fallen asleep wrapped in a blanket. She opened the door. "Didn't I tell you not to come out in this storm, Paula? It's too dangerous for you to be driving."

"Oh, don't you be silly. I've been out in worse than this. I remember when neither one of us ever worried about any ol' storm." She took off her coat and reached for Amanda. "Now let's take a look at you. My God, you look like shit!"

"I feel like shit."

"Have you eaten anything today?"

"Hell no. Wouldn't be able to hold it down, if I did."

"You got any cans of soup?" Paula asked.

"Some tomato and chicken noodle in the cabinet."

"Okay, you go lie down. I'll fix some crackers and chicken noodle. That'll do the trick. You got any tea?"

Amanda pointed with one hand and held her belly with the other. "There's some green tea in the basket on top of the refrigerator."

Paula immediately brewed tea and poured a can of Campbell's soup in a pan on the stove. She stepped back in the kitchen doorway to look at Amanda lying on the loveseat in her blanket. "Hon, you don't look too good. Maybe we ought to take you to the doctor."

"No, I'll be all right. It's getting better, really. You know I don't like doctors."

"Well, I don't know. Your face looks drawn and it looks like you lost some weight and you can't afford to do that. You're skinny as a rail as it is."

Wanting to change the subject, Amanda said, "You look like you're ready to pop that child, Paula."

"Yep, you got that right. Come hell or high water you're gonna get a nephew this month."

"Looks like it might be high water if this storm keeps at it." They both laughed.

Paula stepped back into the kitchen to prepare the soup and the tea. She carried out a cup and saucer for Amanda. "Okay now, sip on this. I put some honey in it. It's good for you when you're sick like this. It'll give you some energy. You need to get some liquid in you since you've lost it all."

"Actually I feel better than I did when we talked on the phone. Must be the capsules I took."

"Well, the soup will help, too. I'll have a cup of tea with you." She went back to the kitchen for the tea and stirred the soup. "Have you heard from Richard?"

"He's coming down on Monday. We're going out to dinner at the Woolgrowers."

"He's such a nice guy, isn't he? And he really does like you, hon. I couldn't believe how much he watched you when y'all were at the house last week. He couldn't take his eyes off you. Drake remarked about it after you left. And talk about getting along with Drake! I mean, they're like two peas in a pod. We couldn't ask for a better brother-in-law."

Amanda smirked. "We ain't getting married. I'm already married."

Paula waved a hand dismissively. "That doesn't matter. You can't go back to living with Arlie even if he did come back. You wouldn't *want* to, would you?"

"Hell, no."

"Well, you can annul that one. You said Richard wants to marry you." Paula sat in the chair next to the loveseat with an inquisitive look on her face.

"I didn't say I would."

"Why not? You like him and he's good to you. It's obvious he's crazy about you."

"The soup's boiling over, Paula."

"Dammit!" She lunged for the kitchen and the pan of soup. "It's okay. Not much of it boiled over."

"You never were much of a cook." Amanda laughed.

"I didn't have to be, I had you and Grandma to do it all for me."

They both giggled as if they were little girls again.

Paula reached for a soup mug. "Remember the first time I made spaghetti, wanted to surprise you and Grandma? I put a half cup of salt instead of sugar in the sauce?"

"Oh yes. I remember that. It was awful." Amanda grimaced at the memory. "And Grandma ate it anyway, like it was supposed to taste like that. Told you it was good while you and me were spitting it out on our plates."

"I miss her," Paula murmured. "I really do."

"I do, too."

Paula returned carrying a tray. "Okay, here you are … a nice hot cup of chicken noodle. Just like we used to have when we were sick." She set the tray on Amanda's lap.

"Thank you. It looks good. You didn't put any salt in it, did you?"

"No, I didn't put any salt in it. Now you just be grateful and behave yourself."

"Just wondering." Amanda grinned as she blew on a spoonful before putting it into her mouth.

Paula returned to the kitchen and poured more tea for both of them. She was worried. Worried that Amanda would make the biggest mistake of her life by rejecting Richard. She only wanted the best for her little sister. She wanted her to be loved by a man that could take care of her. And she knew in her soul that Richard was that man. Drake thought so, too.

Chapter 13

Allan George Livingston was delivered to Paula and Drake on February 22, George Washington's birthday so they gave him George's name. The happy parents adored the little fella from the moment he popped into the world.

At the first sounds of the baby's cries announcing his arrival, Drake beamed as he looked at Amanda and said, "Listen to the noise A.G. is making. That child has got some strong lungs on him if you ask me."

Three months had passed since A.G. was born.

It was the last Sunday in May when Amanda drove out to a barbecue at her sister's house by the river. Drake had given Amanda a brand spanking new red Ford 150 super cab pickup truck on her birthday the month before. Although she hadn't wanted him to do it, she was grateful she hadn't had to use her savings to buy a car, and it was obvious she adored her truck, the first vehicle she'd ever owned. It was her baby to be proud of, and it was in her name. She wondered what Arlie would think about her owning such a fancy truck and learning how to drive.

Nearly a year and a half had passed since Arlie had disappeared, and they weren't any nearer to solving the mystery than they'd been the week after he was gone. Amanda had resigned herself to the fact that he was probably dead. She just couldn't imagine he could still be alive and not trying to contact her, regardless of his reasons for leaving. Surely he would want a divorce if he were alive after all this time.

Richard had been pressuring her to marry him every time they were together. She hadn't given in to his frequent sexual advances and was feeling guilty about it, but she just couldn't go all the way with him. She used the excuse of still being married, but that was fast becoming a lame excuse for she was beginning to want him in her bed. The desire was building. In fact, she looked forward to the sensual kisses and embraces that almost pushed her past the point of no return. She knew she was falling in love with him and was fighting it with all her might.

As she drove, she recalled seeing Richard a couple weeks before. He'd knocked on her door and when she opened it and saw him standing there grinning, holding a guidebook on traveling in Europe in one hand and a bouquet of yellow roses in the other, she couldn't help but feel love for him. He was perfect. She could find nothing wrong with him.

That evening she had made dinner for him, they sipped wine, and as they cuddled on the sofa, he asked her to marry him once again. With tears in her eyes she had put her arms around his neck and kissed him passionately, not giving him an answer.

He picked her up and carried her to the bedroom and they lay on the bed together for the first time, but fully clothed.

"I love you, Amanda," he said hoarsely as he brushed her hair back from her face. He cleared his throat, embarrassed at the sound of his voice. "I want to make you happy and give you everything you want, darling. I'll never leave you." His fingers traced the arch of her eyebrows and he kissed her nose. "Do you love me a little bit?"

Instead of replying, Amanda pulled him to her and gave him a long, deep, wet, passionate kiss that left them both dizzy and weak. Then she moved from the bed and took his hand, leading him back into the living room.

"It's time for you to go back to the hotel now. It's after three. Paula will be here in six hours to go shopping, so I've got to get some sleep."

He was hurt that she couldn't tell him she loved him, couldn't say she'd marry him. Something kept holding her back, but he wasn't going to let that stop him. He believed he could persuade her eventually.

"Where's my little A.G.?" Amanda called out as she burst into the Livingston house through the back door into the service porch that led to the kitchen.

"We're in here!" Paula answered from the family room. "Watching the game."

Amanda took off her coat and left it in the kitchen draped over a chair. "Gimme that little bear!" She reached for A.G. in the playpen and picked him up; giving him enough hugs and kisses to last a lifetime. "You little baby bear … baby, baby bear … you're my favorite little cub, yes, you are. I'm going to eat you all up. Yum, yum, yum."

A.G. began giggling as she nuzzled under his chin and blew on his neck.

"So, where's Richard?" Drake asked. He guzzled his beer and got up from the leather recliner to get another one.

"He's driving out by himself. Called and said he wasn't sure when he'd be through with the meeting."

They all heard the horn honk.

60

"There he is now." Drake rushed towards the back door.

"Well, I guess he's excited about seeing Richard," Amanda said as she put A.G. back into the playpen and then sat down next to Paula.

"More excited than you are, little sister?"

Amanda smiled at Paula.

"What's going on, Amanda?"

"I'm making an announcement today."

"Oh, Amanda!" She reached over and hugged her before Amanda could respond.

"Where's my little darlin'? Where is she?" Richard didn't take the time to take off his sheepskin jacket as he barreled through the kitchen and set a cooler box on the table. "It's been two weeks since I've seen my woman. There you are! Come here, you little angel." He headed straight for Amanda.

She stood up and he smothered her with an embrace and a kiss that would melt the thickest glacier in the Swiss Alps.

"I don't think I could have made it one more hour without you in my arms. I'm never going to be away from you that long again. Never." He turned towards Drake and Paula. "I love this woman, you know that. And I want to make this formal right now." He reached into his pocket and withdrew a red velvet ring box. He opened it and took a 10-carat ring from its perch and lifted Amanda's left hand. "Will you marry me, Amanda?"

Amanda's face flushed and her pulse quickened. She was having trouble breathing, gasping.

"She's going to faint, Richard!" Paula rushed to her side and they guided her to the sofa.

"No, no. I'm all right. It's okay. Could I have a drink, please?" She turned pale as she leaned her head back on the sofa and looked up at Richard, tears in her eyes.

"The champagne is in the cooler I set on the kitchen table, Drake. Let's have a toast."

"You got it!" Drake hurried to the kitchen.

Richard reached again for Amanda's hand.

"Richard, sit here beside me." She patted the seat. "I have something I want to say. C'mon, sit down." She took a couple deep breaths, looking back and forth at the faces of Richard and Paula.

Drake returned with four flutes and the open bottle of champagne. "Here we go, time to celebrate." He began pouring and handing out the glasses.

Amanda hesitated while the three happy faces stared at her, waiting. She lifted her glass. "A toast to this lovely man who I adore more than any other. To you, my dear Richard."

They all took a sip.

She looked down at the glass she held in her lap. "But … I'm going to Bruges, Richard. I have my plane ticket," she continued as her eyes met his, "and I've taken a leave of absence from work. I'll be leaving on Thursday and will be gone at least two months. So I can't commit to marrying you just yet." She reached for Richard's hand and looked at Paula. "I don't know what lies ahead for me; y'all can understand that, can't you?"

Richard was paralyzed. Paula was wide-eyed and Drake's mouth fell open. They all stared at Amanda. No one spoke. The silence was a departure for them. Even A.G. was quiet; it was as if he understood that now was the time to be silent.

"I made the decision and finalized it last week. I'd planned to tell y'all today. Wanted to surprise you. You know this is what I've always wanted to do. All three of you know that. It hasn't been a secret. And, Richard, I didn't know you were going to do this today. I'm so sorry. I don't want to hurt you. But it's been my dream since I don't know when to go to Belgium. I just have to. Paula, you know how I feel." The tears were spilling from her eyes. What she'd hoped would be a happy announcement was turning out to be a fiasco.

Richard blinked back his own tears and squeezed her hand. "Well, we can get married on Wednesday and I'll go with you. I'll take the time off. We'll make it a honeymoon, darling. I'd love to show you Europe. Venice, Paris, the Swiss Alps, and all the places you want to see. I'll take you."

"No, Richard. I have to do this by myself. Please try to understand. Please?" She stood up and walked towards the window and watched the Kern River flowing by through the trees.

Richard had recognized the determination and sincerity in her eyes, and the pain. Of course he realized what going to Bruges meant to her and he suddenly felt he'd managed to make it harder for her to be joyous. He went to her and turned her to face him.

"My darling, I do understand. I shouldn't have sprung this on you like I did. I know you need to do what you've got to do. And I'll be right here waiting for you when you get back. You can bet on that. Drake, pour us some more champagne, let's celebrate! My baby's going to Belgium!"

Drake snapped out of his stupor and topped off the glasses.

"I want you to hang on to this ring, darling. It's yours, regardless of what happens." He slipped the ring on her finger and closed her hand in his. "I know that one day you'll be my bride. I can wait for that day." His voice cracked and he used his fingers to wipe his tears.

Amanda covered her face and began weeping.

Richard drew her to him and held her close. "No, no, my dearest Amanda. Please don't cry. I don't want you to cry. Come on, now. Let's celebrate your dream trip. Okay?" He held her at arms' length and grinned at her. "I mean it, darlin'. No more tears. You don't want to make a grown man crumble at your feet, do you?"

Paula reached for her, too. "Now, come on, honey. You just sit down and tell us all about your plans. How're you gonna get to the airport? This is really good news, you know. Ain't it, Drake? She's finally going to Europe. Can you believe it? Your dream is comin' true, Miss Amanda Jeffries— I mean Conroy! We ain't gonna mention that scalawag Arlie's name anymore!"

They laughed.

She pulled Amanda to the sofa and sat down next to her. "Now, show me that monstrous rock on your finger. That's the biggest dad-gummed diamond I've ever seen in my whole life! Drake, how come you never gave me one of these? Huh?"

The laughter grew and they all began celebrating Amanda's dream that was finally coming true.

Chapter 14

For over eighteen months Arlie had lived in the small copper mining town of Miami, which was situated between another mining town called Superior and the county seat of Gila County, Globe, Arizona. The area was generally referred to as Globe-Miami.

Miami is in the Tonto National Forest with a population of around 2,000, a residential community, not much going on otherwise.

The original downtown area consists of boarded-up buildings, shacks, and dozens of antique stores. As for bars and eateries, in a three or four block-square area, there is an art gallery/coffee shop on Sullivan Street, an outdoor bar shaded between its neighboring antique shops on Miami Avenue, but most of the locals frequent the Shamrock Bar which is on the main highway and Judy's Cook House toward Globe. Mexican restaurants are also spaced on the main drag between Miami and Globe. Miami is a collector's paradise, not a culinary haven.

The two men who had found Arlie – Scott and Jimmy – were employees of the Miami copper mine. But after Arlie's lengthy stay in the hospital and his slow recovery, their failed attempt to get him a job at the mine without I.D. or memory turned out to be a godsend. Scott decided to start his own construction company, something he'd wanted to do for years. So Arlie became his partner, for he proved himself to be as talented a carpenter as he was an electrician. Jimmy stayed with the mine, unable to afford the drop in pay for a new enterprise.

Scott was divorced and owned one of the larger shacks in downtown Miami on Gibson Street. So Arlie bunked with him.

A small town seemed right to Arlie. He didn't want to go anywhere else. It felt comfortable. He felt as if he'd always lived there, but he still couldn't remember who he was or where he came from.

Although his lower back had been broken, it mended after being in traction for seven months. His legs and his left arm had healed miraculously, but he was left with a slight limp.

Now Arlie was known as John Cramer, a name the hospital staff had given him when he couldn't remember his own. His wallet wasn't on him when he was found. There was nothing else in his pockets, no car keys, no money. It was as if he had been dropped from the road with a bullet wound through his shoulder. Nothing else was known about him, except that he must have been married, he wore a wedding band. That bothered Arlie more than anything else. Somewhere he had a wife. He wondered if he had children.

The new John Cramer had been examined and tested by a neurosurgeon and was told he had suffered memory loss due to the concussion. The doc said his memory would eventually come back, that he needn't panic. Most amnesia victims begin to regain bits and pieces if not in a few days, then in a few weeks. But it had been a year and a half and no bits and pieces had surfaced in Arlie's memory.

The gunshot wound had raised questions from the sheriff's department when he'd been hospitalized. They'd taken his fingerprints, but nothing came up in the system. He was truly a John Doe, or rather a John Cramer.

Little did they know, the pickup truck had been hauled off by a desperate passerby teenager. The shooter, being the professional that he was, had picked up the bullet casings. As for Arlie's wallet with his I.D. and money, it was never found.

So eventually life went on as usual, as it does in most small towns.

Arlie Jeffries was dead and gone. John Cramer was alive and well.

Rebecca Randolph Buckley

PART TWO

"Your thoughts and your feelings create your life. It will always be that way. Guaranteed!"

Lisa Nichols
The Secret

Rebecca Randolph Buckley

Chapter 15

RACHEL O'NEILL

Another beautiful summer day, Rachel O'Neill thought while stepping from the shower and glancing through the open French doors at the view from her bedroom to the garden and the sea beyond.

The aroma of roses, carnations, and hyacinths mixed with the crispy, cool salty sea air gave her a euphoric high as it always did. This was her favorite part of the world. She looked up into the sky where black clouds were overtaking the white ones, forming billowing picturesque subjects over the ocean. *Perfect watercolor paintings* she thought, remembering art classes she'd taken years previously. Storm clouds were the best subjects.

Storms weren't unusual on the southwest coast of England in the summer. Glorious summer storms were especially of the norm in the Newlyn and Mousehole harbors, which was one of the reasons Rachel bought a cottage in

Cornwall. The first time she had visited the area with Ethan Philips it had been a stormy Christmastime, and she was immediately hooked by the dramatic and romantic ambiance of her favorite author Daphne du Maurier's world, creator of *Rebecca, My Cousin Rachel*, and *The Birds,* to name a few … du Maurier was the most successful Cornish novelist of all time.

Rachel agreed fully with Daphne's description of Cornwall: *"Beautiful, mysterious, Cornwall exerts a potent spell on all who visit it."*

For hours Rachel would sit at her window spellbound, much like Daphne, watching violent lightning and thunder storms move from the sea to hover over the southwestern coast of England. Sometimes she would open her French doors and breathe in the fresh cold air that gave her an abundance of energy and fueled her creativity.

In the summer the Cornwall coast was also full of blossoms and butterflies and chirping birds, in spite of the occasional storms.

Not only did Rachel love her cottage on the cliff, she loved the fishing boats in Newlyn Bay below, with their clanking lines battering the masts making mysterious night music.

Newlyn was one of the few working fishing ports remaining in the UK, and hosted the second largest fishing fleet in the country – vessels of all sizes. The Pilchard Factory had recently closed, which was a sad event. It had been in operation for ninety years. When Rachel first arrived, the Pilchard factory was still in operation. She had spent many mornings soaking up the local color at the factory, watching and listening to the fishermen and the factory packers at work.

In the summer the primary catch was silver mackerel. How she loved walking to the Newlyn Fish Market where the fish were sold. The fish were held in rectangular baskets of all colors, neatly stacked, and ticketed waiting for a buyer in the auction - from dovers to hand-line caught tuna to monk to lemons to John Dorey.

She was thinking she might make a quick trip to the docks and see what fish were available that morning. She was feeling she might want to cook some for dinner.

Reaching for the plush towel she'd thrown over the white wicker chair near the French doors that opened onto the patio, she began humming George Gershwin's "Summertime" while rubbing the water from her hair and face, followed by a quick, brisk drying of her body from her neck down to the soles of her feet. She was feeling that life was grand.

"You are lovely as a 'n noeth angel." Pete's voice startled her."

"Oh! I didn't hear you come in." She laughed as she dropped the towel and went to him, standing on tiptoes to reach her hands up around his neck while pressing her nudeness against his fully-clothed body. She'd come a long way from the days she couldn't bear to let anyone see her naked, including her first two husbands, not even Ethan. With Pete it had all gone by the wayside. He made her feel sexy and free. She adored him and wanted him to have every bare inch of her. He made her feel proud of the body of which she once felt ashamed.

Pete swept her up into his arms and carried her into the bedroom.

"No, no, no," she giggled. "I have to get dressed, darling. I have an appointment this morning."

"All arhosa!" he replied in his native Welsh.

"Pete, speak English. What is all arhosa?"

"It means it can wait, my luv, it can wait." He grinned widely, tossing her onto the bed and following after he pulled off his clothing as fast as he could. "You drive me mad, woman, 'n arbennig pryd 'ch re 'n noeth."

"English!"

"Especially when you're naked," he whispered as he nuzzled her neck.

She loved Pete's eagerness and his passion. He had made her believe her body was beautiful and he'd helped remove her shyness and terror of being nude in front of a man. He'd taught her that making love was the ultimate experience between a man and woman. She'd lived her whole life afraid of sex and the vulnerability it presented. It took Pete to change her feelings.

She couldn't help but notice the franticness Pete was showing in this morning's lovemaking. He usually was more gentle and a genius at foreplay. But not this time, it appeared. The passion was there, in fact it was at a frenzied high, and she had to admit she was enjoying it for a change. It made her giggle.

"My luv, my luv … " He was devouring her breasts with his hands and his lips. He slowly flicked his tongue down her body past her navel, teasing her till he reached her female softness where he found what he was looking for. She sighed and squirmed with utter rapture.

Suddenly he rolled over on his back, placing her on top of him, pulling her hips to his. His huge hands held her buttocks in place as he entered her with ease and began the slow, rhythmic movements that she loved so much.

Later Pete sat on the edge of the bed beside Rachel and lifted her hand to his lips. "I have to leave for London in a couple of hours, luv." He searched her green eyes for the reaction he knew was coming.

She frowned and stared into his eyes, not saying anything.

"You knew it would be soon, doll. You knew I'd be leaving again."

"Where to this time?" she asked quietly, turning away.

"The Amazon."

"Not again!" Rachel looked at him with a frown and sighed deeply.

"Yes, luv. The deforestation is happening at an alarming rate now, and we have to get in there to rescue samples before plant life as we know it will be completely destroyed. The country is being plundered, Rachel. These are critical times. We've discussed this."

She looked down at their clasped hands in resignation, "I know. I know."

"Be happy for me, Rachel. You know I love doing what I do. Please don't make it difficult for me. I love you and I need your support."

She stood in front of him and put her arms around his neck, while he remained seated on the bed, his face pressed against her breasts.

"I don't mean to be a shrew, darling. I'll just miss you, that's all. I'm so afraid something will happen to you again. I couldn't go through another plane crash, wondering if you're alive or dead, and that jungle is treacherous."

"There won't be another plane crash, luv. The chances of it happening again are next to none. Besides, we're flying into a major airport, not taking a puddle-jumper this time. And we're going up river by boat, so there won't be any small planes involved at all. I'll be safe."

"So how long will you be gone, then?"

"I'm not sure exactly. Three or four months. I'll know more after we get there. Might be up to six, I won't lie to you."

"Why didn't you tell me before now? That's not fair, Pete."

He stood and held her close to him, tightly. "I didn't have the heart to tell you. I knew how you'd feel and I couldn't bear seeing it in your eyes. This way I only have to bear it for an hour or so."

"Not fair, Pete! Not fair at all!" She pulled away from him and grabbed her towel on the way to the bathroom and slammed the door. In the next instant she re-opened the door and flew back into his arms, crying. "I'm sorry, I'm so sorry. I don't know why I act this way. I love you, my darling, and I will miss you so much." She held on to him as if it would be the last time they'd be together.

"I love you, too. And when I get back we'll take a holiday to Paris, if you'd like. How's that, does that sound good to you?"

Trying to hold back the sobs, she looked up into her tall lover's kind eyes, more in love with him than ever. She kissed his chin. "Yes, that would be perfect. Yes. I'll make sure the house is ready for us, Montmartre will be perfect for an anniversary getaway – we can go to Maxim's, reserve the same table where you proposed to me. We'll invite Robert and Janet, too. Maybe Shellie and Adrian will be in town. Yes, that will be fun. I'll get dressed and we can have a cup of coffee together before you go, then I'll take you to the train station. I'll cancel my appointment."

"All right, luv." He patted her on the bottom and gave it a loving squeeze as she turned away.

"Hey, stop that."

They both laughed until she disappeared into the bathroom and he began putting on pants.

He called out to her, "Why don't we get married this Christmas, luv? Don't you think we've been engaged long enough? Two years is plenty of time, don't you think?" He held his breath, waiting for an answer.

Rachel immediately appeared in the doorway, grinning from ear to ear. "Do you mean it? You really want to?"

"It's time, luv. That ring on your finger needs its matching mate."

"You're sure you want to? I mean, you're the one who said there's no rush."

He walked to her and put his arms around her, "Do fi m 'n ddiball , 'm cara."

"English, English!"

"Yes, I'm sure, my luv."

"Oh, I am so ready to marry you, Pete Bell. I am so ready!"

Chapter 16

The next day went by fast. Rachel didn't think of Pete as much as she thought she would, but then it had only been a day and night. Her thoughts were taken up with the subject matter of her next novel. After a two-month break since she'd submitted the previous novel to her agent, she was ready to get back to work on another one. She'd already decided where the setting of her new novel would be. So she figured she'd go there for a couple of months, or however long it would take to write the first draft. The timing was perfect since Pete would be away for a while.

As she walked from her cottage down the alleyways to the bus stop in the center of Newlyn (she liked taking the bus to Mousehole instead of driving the two miles), she was thinking how happy she'd been in Paris with Shellie and Janet just two years before when Pete had made the last trip to South America. His plane had crashed and he had gone missing for weeks before he and the pilot were found close to death.

Tears came to her eyes as she thought about almost losing her beloved Pete. She was grateful for the time they'd had together over the past couple of years, although their individual business travels often took them to separate destinations. Now they were to be married. She wondered if that would change anything. Probably not. They both still had their work—Pete had the Eden Project, she, her writing—and the travel that came along with it all. There shouldn't be a problem.

She stopped to smell a rose along the alleyway. Tears pricked her eyes again as her thoughts shifted to Ethan and the tragic way he had died. That was before she and Pete were engaged. She'd known Ethan before she met Pete.

Several years before Pete came into her life, she had come to England to help her friend Ethan with his business. He'd wanted to marry her, but she couldn't do it. She just didn't want to have to deal with a man and his demands - any man.

Then when Pete and Rachel had grown apart due to commitment issues, Ethan had stepped back into her life for a moment. Only a moment, for he'd crashed his car near Penzance on the way to see her and hadn't survived. It took a long time for Rachel to get over the guilt she felt for his death. She wasn't sure she was over it yet.

A foreboding feeling was increasing as she walked along the street and crossed the bridge by the post office to the bus stop. She shook off the feeling and deliberately began concentrating on the novel she was going to write. Her thoughts were about the novel the rest of the two-mile trip on the bus to Mousehole.

Rachel couldn't wait to get to Belinda's studio and tell her the good news about the December wedding. Hopefully Paul would be at the shop, too. She'd tell them both at the same time. She knew it would be difficult for them to go to Paris for the wedding with the two children, but she was going to invite them anyway. Maybe the timing would be right for them to check on their artworks at the gallery in Montmartre. They were her dearest friends, her closest friends, and they'd been through so much together in the past few years. It was as if she was a magnet to drama and tragedy – her own as well as that of her friends. She chuckled at the thought of a *drama magnet* and opened the heavy door leading into the shop.

Paul and Belinda Newland had named the shop *Newland Gallery near Newlyn,* even if it was in Mousehole. Rachel was amused every single time she saw the sign above the door.

"Hello, anybody home?" She glanced next door through the opening they'd cut through the thick wall to join two shops. Dudley wasn't in his rock shop, either. "Yoohoo, where are you? I'm a thief and can steal everything in sight!"

Paul came bounding down the stairs, laughing. "Well, you can try to, if you want. But you won't get far." He reached for Rachel and gave her a big bear hug.

Rachel never ceased to feel a thrill when Paul hugged or kissed her. It would immediately take her back to the first night they met, a kiss between strangers at the stroke of midnight on New Year's Eve in Trafalgar Square four years before. She would never forget that kiss and how she had felt. She just adored the guy, and she adored Belinda and their two sons.

"Well, I could have been a couple of guys, you know. They could have stolen all the stuff."

"Nah. I would have heard them. So what brings you out today? You ride the bus?"

"Of course."

"I'll take you home when you're ready," Paul offered. "No sense in taking the bus back."

"I don't mind."

"I know, but I'm going into town anyway."

"Where's Belinda?" Rachel asked.

"Took the boys to the doc for their regular checkup." Paul reached under the counter and pulled out a ledger.

"They're okay, right? Nothing wrong?"

"It's just a routine check, nothing's wrong. She said she wanted to get a checkup, too, while she's there. So I guess that'll take all day by the time she runs errands and goes shopping. You know. And whatever else you girls do when you go to town. I'm meeting them for dinner at the Queen's Hotel ... another artist friend and her family are joining us."

Rachel nodded and grinned. "Well, I just came by to tell you both that Pete and I are getting married in Paris this Christmas."

Paul's eyes widened before his grin did. "Are you kidding me? You're actually getting married? To Pete?"

"Well, who else would it be, if not to Pete?" Rachel was laughing at his response.

"I mean—I just—I can't believe it's finally going to happen. The bugger didn't tell me."

"He barely told me before he left."

"Christmas, huh?"

"Yes. And I would love to have you and Belinda there if you can do it."

"Of course we'll come. Yes. You can count on that. Belinda will be thrilled." He hesitated, then moved to Rachel and reached for her shoulders, gazing into her eyes. "Are you happy, Rachel? Is this what you really want?"

For a second Rachel couldn't answer the question. Whenever Paul touched her, it always rattled her. Then she blurted out, "Yes, yes, of course I'm happy." She backed up toward the door.

She wasn't as convincing to Paul as she thought she was.

"I've got to run ... starting my next novel, you know ... I'm going to Brussels on Friday."

"Brussels?" Paul leaned back on the desk and sat on its edge.

81

"Research for my next novel."

"Sounds heavenly. I miss traveling as much as I used to when I was a single man." He grinned, his blue eyes sparkling in the reflection of the sun streaming through the windows.

"Well, it might be a quick trip this time. Maybe just a month, I don't know. Or two. Anyway, I'll be back in time to get everything together for Paris."

She admired this man standing before her with the faint smell of Calvin Klein's Obsession for Men, a scent he always wore. He was just the opposite of Pete. Pete was a rugged handsome. Paul was romance novel book-cover handsome. He wore his long, thick blond hair tied back at his neck, had smooth, tanned skin, wasn't overly muscular, just toned. She'd been attracted to him since the first moment she had laid eyes on him, long before he married Belinda and before she met Pete.

They had first met on a New Year's Eve when she and Ethan were in London. She first saw Paul after she and Ethan were leaving dinner at the Ritz to get to Trafalgar Square before the midnight festivities. Paul was ushering a group of Japanese clients from the Ritz into a limo next to the taxi she and Ethan were about to enter. At that time Paul was a creative director for an advertising agency.

That night outside the Ritz her eyes had connected with Paul's and a thrill shot through her. Then at Trafalgar Square in the midst of the New Year's Eve celebrations, just a few minutes after seeing him at the Ritz, Rachel was thrust into the back of him on the front lines of the crowd at the Trafalgar fountains. Hundreds of people attempted to enter the crowded square. He managed to turn around and they kissed when the countdown hit midnight. She never would forget that kiss and the way he had slipped his hand around her waist and held her close.

Their paths had crossed two more times during that weekend; it was uncanny, it was as if they were destined to be in each other's lives, but in a configuration she would never have guessed.

A couple months later, after the coincidental (or was it?) meetings on that New Year's weekend in London, they ran into each other on the south coast of Cornwall and began an actual friendship.

During that year, four years ago, it was Paul who had had to deal with his own demons. It was Paul who had fallen in love with Belinda after a cruel and merciless gang rape she had endured and survived. It was Paul who had saved Rachel in California from a sure death. It was Paul who was the pivotal male in the two women's lives.

Rachel crossed the room to Paul and gave him a quick goodbye hug. "Tell Belinda to call me when she gets back, will you?"

"I will. So you're leaving on Friday?"

"Yes, and I'll give Belinda the hotel number where I'm staying, and of course I'll have my cell phone with me."

"Then how about dinner on Thursday night before you go? Belinda would love that. We'll get a sitter for the boys and drive over to Marazion. I'll call Margaret and let her know we're coming."

"That would be fabulous, Paul. Thank you."

"We'll pick you up at 6:30."

"Okay. Bye then." She opened the door.

"Wait a minute," said Paul, "I'm driving you home. I'll get my keys."

"No, no, no. Please. It's still early and I do love that bumpy bus ride back to Newlyn. I want to go into a couple of the shops here before I leave, anyway. Next time, Paul. Thanks. Really."

She was relieved to be out of Paul's reach. There was just something that took hold of her when she was around him, when it was just the two of them together.

She shook her head as she ambled down the lane towards the bayfront shops in Mousehole. She felt exhilarated and energized. Not only did the sea air do that to her, Paul did it, too.

She forced thoughts of Pete back into her mind. He was the one she should be thinking of, she told herself, not her best friend's husband.

Chapter 17

It was Thursday evening and the five-mile drive to Marazion, the oldest chartered town in Cornwall dating all the way back to the 1300s, was quick and full of excited conversation between Rachel and Belinda. They hadn't seen each other for days and it was catch-up time.

Paul grinned while he listened to the chatter of the two women he adored most in the world. He would turn and look at his lovely, fragile wife periodically, whose animal sculptures were as popular as his gigantic contemporary paintings. When he would approach a new gallery to show their works, the sellers were always as impressed with her metal works of art and their iridescent Ammolite stones used as eyes as they were with his colorful nude interpretations on canvas.

Paul and Belinda Newland were the perfect team, something he realized soon after Belinda quit the international advertising firm where he was creative director and she was a graphic designer. Then when they fell in love, he left the corporate advertising world himself, left London, and both he and Belinda opened the studios in Mousehole. His studio was

85

upstairs, hers at street level next door to their rock shop friend, Dudley.

As they rode past Penzance, Paul was thinking of their first days in Cornwall after they were married, and how their lives had become entwined with Rachel's.

"So what did the doctor say, Belinda?" Rachel's question severed Paul's train of thought.

"What part do you want to hear?" Belinda asked.

Belinda's frown and quick glance at Paul was obvious as Rachel leaned forward from the back seat. "Is everything all right?"

"Yes, of course. We all have a clean bill of health. No need to worry." Belinda turned and looked out the passenger window a bit too quickly in Rachel's estimation.

Rachel felt something not ringing true in Belinda's behavior and words. She decided not to press it any further for the moment; she'd drill her on the way to the station tomorrow. Belinda was taking Rachel to the train station the next morning.

"So, Rachel, tell us about the book you're going to write in Brussels," Paul said as he looked at her in the rearview mirror.

She leaned back against the seat and took a deep breath. The mood had changed in the car. It felt awkward. Something was amiss, she was sure of it. "Well, it's a murder mystery about a Belgian hat maker who falls for an American spy in Brussels."

Belinda turned quickly toward Rachel, delighted with the possibility. "So which is the woman, the spy or the hat maker?"

Rachel laughed. "Which do you think she should be?"

"Make her the spy."

"Good idea. The woman is the spy then."

"How does she meet the hat maker?" asked Belinda.

"Well—"

Belinda quickly inserted, "I got it … have her meet him in one of those shops on the way to the Grand Place in Brussels.

Maybe next to a chocolate shop, or a lace shop, there are so many of them. Maybe she buys chocolates and then stands outside his hat shop window, watching people and gorging. Then she turns and looks at the hats displayed in his window. He sees her, notices how beautiful she is, of course she's drop-dead gorgeous. Then he comes to the door and invites her in to try on a hat that he thinks will be perfect for her. And maybe he's a spy, too. A Russian spy."

Rachel laughed. "You should be writing the story, Belinda."

"I've always wanted to write. I've definitely read tons of romance novels in my lifetime, if that counts for anything."

"I can attest to that. Our library is half-filled with the romantic novels she's read," Paul added.

"It was all I did in my spare time. I never dated. After university I got the all-consuming position with the agency and when I wasn't working, or sculpting, or helping my mother with the B&B, I was reading. That was my love life – romance novels. I lived vicariously through the heroines. But I don't read so much anymore now that I have my own Prince Charming and two wonderful boys."

"I was hoping you'd say that, luv." Paul reached over and squeezed her knee. "You had me worried there for a minute." They laughed.

Quietness filled the air space, still an obvious awkwardness felt. At least Rachel and Belinda felt it.

Their attention was soon drawn to the magnificent view of the approaching Mount St. Michaels at the end of the causeway that led from Marazion through the waters of the bay.

Dinner would be at the Godolphin Inn with the best view of the bay and St. Michaels Mount straight out from it. On the beach below the inn the causeway led thousands upon thousands of annual trekkers from the mainland to the medieval castle and its hanging gardens and the remains of a village at its base – now occupied by food and tourist shops.

Marazion was one of Rachel's favorite places. Before she moved to Cornwall or had even seen Marazion, she had dreamt that in a past life she was a school teacher of another century, living in Newlyn, and would boat to St. Michael's Mount to teach the children in the village. It was below the Godolphin Inn, in her dreams, where she had met a lord from Charlestown who became her husband centuries before.

Those thoughts filled her mind as Paul pulled up to the inn. She and Pete had actually found the estate in her dreams after she moved to Cornwall and had discovered that she was identical to a female subject in one of its paintings, still hanging.

Paul quickly hopped out of the car and opened the doors for the ladies. "You girls go on in, Margaret's waiting for you. I'll find a parking space."

Tears filled Rachel's eyes as she remembered the same exact words being spoken by Pete on their first date at exactly this same spot. It seemed so long ago. She was beginning to miss him.

Chapter 18

"So tell me what the doctor said," Rachel blurted out as soon as Belinda picked her up to take her to the train station.

"He said the boys are in perfect health; they're the correct weight and height for their ages, and—"

"That's not what I mean, and you know it." Rachel shifted in the passenger seat, half facing her best friend behind the wheel.

"No, I don't know what you mean." Belinda still didn't look at Rachel. She started up the engine and headed back down the lane to get on the coastal road to Penzance.

"Belinda, something is wrong, I feel it. You know I sense things, and I sense that something is wrong and you're not telling me."

Belinda glanced at her for a moment, and then pulled over to the side of the road. "Okay, if you must know, I'll tell you. But I haven't told anyone else, not Paul, not my mother. It's between you and me, promise?"

"Yes, I promise."

"I'm pregnant again."

"And?" Rachel held her breath.

"And the doctor said he wants to run some tests because there's an abnormality in the blood tests he took several days ago. I didn't tell Paul I've been having some unusual symptoms."

"Like what?"

"I have a lump under my left arm, and another one, here, at the base of my neck. And I have been so tired in the past couple months. It's such a chore to get out of bed every morning. By noon I can hardly hold my head up. I'm always tired."

Rachel gasped. "What did he say about that?"

"Well, he's not sure, but he's testing me for lymphoma."

"No! No!" Rachel reached over and hugged Belinda as they both began to weep.

"He's not sure, Rachel. So I'm not going to say anything until I know. Please don't tell Paul." Belinda wiped her eyes with tissue. "It's so hard keeping it all inside, but I'm glad you pulled it out of me. I feel much better now."

"What about the pregnancy?"

"He said if I do have lymphoma, it would be best to abort the baby. But I don't want to think about that right now." She pulled the car back onto the road.

"You'll take chemo, definitely," Rachel said. "You have to do that if it turns out you have it."

"If I take chemo I'll have to abort the baby first. If I don't take chemo, I can carry the baby, and then do the chemo after it's born."

"We shouldn't talk like you have it. There might be another explanation for why you're tired and have those lumps."

They both knew there wasn't.

"I hate to leave you like this," Rachel murmured. "Maybe I shouldn't go away just now."

"Don't be crazy! I'm going to be fine. As soon as I find out I'll tell Paul and Mother. If it is lymphoma. And then we'll decide. But whatever it is, you'll only be away a month or two."

"Okay, but please call me as soon as you hear the test results. Promise?"

"I promise."

Rachel hurried down the platform to get on the train to Exeter where she would be catching the plane to Brussels.

"Call us when you get there!" Belinda yelled.

"I will!" Rachel called back. She boarded the train five minutes before it pulled out of the station.

Rachel lifted her notebook from her bag and began making a list of what she needed to do first when she arrived in Brussels. First she would do a thorough research on the Internet about lymphoma.

Her cell phone rang.

"Hello, babe. Are you on the train?"

"Pete! Hello, darling. I'm so glad you called. Where are you?"

"We're in Belem, refreshing our supplies. Tomorrow we're heading back up the river."

"Are you all right?"

"Yes, luv. You needn't worry. There's a bit of trouble with the poachers but we're careful about keeping our distance. It's beautiful here, luv. I wish you were with me."

"I wish I were, too, except I don't think I could take all those insects and reptiles. That will keep me away from South America more than anything else. In fact I know I couldn't bear it there. So it's much better that we meet in Paris, darling. That's more my style."

Pete laughed.

"I miss you so much, Pete."

"Miss you, too, doll. I'll call you when you get to Brussels. Love you."

"Love you, too," she whispered, tears gathering in her eyes. She wanted to tell him about Belinda, but she'd promised.

"Have a safe trip, doll."

"You, too." She closed her phone and leaned her head back and shut her eyes, suddenly feeling depressed and very, very tired.

PART THREE

"When you visualize, then you materialize."

Dr. Dennis Waitley
The Secret

Chapter 19

It had been a warm, cloudless June day when Amanda arrived at the Brussels National Airport near Zaventum. She felt lost and at a complete disadvantage not knowing any of the languages that the people around her were speaking. The overhead signage was not in English, but she could make out what some of them meant by the graphic icons next to the wording. She knew she had to take a train to Bruges, but didn't know where she was supposed to catch it. After she cleared customs, she saw a train symbol and followed the arrows along with droves of other people doing the same. She figured they all couldn't be wrong.

Having gone through a rather lengthy combination of flights to Belgium, Amanda was thrilled she had finally landed in Europe. Luckily the connecting plane from Chicago was not full and she didn't feel as if she was a sardine in a tin as she had felt on the flight from California to Chicago.

That flight had been implausible. She'd wondered why the seats were so close together. Her knees were hitting the seat in front of her and she couldn't use the communal armrest because a man sitting next to her hogged it. It was a miserable flight. So she had tried to sleep most of the way, crammed into her corner against the window. Good thing she'd been tired to begin with.

The second leg of the flight had been much better. She'd had an extra seat to spread to and had caught up on some sleep, since she'd stayed awake with excitement the night before she left.

Richard had taken her to dinner the night before, so that had killed some of the waiting time. And she'd invited him into her apartment afterwards where they'd looked through magazines and talked till the wee hours of the morning. She was still keeping him at bay sex-wise, and he didn't seem to mind at all. At least he wasn't pressuring her. She was grateful for that. But she had to admit she wondered how it would be to make love to him, although she dismissed the thought from her mind just as soon as it appeared.

So here she was in Belgium at last! As it turned out the train station in the airport was relatively easy to find, she was right about the train icon and arrows.

She'd read that French was spoken mainly in Brussels, and Dutch in Bruges, but people were friendly and helpful enough, even in gesturing, so she was able to get where she wanted to go.

After leaving the airport she changed trains once in the center of Brussels, at Brussels Nord, and then found a comfy seat at a table on the second train where she settled in to enjoy the remainder of the trip to Bruges, or Brugge … she noticed it was spelled both ways. However, that comfort was short-lived, for the conductor came through and told her she would have to go to the second class car because she was sitting in first class.

She apologized and moved her luggage, two pieces, to a space in between the cars and that's as far as she got … the second class cars were packed. More sardines. She opted to stand up for the duration of the trip in the space between first and second class; making her a no-class passenger ... she chuckled at her self-description. Standing felt pretty good to her, anyway, since she'd been sitting for over thirteen hours as it was.

The train ride through the Belgian countryside reminded her of the photographs and movies she'd seen of the Austrian countryside. Very green, dotted with stone houses and farms, although no mountains as in Austria. The Belgian terrain was flat.

Other than the occasional visits the passengers were making to the toilet (as it turned out she was standing by the toilet in the in-between-cars space), she was alone to take in the lovely views through the narrow panes in the doors. She was happy.

Once in Bruges she headed directly to a coffee concession in the train station. She hadn't had a cup since leaving Chicago. The flight from Chicago didn't have potable water, as it turned out, and they were unable to serve tea or coffee. They even asked that the passengers use the sani-wipes they provided in the restrooms for their hands, asked that they not use the water from the faucet. Evidently there'd been a problem and they hadn't received fresh water before leaving the States. There was bottled water to drink, luckily, but staff had to make a last minute trip into the terminal to get enough of it for the duration of the flight.

So, the coffee in the little Belgian concession stand in the train station tasted a very welcome *perfect*. She sat there and enjoyed every drop of it while she got her bearings and realized where she was. She was in Belgium.

What am I doing here? the question surfaced without a moment's notice. She was suddenly feeling alone in a strange country, not knowing a soul. Sitting with a cup of coffee and two suitcases and all the money she had in the world. This was it. This was the entire package.

She shook off the fear that was beginning to emerge, took a deep breath, and decided to leave the safe spot at the coffee stand and venture out into Belgium. After she bought another cup of coffee to go, the first thing she noticed was how warm the weather was, and then she saw the uneven cobblestoned walkways and streets all around her as she made her way across the huge square to what appeared to be a taxi stop.

She waved to a cab driver and waited for him to pull up to where she was standing. He told her she couldn't drink coffee in his cab and that she'd have to dump it. Sadly she did so.

He turned out to be a very pleasant driver, however; told her a bit about the town as he drove, gave her a map, and took her through the center of Bruges and the Market Square, indicating other points of interest that were within the ring road.

The driver told her that most European cities are situated within a ring - a road encircling the city. When you reach that road from within, you know you're moving into the outer limits. It comes in handy when you're a city-walker.

She noticed that the B&B where she'd be staying was within the ring. The town center was maybe a ten-minute or less walk according to the map, over and alongside canals and shop-lined cobbled streets.

Her hosts Robert van Nevel and Lievetje Gevaert turned out to be pleasant and energetic hosts. Robert spoke English as well as French and Dutch and who knows how many other languages. His appearance reminded her of a bearded, long-haired professor, an intellectual like some of the ones who came into KC's Steakhouse on occasion. Lievetje was a charming woman, still learning English.

Robert built all the furniture in the guest rooms – two bedrooms in their home that they rented out to tourists. It was set up just like a small hotel, however. In the parlor were antiques and collectibles - an antique camera collection that caught Amanda's attention. She'd never seen anything like it.

Carmersstraat appeared to be a very quiet street, with a small grocery store across the lane from the B&B, more like a tiny version of a stateside convenience store, Amanda noted. The Nevel house was a brick and stone sixteenth century building with high ceilings and tall windows opening onto the street below. She was paying 265 euros for five nights. She figured that would give her time to find a place for a longer term. This place didn't have an elevator and the stairs were very steep, so getting her luggage up to her room posed a problem. It took both Lievetje and Amanda to carry the heaviest suitcase because Robert wasn't there when she had arrived. Lievetje did her best to go over everything with Amanda in broken English.

Amanda was very happy to finally be left alone in her comfy room with a bed she immediately sprawled across. At that moment she felt like she might never rise again. Felt like maybe she would spend the next five days in that bed.

Chapter 20

Two days had passed since Amanda arrived in Belgium. She'd slept through the first afternoon and night and the next day and night, only awakening to drink water and to go to the toilet.

The afternoon of the third day she went across the street to the little neighborhood grocery and bought some food that could be eaten without cooking – she was starving. But she still wasn't up to par. The time of day was confusing to her; it felt like it should be nighttime. That was because she was still on California time, and wasn't adapting very well. No one had warned her of jet-lag.

As she sat in her room at a window eating a jar of delicious white asperges (as they spell it in Bruges, *asparagus* in the U.S.), she glanced out the tall open windows to the rooftops of the neighborhood houses lined up across the lane. The front rooflines, or façade, were shaped like stair steps starting from the eves of the building on each side, stair-stepping to meet at the apex in the middle, topped with a chimney-like crest. She noticed that one of the pieces of furniture in her room that Robert van Nevel had built had the same motif on its top edge, same as the roof facades. It was a design used throughout Belgium for furniture as well as roofs - she'd learned in one of her travel books.

That afternoon she was going to venture out and get to know her surroundings. She decided to first take a boat ride through the canals she was dying to see.

So she finished the tasty *asperges* and drank some bottled water and grabbed her shoulder bag. She opened the door to the carpeted stairwell and caught a glimpse of Leitive as she was climbing to the next floor up the narrow staircase.

"How are you, this morning, Lievetje?"

Lievetje backed down a couple steps and bent to see and respond to Amanda's greeting. "Oh. Hello, good afternoon!"

"Y'all are right, it is afternoon. This time change is confusin' the heck out of me. Well, I'm headin' out to check out the town."

"Is good for you in the room?"

"Yes, it's perfect. I just love it."

"I am happy to hear. I will clean while you are away. Bye, now." She continued to climb the stairs without waiting for an answer from Amanda.

Amanda happily sauntered down Carmersstraat toward the canal she could see just up the lane. The narrow lane felt almost like an alleyway with the three- and four-story houses looming above each side of it. It seemed strange walking on cobblestone streets, and pretty tricky. She stumbled a time or two and caught her balance, but didn't fall.

She reached the waterway and breathed in the fresh air as she stood on the middle of the bridge leaning over the balustrade. She could see the boat rental docks on both sides of the canal from where she was standing. Her excitement level was rising.

She hurried to get in line at the first one she reached that was boarding at that moment. The sun was shining and the other people on the sightseeing riverboat were jovial and having fun. Amanda was elated. The tour guide was hilarious and informative. Amanda thought he must be an actor, maybe a comedian. She never dreamed she would be in such a town taking an open boat ride through the canals with other tourists, viewing the buildings from the water's perspective. It was beautiful, just as it was in the magazines she'd treasured for so long. Along the green-bordered canal where professional photographers congregated to snap the abundant foliage, Amanda marveled at the quaint houses and café patios that lined its edges.

The boatman sitting up front steering the boat, as the passengers sat on built-in benches in what resembled long, wooden rowboats, reminded her of the French actor Gerard Depardieu. She'd seen the movie *Green Card* with her sister the week before she left. The boatman's size and looks were almost identical to Depardieu, except that his lengthy unruly hair was sun-bleached and he was tanned from being exposed to the daily elements of his profession. He spoke four languages during the "cruise." Said that most of the elementary school children in Belgium, and all of Europe for that matter, usually learned several languages in school, said it was standard.

Amanda wondered why the American children are only taught English in school. She was thinking what a shame it was. *In Belgium they learn two, three, and sometimes four languages in their elementary school years; they even learn their neighboring country's languages.* She remembered hearing some of the teachers that came into KC's complaining how they were having to learn Spanish to be able to teach the migrant Mexicans infiltrating the California school system. They were downright irate, she recalled. *What is so wrong with learning a neighboring country's language? Wouldn't that be to everyone's advantage?* she thought to herself and then gave her full attention back to the guide. She was so happy.

After the boat ride, Amanda followed her map's suggestion on getting to the town center, the central square called the Markt (without the *e*). From the Markt Square she planned to branch out to view the city each day. That was her plan. She would go to the Markt each morning for coffee and then plan her day as she sat there. But this first afternoon, now quickly becoming early evening, she was heading to the historic Craenenburg Tavern set on the site where at one time Maximilian of Austria, the Holy Roman Emperor, was held captive. The history mesmerized her. She couldn't absorb enough to satisfy her.

She entered through the Craenenburg's front courtyard full of patrons, drinking and soaking up what was left of the late afternoon sun. As she entered the building through tall glass-paned double doors she was immediately drawn to the elaborate amber stained glass windows around the perimeter of the restaurant. The walls and woodwork were in shades of gold to brown.

A friendly waiter welcomed her and gave her the option of sitting wherever she wished. She selected a table along the wall and sat on the long bench that serviced all the tables along that side of the restaurant. Three chairs were added to each in the row of tables to enable them to accommodate four patrons at every table. Throughout the rest of the room, tables were set with four chairs surrounding, and in some cases tables were pushed together to seat even more customers.

The waiter handed Amanda a menu, grinning widely. "What would you like to drink, mademoiselle?"

"Uh, well, I don't know. Let me see ..." Finally she looked up from the menu. That was the first time Amanda actually paid any attention to the waiter, and she was taken aback at the brightness and clarity of his brown eyes, the size of them, and the thick, dark lashes that protected them. His smooth black hair was short and well-groomed, unlike most of the long tousled locks the majority of other young men displayed.

"Well, I suppose I should have a glass of wine to celebrate my first outing in Bruges, wouldn't you think?"

He flashed a big smile. "Yes, of course! So this is your first visit to Bruges?"

"It sure is. First time in Belgium, actually. First time anywhere, other than the U.S."

"How long will you be here?"

"Forever, I hope." She giggled.

"Then yes, of course, you must celebrate. May I suggest a glass of champagne?"

"Oh my goodness. I forgot all about that drink. Yes, that's what I want. A glass of champagne. Thank you for remindin' me." As the waiter left the table, she thought about all the times at KC's when she would watch the couples come in and order bottles of champagne. At the time, she'd wished that she was the one sitting at the tables ordering. Champagne represented romance to her.

Thoughts of Richard crept into her mind. She had such mixed emotions about him. He was a good man, she knew that. And when she was with him she felt she could love him, but away from him she didn't know how she felt. She hardly gave him a thought – out of sight, out of mind, maybe. And she hadn't thought about Arlie at all. That made her feel guilty. How could she not think about her husband, even though he was missing? Shouldn't she feel sad or upset? She had asked herself that many times over the past few months. Her answer was always no, he had run off and left her. So how could she have any feelings for someone who did that to her?

The waiter returned with a bottle of champagne.

"Is that a good one?" she asked, wanting to seem more sophisticated than she was.

"Yes, of course." He popped the cork.

"You did that good!"

"Yes, of course. I am Antoine. You are?"

"Amanda Jefferies." It was too late to correct the mistake, she should have said *Conroy*. It would take some getting used to, she decided.

"Ah! Both A's, Amanda and Antoine." He laughed as he poured, and then set the bottle in an ice bucket nearby. "I'll give you more time to decide what to order. You are having dinner, yes?"

"Yes, of course." She repeated, using the exact inflection Antoine had used.

He nodded and walked away, thinking she definitely was an A in his book. He wanted to get to know this lovely American woman.

Chapter 21

Amanda spent the next few days walking through the neighborhoods, searching out the historical sites and following the streets indicated on the maps. She spent time roaming through the Saint Saviour's Cathedral and stopped in the main chapel to listen to the sounds of its huge pipe organ. The terrific, eerie sounds consumed the airspace and she felt as if she was hearing the actual phantom of the opera playing. She and Paula had driven to Los Angeles to see the famous *Phantom* show at the Shubert Center in West L.A. She'd never seen anything like it, had never been to a stage show. And now the exciting sounds coming from this organ brought back that wonderful experience.

But this was incredible, even more astonishing than the show. She felt that maybe this guy was playing a jillion extra notes that weren't supposed to be in the number. It sounded as if he was pounding on all the keys at once. Incredible! She wished she would have arrived sooner, for it had been a concert and that was the last song.

Amanda learned that the church was built in the gothic style of the fourteenth century and had been continually added to and restored ever since. After a disastrous fire in 1839 a major restoration had been necessary, but the original rusticness still remained. She couldn't help but stand there and feel in awe for the years the building had been in existence and for the multitudes of people who had passed through its doors.

She also visited an even older church, smaller, in Burg Square which was right next to Markt Square. Its huge rustic-hewn pillars were fascinating. Once inside she touched the irregularity of the stones that had been cut and mortared into place to create the columns that held up the church all those years. If they were flattened out it would resemble the pattern of the cobblestone streets. The columns were huge, she thought they had to be at least five feet in diameter. *Solid as a rock certainly applies to the Belgian churches*, Amanda thought as she ran her hands over the columns.

Another day during her explorations she was on her way to the Jerusalem Cathedral in the St. Anna section, near where she was staying. The lace museum was at the Jerusalem church where the nuns ran the center and the classes.

But first she wanted to stop by the Craenenburg to have a cup of coffee and talk to Antoine for a few minutes. She'd been going into the establishment every day to visit with him, sometimes twice a day, sometimes over coffee, sometimes over champagne, sometimes over a meal. Sometimes she would sit outside in the courtyard.

Antoine told her about his two little girls, ages seven and nine. His wife had left Belgium, leaving the girls behind with him. They lived in a building down the side street behind the Craenenburg, in an upstairs flat, so he was close by if they needed him. His mother had a house further down the lane and she took care of them while he was working.

Because it was so warm, the doors were wide open at the Craenenburg, so Amanda decided to go inside instead of sitting on the patio on this particular day.

Antoine was busy tending a large group of diners at the back of the room and didn't see her as she headed for her usual table along the right wall.

When he turned to take the order to the kitchen, he saw her and his face lit up. He waved and hurried into the kitchen.

Antoine brought a smile to Amanda's face, too. He was always so exuberant and cheerful. She'd not seen him in a bad mood at all. She felt he loved his job and she noticed that he treated all his customers accordingly.

"Amanda! How good to see you!" he called out as he hurried back toward her from the kitchen. He bent down and they kissed cheeks, as was the custom. Amanda was a quick study.

"How did the visit turn out last night?" Amanda asked as she watched his expression change from happy to sad.

"Well, it wasn't as good as I had hoped it would be. She spent an hour with the children and then left. It's the girls I'm concerned about, you know. Not Nadia. Nadia is in a world of her own. We were lucky she even came for an hour. The girls cried when she left." His shoulders slumped and his eyes were vacant for a moment.

"I don't see how she can do that to them. She's their mother, ain't she? Doesn't that bother her at all?" Amanda asked.

"No, not at all." His shoulders were slumped.

"I'd love to meet your daughters, Antoine. I miss my little nephew. Maybe on Sunday we can go to the park at the end of Carmmerstraat, where the windmills are—"

"You would do that?

"Yes, of course. I love children."

108

"Perfect! We'll go on Sunday. That is a wonderful idea." His countenance perked up and he was his usual happy self again.

Chapter 22

Before Amanda headed to the St. Anna's quarter, she decided to go back to one of the streets that led in the opposite direction from the Markt that was lined with fashion shops - shoes, clothing, jewelry - to find a flat iron. Hers wasn't working and the adaptor wasn't helping any at all. She needed one that she could plug directly into the Belgian wall sockets.

In watching the people pass her on the lanes, she had been surprised that the fashion trend was gypsy-like. Layers of colorful fabrics, tufted pants and skirts with vests, scarves and other adornments combined to create the masterpieces. The wearers were walking works of art, actually. Then there were the simply dressed: non-trendy dressers, but stylish, too. Monotoned ensembles in beige, brown, and olive green. She could guess who was affluent and who wasn't. Most times. Not always. And tans! They all had tans. She'd heard they usually went to Spain and the south of France to beaches to get their tans. Some would go to Florida.

It took her a while, but she finally found a flat iron for her hair. It was very expensive - $70. But she needed it, so she bought it.

The Jerusalem Cathedral was straight ahead of Amanda. She took a right off Carmmerstraat on Jeruzalemstraat and walked a short distance towards the Kantcentrum where the lace-making took place. The building attached to the church had the same familiar roofline as most others in Bruges, she noticed. Only this one had ten steps from the top edge of each side wall towards the apex of the roofline.

All the buildings in the St. Anna part of town were of drab stone, not much color. Bruges was certainly a town of stone – streets and buildings. But the original Jerusalem Cathedral had been built of wood, and in the fifteenth century the crumbling wood had been replaced with stone.

What amazed Amanda more than anything about Bruges was that the buildings dated back to medieval times. To her it was astonishing that she could be standing and looking at a house that someone else had been standing and looking at over half a millennium before. She could be touching a stone wall that someone five-hundred years prior had been touching.

She walked through the door leading to the Kantcentrum, whose name meant "lace-making." The Kantcentrum started up in 1970, as late as that, to preserve the lace-making industry that had begun there in 1717 by the Sisters Apostle.

After she viewed samples and supplies, as well as catalogs and books on lace-making, in the reception shop, she followed the arrows which guided her through rooms of completed pieces of antique lace. She couldn't get over the intricate work that went into the making of all types of cloths and garments.

The Chantilly laces captivated her most. Their outlined patterns with a flat, untwisted strand of thread, the placard explained, lace made of silk mostly, and usually black. Chantilly lace was originally made in France, but now it was made in Belgium. There were classic Chantilly shawls on display.

What caught her eye next was the Binche lace. And she'd noticed that the center was giving classes on making it, beginning the following week. The patterns were very detailed with animal scenes and figures. And they weren't outlined as Chantilly patterns were.

Next came the room where the lace-makers were working. There were at least a dozen women of all ages, mostly older, sitting at tables tossing their bobbins, weaving the tiny intricate patterns. One woman was tossing them back and forth so fast Amanda couldn't believe she knew what she was doing. It looked like she was shuffling the bobbins on the flat cardboard that held the thread and moving her hands lightning-fast just to be impressive. She definitely was impressive. The pattern was taking form right before Amanda's eyes. She wondered if she'd ever be able to do that. They gave classes to school children, so surely she could master it if they could. She overheard a conversation that one of the makers had just passed away at 102 years of age.

Before she left the center, Amanda enrolled in the class that was to start the following Monday. Happy as a lark, she left the Kantcentrum and walked towards a café on Carmmerstraat near the B&B for dinner to celebrate her decision to learn lace-making.

As she walked she thought of her mother sewing and mending clothing for a living in Arkansas. She thought of when she was a little girl and watched her mother use a needle, weaving in and out of the cloth to make such beautiful hand-sewn dresses for other people. She and her sister's clothing were made from the scraps and leftovers of those dresses. Their mother would piece assorted materials together and come up with such pretty garments for the two of them. But she didn't do it often, because all her time had to be used to make clothing and to do mending for others so the girls could have food on their table. And sad to say, their mother was not well. She was sickly most of their young lives until the day she died and their grandmother stepped in and took care of them till they were teenagers. Then they married their high school sweethearts and left Arkansas after their grandmother died.

Amanda opened the single door of the small café and was met by a friendly elderly gentleman, who ushered her to a table in front of one of the two windows facing Carmmerstraat. She was the first customer of the evening.

Chapter 23

Rachel O'Neill's arrival in Brussels brought back all the memories of the last time she was there. Only that time she had boarded a train to Bruges immediately, not taking in the sights of Brussels City. This time she checked into the luxurious, art nouveau, French Renaissance Metropole Hotel, built in the 1800s near the Grand Place—the most scenic market square in the center of Brussels.

The hotel listed among its famous clients Caruso, Albert Einstein, Madam Curie, Albert Rubinstein, and many more ... actually dozens and dozens more. Rachel was amazed at the endless list of famous guests on the hotel's website. She hadn't seen a list like that on other hotel sites. And of course the Brussels Metropole was a political haven, since Brussels had become the administrative center for the EU, with over a million inhabitants. Including the surrounding suburbs, the population was nearly three million.

She'd always been drawn to the Metropole hotels and preferred staying in them when she traveled throughout the world. It was romantic ambiance that determined her choice of hotels. And the Brussels Metropole was no exception, it was just as she'd visualized. She immediately felt inspired as she stepped through the revolving entrance doors to the right of the well-known sidewalk Metropole Café where sippers and diners were on display in fashionable attire and sunglasses during the warm months and fur coats in winter. A Mecca designed for the beautiful people.

Rachel felt in high spirits and energetic as she always did when she traveled, not a worry or a care in the world. Nothing else mattered but where she was and what she felt at the moment. It was heaven. She was happy to be there.

Chapter 24

Sunday rolled around very quickly for Amanda. Antoine and the girls were going to walk to her place in the St. Anna district and then they would all walk the rest of the way to the park and the windmills, where the old city wall used to be at the end of Carmmerstraat. The medieval city wall had been taken down in the nineteenth century, but two of the gates still remained.

As they walked over St. Anna's Brug (bridge) Antoine gave his daughters a history lesson. He told them about the St. Anna district that they were entering, about the churches, the nuns. Told them about the Alms houses where the elderly lived.

He told them that poverty overtook the town after the Fifteenth century when silt had filled the seaport separating Bruges from the sea and world trade, and Bruges almost became a ghost town. The very rich came to the rescue for the widows and elderly and built Alms houses for them on abandoned properties, the houses were enclosed in a courtyard with one main gate as the entrance. He pointed out the entrances as they walked, marked by small statues of the Virgin Mother. They peeked into one courtyard and saw the rows of charming white houses, petite and quaint, surrounding the gardened courtyard. He told his girls that there were still between thirty or forty of the compounds throughout Bruges.

They walked by the Jeruzalemkerk (church) and he pointed out the Kancentrum, explaining its history. The oldest daughter spoke up and told him that they knew all about the Kancentrum, they'd learned it in school.

He raised his eyebrows and decided the history lesson was over. His desire to teach history had gotten away from him.

As they rounded the corner onto Carmmerstraat they saw Amanda waiting on the front stoop of the B&B.

Amanda had been watching Robert paint the trim on the house. She enjoyed talking to him, for he always shared the history of Bruges with her.

She saw Antoine and the girls turn the corner and head up Carmmerstraat. "Oh, here they come!" she said to Robert.

He stopped painting and looked at the trio sauntering towards them. "A lovely family. You say their mother abandoned them?"

"Yes, isn't that the awfulest thing you ever heard of?"

"Those adorable little girls? Yes, that is awful."

Antoine grinned and called out to Amanda as they came nearer, "Hello, Amanda. Here we are, right on schedule."

She stepped down from the stoop and met him on the lane. They hugged.

"This is my oldest, Elwina, and little Drulette. Girls, this is Amanda, my friend."

"Hello, Elwina, Drulette. You both look so pretty in your yellow dresses! I wish I had one as nice to wear. This is my landlord, Robert Nevel, Antoine."

Antoine reached out and shook Robert's hand. "Hello. Looks like you've taken on a painstaking Sunday job."

"Oh yes. The weekend work of a landlord. Perfect day for it."

"So shall we get on with it?" Amanda motioned up the street. "Oh, almost forgot." She opened the door and fetched a basket of goodies she'd prepared to take to the park. "Okay, I'm ready. Let's go, girls."

When they arrived at the park at the end of the lane, the area was full of boats cruising the waterway, bicycles following the paths, people stopping to view the magnificent windmills originally built in the 1700s. Three of them.

There was a pub near them with tables and benches outdoors. So they stopped for a drink and to get their bearings. The girls went ahead and played on the grassy mounds, chasing each other and tumbling.

"They are absolutely adorable, Antoine. You have done such a great job with them. They're so polite and seem to be very well-adjusted." She was amazed at how normal they seemed.

"A lot of it has to do with my mother. She has them while I'm working, you know, when they're not in school. Between the two of us, we do all right, I suppose."

"You suppose? You do fantastic! I mean it." She touched his hand and looked into his eyes. "You're amazing."

He picked up her hand and gently kissed it. "I find you amazing, Amanda. Do you mind if I call you Mandy? You're more like a Mandy than an Amanda. Amanda seems so old and great aunt-ish."

She laughed. "My mother used to call me Mandy. I don't mind at all."

"Tell me, would you go out to dinner with me one night when I'm not working?" He seemed afraid of what her answer might be.

She hesitated, not sure if she should or not. But then again, she was a grownup, she told herself, she was on her own, she was living in Bruges in another country for God's sake, all by herself! So why shouldn't she go to dinner with whoever she wanted, when she wanted, especially with the cutest guy in town? Richard's and Arlie's faces flashed through her mind, but only for a few seconds.

"Yes, I will go to dinner with you. Anytime you want."

Chapter 25

Just one more … Rachel popped another Belgian chocolate into her mouth. She'd purchased a box of them from one of the many chocolate shops along the route she'd walked from the Grand Place that morning. But they were putting her to sleep now. Ever since she could remember, chocolate made her sleepy.

The day before, she had taken a long nap in the afternoon after eating six delicious pieces. The milk chocolate was her favorite, solid chocolate. But the shops had everything, crème-filled, nuts, chewy, dark chocolate … you name it, they make it all in Belgium. She observed that the chocolate and the lace shops made up a good percentage of the business in Belgium. Chocolates and lace. What a romantic combination!

After the walk, she came back to the hotel and wrote ten more pages of her new novel. Inspiration was everywhere. She certainly had chosen the right city to trigger her imagination.

She'd been in Brussels for two weeks and had already written 22,000 words. Only 80,000 more to go. Or, actually, 78,000. She liked to keep her novels at 100,000 words, give or take. She would divide the novel into three parts: 20,000 words in Part One; 60,000 in Part Two; 20,000 in Part Three. The *meat* of the story would be in Part Two.

She'd just begun writing the *meat;* an idea came to her that morning while she was having coffee in the Grand Place. Plus she'd been on the phone with Belinda several times and they'd exchanged ideas about the plot. Belinda was full of ideas lately; it tickled Rachel that she wanted to contribute.

As she lay back on the bed closing her eyes and the chocolate began to take effect, she wondered why she hadn't heard from Pete in the past few days. He was usually pretty good about calling every other day. It had now been four days since she'd heard from him last. She drifted off to sleep in mid-thought.

The dream was of Pete in the jungle, in an open boat with a canopy traveling down the Amazon River reminiscent of the boat Bogart and Hepburn used. Then it became a Chinese Junk. She and Belinda were with him. They were sitting at a table with a white tablecloth, drinking champagne and eating giant shrimp cocktails in crystal. It seemed the normal thing to do on a Chinese Junk.

Snakes were slithering at their feet; natives were chucking spears at them from both sides of the river; alligators and piranhas were swimming around the boat. No one seemed to be alarmed. Pete was laughing, saying what a beautiful place it was, saying that he wanted to live in Brazil, wanted Rachel to come live there with him when they were married.

Rachel said "No way!" and stood up from the table to get another bottle of champagne from an ornately carved cupboard that was definitely not the usual boat fixture. She tripped on a pile of snakes and fell over the edge of the boat into the river. Belinda jumped in to save her.

Pete watched them as he continued to drink and laugh. He told them to swim faster, swim to the boat and climb back on. Then he stood and leaned toward the water to pull them aboard, but the boat was moving faster and farther down river until it was out of sight. Belinda was going under. Rachel had to save her. Pete wasn't there, he was gone, out of sight ...

Rachel woke up in exhaustion. It had been a while since she'd had such a vivid dream. One of the reasons she'd come to the UK in the first place was because of her dreams. And she settled in Cornwall because her dreams led her there. She'd been guided by them most of her life.

Also because of her dreams, she had found her mother on an Indian reservation in Montana after years of believing she had died when Rachel was three years old. Rachel also discovered she was British in a past life because of her dreams, and discovered who she was and where she had lived on the south coast of England. Pete and her friend Margaret were believers of past lives, Paul and Belinda too.

Now she wondered what this latest dream could mean. She was expecting a call from Belinda regarding the results of the tests. That had been worrying Rachel. Maybe that was the reason for the dream.

The phone rang.

"Hello?"

"Rachel, luv!"

"Oh, Pete! I'm so glad it's you. I've been so worried."

"No need to worry, doll. I couldn't call because of where we were. No worrying, luv. Promise me."

"But I had such a horrible dream just now. You know how I feel about my dreams.."

"Just be patient a little longer, doll. We're making such progress with the gathering of the plant life. Found some we've not seen before. It is beautiful here. Maybe you'd change your mind about this place if you would come see it. Belem is very modern, luv. We could build a home here, there's enough work to keep me here indefinitely."

Rachel was silent.

"Doll, are you there?"

"I've got another phone call, Pete, am expecting a call from Belinda. Can I call you back later?"

"Yes, I'll be here for a couple more hours."

"Okay, bye now."

Rachel pushed the call waiting key as she answered the knock at the door. Room Service was delivering coffee and toast.

"Hello? Oh, good. Wait a minute, Belinda. Let me pour a cup of coffee and sit down. Hold on." Her heart rate increased already knowing that the news was going to be bad. She couldn't shake the feeling. She tipped the waiter and poured herself a cup of coffee. "Okay, so tell me what the doctor said. I'm all ears."

"Well, it's as he suspected. Lymphoma. No doubt about it."

They both were silent. Both were tearing up. Both were ready to cry.

"I'm coming home. I'll leave today." Rachel's voice quivered, she couldn't hide her feelings.

"No you're not. Now don't do anything foolish. You stay there and write that book. I have plenty of people here to drive me nuts. My goodness, my mother is coming back at the end of the week; Paul is here; Dudley is already suffocating me and he takes Jake off my hands more than usual. So don't you worry. I'm alright.

"We're trying to decide what to do about the pregnancy, Rachel. Paul wants me to abort, and so does the doctor. Sounds like it might be the best thing to do because they want to start the treatment right away. They don't think I should wait till after the baby is born. What do you think, Rachel?"

"Look, I know how much you want your baby, especially since you thought you'd never have any children after Baby Jake, but you do have Paul Junior now. Two beautiful boys. What's most important is that you're around to raise those two boys, you know? I—" Rachel couldn't control her emotions. She couldn't talk anymore.

"I know … I know … but I just can't bear to think that I'd be killing my baby girl. She's a girl, Rachel. My girl."

They both wept.

After a few moments, Belinda continued, "But I know I must think of Paul and the boys, they're the most important people in my life and I can't let them down. So, I will abort. I must. Thank you, Rachel, you've helped me decide. I'll talk to you later, and I'll be all right so don't you worry. The abortion procedure is simple the doc says. So you stay there … and write that novel … you understand me?" Her sobs were intermittent.

"Oh honey, I will … but I'll be home as soon as Pete comes back, or maybe even before that. You take care. Love you."

"Love you, too. Bye."

Rachel closed the phone and sighed heavily. "How can one person go through so much?" She grabbed a tissue.

How can Belinda have all this tragedy in her life time and time again and still manage to come through it all and be the wonderful, loving person she is, and the most talented and creative person that I've known? What is it that singles out one person to dump the hell of the earth on?

First Belinda lost her father to the mines when she was very young. She and her mother both struggled all those years, her mother slaving to put her through college. Then Belinda had been brutally gang-raped and nearly died. Then she became pregnant by one of the rapists, and then had been faced with having to choose between a hysterectomy, aborting her second child after she was married to Paul, or spending several weeks in bed – she'd chosen the latter and luckily made it through to have a glorious second son.

Now this. Every time life got better, something stepped in to threaten it.

How does she get through it?

Rachel needed to talk to somebody, but didn't know who. Instead she decided to take a break and hop a train to Bruges. Yes, that's what she needed, a break from the usual routine in Brussels.

She quickly packed a bag with a couple changes of clothes and left the hotel. She took a cab the short distance to Gare Centrale and only had to wait fifteen minutes for the one-hour ride to Bruges.

It was a lovely afternoon, the rain had stopped and the sky was sparsely dotted with fluffy white clouds. The landscape sparkled clean and green.

Rachel took a deep breath and sighed. She felt relieved and uplifted when she rode trains. She didn't know why, it was just a feeling she'd get. Better than a tranquilizer. In England she rode trains back and forth to London as often as her schedule permitted. She traveled by train all over the country doing research while getting R&R when it was needed.

She loved taking trains to Paris, too. There was something about Paris that inspired her more than any other city in the world. She could go there feeling emotionally depleted and almost ill, and within a few hours would be feeling exuberant and alive.

Over the past two years she had gone every two months, or as often as she could, to enjoy the house in Montmartre she and her friend Janet Corrigan, from the States, had bought together. Janet was there most of the time now, and Rachel would spend a couple of weeks in spurts in her favorite Montmartre section of the City of Lights.

It dawned on her ... that's who she could have called. Janet. And maybe Janet had heard from Shellie - their previous roommate and cohort in Montmartre. Shellie was living in Switzerland now with Adrian and their little girl. What a fairy tale that had turned out to be!

All three Americans – Rachel, Janet, and Shellie – had been in Paris at the same time, sorting out their lives, making decisions for their futures. All three of them had found their hearts' desires when they were living in the fabulous house atop the hill.

Rachel thought of the good times they had. She'd been there visiting, doing research for another novel. It was that New Year's Eve when she and Pete were engaged. Adrian asked Shellie to marry him and go home to Switzerland, and Janet made the decision to stay in Paris to be with Bob – becoming partners in the construction business. What a good ending for all!

Rachel jotted a note to call Janet and Shellie. She was suddenly missing them, and she was suddenly drowsy—must have been all the remembering that did it. She leaned her head against the train's window pane and dozed off.

Chapter 26

The week had been an exciting one at the Kantcentrum for Amanda. She took to lace-making as if she had been doing it her entire life. In five days she had mastered the basics of making Binche lace, and she signed up for another class beginning the third week of August.

She'd been in Belgium for over a month now, and she was feeling a direction beginning to form. Lace-making would be a part of her future, but she wasn't exactly sure how, yet, though she had some ideas.

After she finished class on Friday, she hurried to the B&B to pick up the two aprons she'd already made of natural linen and had attached wide rows of Binche lace to them. She was sure one of the lace shops just off the Markt would most likely be interested in buying them. She'd been feeling them out, talking to the proprietors and had decided which one she'd go to first.

It was an exciting prospect to sell her first hand-made lace-bordered aprons. She had attached her own labels to them - embroidered "Mandy Malone" on a two-inch piece of ribbon and had hand-sewn the labels inside the waistbands where the ties began.

Not only was *Mandy* her mother's favorite name for her, *Mandy Malone* was a name in one of the romance novels she'd read a dozen times back in Nevada as she sat day after day waiting for Arlie to come back home. She had fallen in love with the name back then, in fact she'd dreamed of disappearing like Arlie and changing her name to Mandy Malone.

She never dreamed that that would be exactly what she would be doing more or less - that she'd be in Belgium, a foreign country, all by herself, finding her own way and learning how to make a living doing what she loved. And now she was about to use the name she had picked out months before.

There were moments she thanked Arlie for disappearing. If he hadn't, she'd still be living a lonely, drab existence in the trailer in the desert outside of Las Vegas. She wondered how she could have accepted living that way day after day, year after year.

But now, aprons would be a start for her; she was thinking of making skirts and blouses and dresses, using the strips of lace she would create, combining them with silks and other fabrics. She'd already begun to accumulate pieces of material she felt would be perfect, and even found inexpensive items of clothing she could cut up and use as fabric. Years of making clothing out of scraps was surely an asset. She smiled as she thought of her mother and how proud she would be of her.

After she sold the two aprons to the lace shop and took an order for six more, she hurried to the Craenenburg to tell Antoine the great news.

Chapter 27

In Bruges the first place Rachel headed after she checked into a small hotel near Markt square was the Craenenburg. This was her third jaunt to Bruges and she always found the Craenenburg a delightful place to sit and watch people on the square.

The patio was already crowded, so she went inside the restaurant and sat at a table on the far wall. There was a young blond sitting at the neighboring table on the mutual bench that stretched along the wall, its back curving up at head height. The girl was drinking champagne and smiling.

"Hello, that looks good. I think I'll have one of those myself," Rachel said to the girl as she made herself comfortable on the bench.

"Oh, you're American?"

"Yes I am. And you are too?"

"I'm an Arkansas transplant to Nevada and California," Amanda answered.

"I'm originally from California, but live in Cornwall now. In England."

Antoine arrived at the table to take Rachel's order. "Ah, I see you two have met. May I get you something to drink?"

"I'll have champagne, too."

He sped off to open a fresh bottle.

"So, my name is Rachel. Yours?"

"Amanda or Mandy. Whatever you want to call me."

"Which do you prefer?"

"I think I prefer Mandy. I think I'll change my name to Mandy Malone in fact." She grinned at the prospect of the name change. "Do you have to do anything legal to change your name like that? Do you know?"

"Well, if it's not to defraud the government, like skip out on taxes or whatever, I don't think so. Writers use pseudonyms all the time. They still pay their taxes under their real names, though. Why do you want to change it?"

"Here you go, champagne for the ladies!" Antoine poured the glass and topped off Amanda's. "Anything else I can get for you?"

"Not at the moment. This is perfect, thank you," Rachel answered.

He squeezed Amanda's shoulder. "Anything more for you, luv?"

"Nothing, I'm fine."

Rachel picked up on the familiarity between the two young people. "Is he your boyfriend?"

"No, no. Just a friend. A good friend," she blushed. "Maybe more than a friend, but that's all. We're not, you know, we're not intimate or anything. Actually, I'm married, but my husband disappeared on me over a year and a half ago. No one knows where he is. He's probably dead in the Nevada desert somewhere. At least that's what my sister thinks."

"What happened?" Rachel's interest was piqued.

"Oh, he just up and disappeared on Christmas Day, year before last. We lived outside of Las Vegas and he abandoned me in our trailer with no car and no money. My sister came and got me and took me home with her to live in California. She got me a waitress job there, in Bakersfield."

"Oh my gosh! I was born and raised in Bakersfield. Small world. So where were you working?"

"KC's Steakhouse. You know where it is?"

Rachel's eyes lit up, "Of course I do. Been there many times. But I imagine it's changed quite a bit since then. Anyway, sorry I interrupted. Please go on."

"Well, I'd never worked before. So when I got that job with KC's, I saved my money to come here. So here I am. And now I want to live here, don't want to go back home. What brings you to Bruges?"

Rachel leaned back and looked at Amanda with renewed curiosity. "Well, the story isn't as dramatic as yours, that's for sure. I'm just here to work on a novel that I'm writing."

"You're a writer? My gosh, I've never met a writer. Wait till I tell Paula. She's my sister."

"So you didn't say why you want to change your name."

"Well, I want to open up a boutique. I'm learning how to make lace, and I design clothing. So I've named my shop Mandy Malone Designs. That is on my labels. I got the name from a romance novel. My mother called me Mandy, so I figured that would work. I'd still have my own first name. But my real name is Amanda Jefferies, my maiden name was Conroy. I like Mandy Malone. What do you think?"

"Mandy Malone is a great name for a label. So when are you going to do this, open a shop?"

"I'm not sure, but I've got to do something pretty soon, I'm running out of money. I'm making aprons to sell to the lace shops. Sold six of them today. That's why I'm celebrating."

Rachel lifted her glass. "Congratulations!"

The two days came and went too fast for Rachel, but she felt she had to get back to Brussels and back to work on her book. The friendship between she and Amanda appeared to have the makings of a lasting one. She was already fond of the girl.

So before she left Bruges she invited Amanda to come to Brussels and spend a few days with her at the Metropole Hotel, told her about all the shops in the Old Town area surrounding the Grand Place, and told her it was a fashion Mecca for new designers. Amanda was eager to see it all, said she'd let her know when she could come.

Chapter 28

September was an unusually warm month in Belgium. Although from May to September warm weather prevailed, it was warmer than it had been the past few years. Everyone was attributing it to global warming. It was being said that the hot would be hotter and the cold would be colder in days ahead. The predictions of this happening later was happening sooner.

Amanda had moved into a small flat in Antoine's building after living longer than she had planned at the B&B. The van Nevels had given her a special rate, but it still wasn't as inexpensive as a flat and wasn't as close to the Markt area, and of course not as large. Plus, now she had her own kitchen.

She was a floor above Antoine and had a view of the street below. The apartments facing Markt square were larger and more expensive and the tenants in those had been there for years, with no desire to move elsewhere. They would have to die before those flats would be available.

At first Amanda thought it might be a bit awkward to live so close to Antoine and the girls, but it turned out to be perfect. They did spend a lot of time together, and she took care of the girls when the grandmother needed to run errands or needed a day off.

Amanda had set up a sewing room in one of her three rooms and she worked day and night putting together a collection of clothing. She'd made up her mind. She was going to open *Mandy Malone's*. She didn't know how she would handle the legalities of it all yet, or where the shop would be, but she still had time to figure it all out. She'd find a way, she knew she would.

In the meantime, she needed to increase the income she was bringing in, the funding from her brother-in-law was running low and she didn't want to have to ask anyone for help. Which reminded her, she needed to call Paula.

She dialed and Paula answered.

"Hi, Paula. Whacha doin'?" Amanda greeted as she sat on the sofa.

"Oh, baby, it is so good to hear your voice. How are you doing in your new apartment?"

"I love it. And I'm sewing up a storm. You should see all the stuff I've made, the lace and all."

"I bet it's pretty. I sure would like to see you, hon. So what is your plan?" Paula asked. "I think you have to come back to the U.S. in six months, you know. I don't think you can't stay there over six months without a visa."

"I'm going to check that out next week," Amanda said. "And if I have to come back for a visit, I will. That would be in January, wouldn't it? Six months since I came here?"

"That's about right. So have you talked to Richard this week?"

"He's called a couple of times and left messages. We keep missing each other."

"You know he calls here all the time and comes over every time he's in town. The guy really loves you, Amanda. He really does."

Amanda sighed. "But I'm not sure how I feel about him, Paula. And he probably wouldn't let me do what I'm doing if I came back and married him. I don't want to give this up. It'd be like living with Arlie again. And then there's Arlie. We're still married, so I can't get married to Richard anyway."

"I'm sure Richard would take care of all that. He'd make it right. And I don't think being married to him would be like being married to Arlie. You don't really think that, do you?"

"It just scares me, that's all. You know I'm seeing Antoine a lot now. And his girls are the sweetest ever. We get along so good."

"Are you in love with Antoine?" Paula asked cautiously.

Amanda considered her answer. "No. I'm not. It's just different, you know? We're friends, helping each other out in a way. He's easy to talk to and be with. I don't feel stupid around him. Sometimes Richard makes me feel so dumb. He's older and smarter. Richer. Oh I don't know how to explain it, but it's just easier with Antoine. He sort of grows on you."

Amanda went to her kitchen area, which was one wall of the living room, and got a can of Pepsi from the refrigerator. "And he's ... well ... we're the same age and on the same level. I think Richard's too good for me."

"He is not! How can you say that?" Paula sounded exasperated. "If anything, you're too good for him. You've got to get that nonsense out of your pretty little head, girl."

Amanda laughed. "I think you're biased, Paula." She took a swallow of the drink.

"Well, you're my baby sister, that's why. And you know that Mama and Grandma would say the same thing. You've always been special, Amanda, you just haven't known it. Why,

135

look at what you've done in the past year. How many people could do what you've done? Huh? How many people would have even tried? You set your mind to it and you did it. I'm just so proud of you, baby. So proud!"

Amanda could hear the emotion in Paula's voice. "Are you crying, Paula?"

"Well, you make me cry, baby." She laughed. "I just want you to be happy, and I just know that Richard is right for you. Please give him a chance. Promise me you will."

"I haven't told him no yet, Paula. I haven't told him anything. And when I come home to visit, maybe I'll know more about how I feel. But don't tell him my plans for the shop over here. I don't want him to know that just yet."

"Okay, I won't."

"Well, I gotta go now, so you give A.G. a big fat kiss for me, and give Drake a giant hug. I'll call you later."

It was Friday night and Amanda was trying on one of her newly sewn creations – a silk dress flowing from a strapless lined-lace band that fit snuggly across the bust line. The sky blue color of the fabric reflected the color of her eyes. Her plans were to cover a pair of shoes with the silk to go with the dress.

As she looked in the mirror she thought of Antoine. Their outings with the girls and the evenings alone after the girls were in bed and their dinner dates once a week were becoming more and more romantic, they'd end each evening with a kiss that became more intimate than the one before. And she was becoming more and more eager to see Antoine each night when he got home from work. He'd spend an hour with the girls, put them to bed and then come upstairs to see Amanda.

There was a knock at the door.

She looked at her watch and saw that it had to be Antoine. After a brief hesitation, thinking of quickly taking off the dress and putting on her jeans and top, she decided against it and opened the door.

"Wow!" Antoine stared at her with his widened eyes and mouth agape.

"Come in." Amanda was pleased by his reaction. She wasn't sure if it was a reaction to the dress itself or how she looked in it. "So what do you think?" She twirled so he could see the identical front and back. The seams were almost invisible, which she took great pride in, had learned how to do that from her mother. "Think I could sell this?"

"Sell it? You should wear it every day and night. It's beautiful! We should go out dancing somewhere."

Amanda giggled. "No, no, no. It's to sell. Do you like the design?"

"Oh yes. I can visualize this in your shop window. It'll cause quite a stir, it will."

"Well, I'll just be a moment," she said as she went into her bedroom to change. "Pour the wine, will you? And there are some snacks on a plate in the fridge. Help yourself."

As she undressed she thought about how far she'd come from the hills of Arkansas to entertaining a handsome young man in her own comfy flat in Belgium. It felt so natural to be making gorgeous clothing and sipping wine with Antoine late at night. She decided to put on an oversized t-shirt that came down to mid-thigh instead of her jeans and top. Less constraining, more comfortable.

The music was on and a glass of wine was waiting for Amanda on the table in front of the sofa alongside the plate of sandwiches. Antoine was leaning back on the sofa pillows watching for her entrance from the bedroom. The look on his face was soft and loving.

"Oh, great! You did good, Antoine. I definitely need a glass. It's been a long day for me, finishing that dress and starting more lace for another." She sat in the middle of the sofa and reached for the glass from the table. "Cheers!"

They clanked their glasses and melted into the fluffy cushions.

"So what was your day like?" She sipped and reached for a sandwich as she waited for his answer.

"Uneventful. Typical day. The Friday regulars came in, sat at their favorite tables. Nothing changes. Once in a while someone new and interesting comes in, like the day you first walked through the door." He grinned and took a sip.

"So you're saying that happens a lot?" she teased.

He laughed. "No, I'm not saying that." He reached over and touched her knee. "You look as good in a t-shirt as you did in the fancy dress."

"Ha! Now I know you're putting me on."

Antoine set his glass on the table and moved closer to Amanda. "You know how much I care for you, don't you, Mandy? I mean after all this time, you've got to know."

She felt uneasy and moved her knee from his touch by placing her foot on the floor and sitting erect. He put his arm around her shoulders and pulled her towards him, leaning in for a kiss. She relaxed a little and let him kiss her. Kisses felt nice, and they were harmless.

He took one of her hands and placed it on his shoulder as the kiss continued, and then he reached for her other hand and did the same. Amanda felt tingly all over as he pulled her closer to him.

Returning his kiss was easy and she was enjoying being held close. But as he began to gently lay her back on the sofa and move his body above hers, pressing against her, she stiffened and tried to sit up.

"Stay in the moment, stay in the moment …" he whispered.

It became easier than she thought it would be. Antoine made it feel natural as he stroked the outside of her thigh and slipped his hand under the back of her t-shirt and pulling her even closer with his hand pressing into the small of her back.

The kisses became more intense and breathless as Amanda felt his hot body against hers. She became even more aroused when Antoine lifted the front of her t-shirt and kissed the space between her breasts as he began kneading them gently. His lips brushed her throat, and the indentation at the front of her neck.

Then he raised his head slightly and looked up at the expression on her face and her closed eyes. This was something he'd wanted to do ever since he first saw her.

Amanda opened her glazed eyes and gazed into his. "We should probably stop, you know."

"Not now." He tickled her nipple with his tongue. "You like that?"

"Oh my God, yes!" She giggled and squirmed as he continued to make an all-out effort to pleasure her in every way he could think of. She had no idea she could feel as good as he made her feel. The thrills were zinging every erotic zone of her body. Antoine was a very talented man at lovemaking, she decided.

After two hours of teasing and gentle lovemaking that culminated in both of them reaching the ultimate high in sexual ecstasy, Amanda abruptly sat up, almost knocking Antoine off the sofa.

"Oh my gosh! Look at the time. I've got stuff to do." She reached for her glass and went to the fridge for some cold water. "Would you like a drink of water before you leave?"

She was half embarrassed and half thinking that maybe it was time she take Rachel up on her offer and go to Brussels for a few days. Having sex with Antoine was much too confusing. She needed to get away from him right away.

Richard's face flashed through her mind. She felt guilty.

Yes, she'd call Rachel in the morning and make arrangements to go to Brussels for a few days.

Chapter 29

It began raining as Rachel headed for her morning coffee. She rounded the corner from the lane leading to the central square and the restaurant on the corner at Number 1 Grand Place. It was her favorite, besides the Metropole Cafe at the hotel where she was staying. It was called the *Le Roi d'Espagne*, named after the bust of Charles II which decorated the façade on the second floor. One of the things Rachel loved doing was finding out the history of the fascinating old buildings wherever she went. This had only become a favorite pastime of hers in later years; she had never been interested in history before becoming a writer. Doing historical research, visiting places, reading about the people, it was all part of a writer's creative process.

She was attracted to The Roy (its nickname) by its ambiance and the history of it. Built in 1697, originally a Bakers Guild, at one point it added a café and a hardware store, then became strictly a café in 1952. According to the waiters, to work there one had to speak French and English in addition to the local languages.

At least three or four times a week Rachel went there for a late morning cup of coffee and pastry, sometimes lunch. She'd sit a couple hours and make notes about her thoughts and for the novel. Sometimes a person she would see, hear, or talk to would trigger an idea and she'd jot it down.

That morning after she ordered she asked her waiter, "By the way, what are guild houses? You know, like the Bakers Guild, where we are."

"Oh, that is easy. During the Middle Ages and after that, every city had guilds or corporations as we would call them today - for instance the Bakers Guild. The guilds or corporations had influence on the governing body of the city. And because guilds were very wealthy and politically powerful and their four- to six-story houses or headquarters reflected the affluence and influence, they would regularly meet in them to discuss new rules or regulations for their specific trade or commerce. They'd pass that along to the city administration to implement. So the Grand Place was the center of government in those days, with all its guild houses. Now it is a tourist attraction." He grinned at her.

"Thank you so much, you've earned your tip today for sure." She grinned back at him.

"That makes me very happy, thank you. I'll turn in your order." He waited on her almost every time she came in, so he knew what to expect in the way of a tip from her. Most Europeans didn't tip, but Americans did. In fact Rachel over-tipped, and he told her so, but he was very grateful and glad to see her come in. And he enjoyed giving her bits and pieces of history, she was always full of questions.

Rachel wrote a note to herself to call Belinda as soon as she returned to the hotel; she wanted to know how the treatments were going.

Her cell phone rang.

"Hello?"

142

"How's my doll?"

"Oh, Pete! I was worried. It's been a whole week again."

"Darling, you mustn't worry. If I can't find a signal, I can't call. Just believe that nothing will harm me. Nothing will prevent me from spending the rest of my life with you. I miss you, luv."

Rachel took a deep breath. "And I miss you, too. More and more every day. So when will you be through?"

"That's why I'm calling; we're going to be here a bit longer, I'm afraid. Maybe till November. But that won't interfere with our wedding at Christmas. Nothing will get in the way of that, doll. I promise."

"Oh dear." She hesitated. "Well, actually, I'm pretty busy here … the book and all … and I've some more side trips to take for research, so I guess I'll be all right. Yes, I'll be all right. I'm sorry, Pete; I don't mean to be nagging. Forgive me?"

"You aren't a nag at all. I've seen some real nags in my lifetime, married one before, you know. So you can rest easy about that, luv." He laughed heartily. "Got to go, doll. I'll talk to you in a few days."

"Okay, take care of yourself for me."

"I will. Bye now."

She sighed deeply and slumped in her chair, staring sadly out the window.

Her phone rang again.

"Did you forget something? Hello? Oh, Mandy! How are you? Yes, I thought you were Pete, he just called. No, he's still in Brazil. Yes, of course, anytime you want. That'll work. Can you take a cab to the Metropole Hotel from the train station? Yes, they all know where it is. Sure. I'll most likely be at the sidewalk café in front. Yes, at the hotel. Okay, see you then. I'm glad you're coming, I desperately need the company."

Chapter 30

Rachel adored Amanda, or Mandy, as the young lady wanted to be called. Rachel had not met as sweet a girl since she first met Belinda and Shellie. Both Belinda and Shellie had become her dear friends who she'd fight for and do whatever it took to help them with whatever they needed, if it was within her power. And now she'd met another young woman who fit the same criteria, and she felt motherly towards this one – like Janet felt towards Shellie. Probably because Amanda was so young and she was all alone in a strange land. Rachel felt a kinship to her, had been drawn to her at the onset. Felt it was for a reason.

She knew one of the reasons. She wanted to invest in Amanda, if Amanda would let her. She'd made up her mind about it the second day Amanda was in Brussels to visit her.

On the third day of the visit they were sitting at The Roy eating lunch.

"Got some good news this morning from my publisher in the States. My latest novel just hit the million mark in sales. I'm rich!" Rachel laughed.

"Congratulations! Which one is it? I'll have to buy it and read it. I love reading novels."

"*Love at the Louvre*. You don't have to buy it, I have a copy at the hotel, I'll give it to you." She hesitated for a second. "Mandy, I also want to give you some money—"

"Oh no, you can't do that. I'm not wanting anything from you."

"I know that, dear. I know you aren't the type to take from people. Believe me, I can pick up on that quicker than most. You are a talented seamstress and designer, and that's what I want to invest in. You have to let me. It'll be just that: an investment. We can work it all out with my attorney, if you'd rather. Make it legal." She was grinning, wide-eyed, at Amanda, excited about the venture. "And besides, now I have the money to do it." She laughed.

Amanda looked down at her plate for a moment, thinking about what Rachel had just proposed. She leaned back and looked at her with tear-filled eyes. "I don't know what to say—" She couldn't continue. She cupped her hand over her mouth and chin to hide the quivering and stop the beginnings of a sob.

"Oh, Mandy!" Rachel reached over and held her other hand. "I'm really excited about this. When you got here and handed me that beautiful silk lace jacket that you made, I mean you even made the lace, I knew right then that I wanted to help you. You need to be seen. Your creations need to be out there. It's your dream, honey, and I can help make that happen for you. Please let me."

"It's so hard for me," Amanda murmured sheepishly.

"So let's just sort it all out and work together on it. Okay?'

"So you really think I should open the shop in Brussels instead of Bruges?" She wiped her eyes that were refilling with excitement instead of tears.

Rachel nodded. "More traffic, more local as well as tourist trade. Definitely here in Brussels. We can find a shop with an apartment overhead for you." She took a bite of her sautéed fish. "Mmmm, this is delicious. So how long would it take you to be ready with enough garments to open a shop?"

"About three more months."

"Okay, I'll talk to my attorney in London and have him email a contract right away. You and I can work out the details before you go back to Bruges, and then I'll write you a check for fabric and supplies and living expenses that will tide you over for the next six months plus. I'll be going back to Cornwall soon. So after the first of the year, we'll meet here in Brussels and get down to brass tacks to figure it all out, find a shop and apartment, all the fun stuff. How does that sound?"

Amanda leaned over and gave Rachel a loving hug.

Chapter 31

It was already October. Rachel couldn't believe how fast the weeks were flying by. She had finished the first draft of her fourth novel and was taking a couple of days away from it. She decided to pack up and take the train to Paris for the weekend, after which she would head home to Cornwall.

First she sent an email to Amanda to tell her what she was going to do. Before Amanda left Brussels to return to Bruges, Rachel purchased a laptop for her and showed her the basics. Amanda learned quickly and although she couldn't type, she used the one-finger hunt-and-peck method that worked just fine. Now they would stay in touch every day, no matter where Rachel was.

Rachel also sent an email to Pete and one to Belinda. She didn't want to call and have long conversations; she wanted to get going. But she did call Janet and left a message that she would arrive in Paris late afternoon.

After sending the emails and reading those awaiting her from others, she shut down her computer and began packing.

Her cell phone rang.

"I don't have time for this," she growled aloud. She thought about letting it go to the message center, but on the last ring she decided to answer. "Hello?"

"Rachel O'Neill?"

"Yes, that's me."

"This is Carl Wilson in Belem. I'm with the Eden Project."

"Yes, I remember you." She took a deep breath and closed her eyes.

"My dear, I'm sorry to inform you ... "

Rachel's heart stopped.

" ... Pete was shot and killed this morning as he and the others confronted a gang of poachers. Three of our men were killed and he was one of them. I'm so sorry."

Her vision blurred. She shook her head. "But that can't be. I just talked to him yesterday. No! You're wrong! He has to be alive. He promised me. He promised! We're getting married at Christmas!" She crumpled to the floor, still holding the phone to her ear. "He can't be dead ... he can't ..."

"Miss O'Neill, Is there someone I could call for you?"

She dropped the phone. It fell next to her as she began to rock back and forth, crying and sobbing.

"You ... you promised me, Pete ... you promised ... I can't do this again ... I just can't ... can't do it ..."

She struggled to stand up, then staggered to the bathroom medicine cabinet.

Chapter 32

Carl Wilson called Paul and Belinda in the UK after telephoning Rachel in Brussels. He told them he'd talked to Rachel at the Metropole and it had sounded as if she'd collapsed at the news.

After failed attempts all afternoon and evening to contact Rachel, and when Janet called telling them she didn't show up in Paris as planned, Paul spoke to the hotel and learned that Rachel hadn't checked out. He told them to go into her room to see if she was there, that he would wait on the phone.

Five minutes later they told him they had found her unconscious on the floor, an empty prescription bottle of anti-depressants on the floor beside her, and they had called an ambulance.

He left immediately for Brussels.

When he arrived at the hotel, the manager said she'd been taken to Cliniques Universitaires Saint Luc, a local hospital. Paul couldn't believe Rachel would have tried to take her own life. Of all people, not Rachel. He broke down in front of the hotel staff. They ushered him to an office till he was able to get control of himself. Her things were still in her room, they told him. So he asked for a key and requested that they switch the name over to his. He would be staying there till he could take her home.

When Paul saw Rachel lying in the hospital bed, her face and eyes swollen from the overdose, she was barely recognizable. He wondered why she'd been taking anti-depressants in the first place. She'd never seemed depressed. She was one of the most cheerful people he knew and always so full of energy and life. He loved that about her.

As he got closer to Rachel, the tears began to build again. He choked them back and shook his head. He lifted her pale hand and brought it to his lips. "My dear Rachel, nothing is worth this grief."

Her eyes slowly opened. "Paul?"

"Yes, dearest, it's me. I'm here to take you home."

"But—"

"No buts. You're coming home with me as soon as I can get you out of here."

She turned away. "He's gone, Paul ... he's gone."

Paul could barely control his own grief over Pete, but he knew he had to at that moment. "But we're not, Rachel. You and me, Belinda, the boys ... we're all still here and we love you. Maybe Pete has left this world, but he'll never leave our hearts—"

His voice broke on that one. That was it. Control gone. He stretched his arm across Rachel, buried his face next to hers on the pillow and gave in to his own sobs.

He adored this woman. Ever since he first saw her and kissed her that New Year's Eve at Trafalgar Square in London, he knew that wasn't the end of it, he knew she would be in his life somehow, somewhere. And now she was. She had become a big part of his life.

This time it was Rachel who squeezed Paul's hand. Her eyes were closed. She whispered, "... it will be all right ... it will ... I'm so sorry ... don't cry ... "

She faded into sleep.

Chapter 33

Two weeks later Rachel was almost back to normal, although still a little weak and fragile. She was embarrassed and regretful that she'd tried to commit suicide. The shock had been too much for her the doctors said.

Being back home in Cornwall with her friends calling and visiting her was a blessing. She was feeling much better.

The memorial service for Pete had come and gone and all she had left were her memories of him. With Paul and Belinda's help, she was learning how to place the memories on a virtual shelf to take them down whenever she needed or wanted them.

She talked to Janet and Bob, they called from Paris the day before the service; they were saddened and grieved over Pete's passing. They were there when Pete had first proposed to Rachel two years before in Paris. His death was breaking their hearts, too. Shellie and Adrian had been there, too. All of Rachel's friends were sorrowful and conveyed their condolences.

As she sat and stared out the window of her cottage, she wished she could relive those six months in Paris with Janet and

Shellie; such happy times culminating with Pete making his surprise appearance on New Year's Eve, proposing to her. She smiled as she remembered.

She hadn't known he'd already arrived in Paris for New Year's Eve. She thought he was still in Brazil recuperating from the deathly plane crash and being lost in the jungle for weeks, almost eaten alive by insects and infections. Then when the girls were picked up by Bob and Adrian in Montmartre, Pete stepped out of the Limo in all his glory to surprise Rachel. Later on the dinner boat Maxim's, where Shellie was performing with a jazz combo, Pete proposed to Rachel and slipped a Brazilian diamond ring on her finger.

But here she was alone again, without him. She couldn't believe that he was gone, out of her life, after she'd finally admitted to herself that she needed and wanted to be with him forever, that she loved him. She just couldn't believe he was dead. How could it have happened? Why did it happen? What was it that always took love away from her? This had been the first time she'd begun to truly believe she had found her soul mate. She *had* found her soul mate. And knowing that they would be together again in another lifetime was of no consolation at the moment.

She shook her head and stood up, running her hands through her hair. She wasn't going to spend her life questioning and grieving and wallowing in self pity. She just wasn't!

Rachel dropped her robe and stepped into the shower.

She had to pull herself together. Death wasn't new to her. She'd survived it many times before and she would do it again.

As she stood under the hot water spray, she decided that the first thing she had to do was get in touch with Amanda. She wanted her to know that she still wanted to help her.

Later that morning when she telephoned Amanda's number in Bruges, no one answered. She emailed, but didn't receive any return emails.

She hoped nothing was wrong. Surely not.

Chapter 34

Amanda was in California. The trip back was even longer than it had been when she had flown to Belgium. First there was a four-hour delay before she took off from Brussels, which made her late for a connecting flight in Chicago. Then she had to wait three more hours in Chicago before taking off for California. So by the time Paula and Drake picked her up at the Bakersfield airport, Amanda was exhausted, she'd been traveling for hours.

It was a sudden and unexpected return to the States. Arlie was in Bakersfield. He'd turned up at Paula's wanting to know where his wife was, demanding that she tell him. Paula was able to calm him down and convinced him to wait till Drake got home that night. She'd invited him to stay and have dinner with them. He always had liked Paula and Drake so he relaxed and waited.

After Drake got home, the two of them told Arlie what had happened and that she was in Belgium. He was stunned. He couldn't imagine Amanda having the guts to do something like

155

that. He just couldn't imagine it since she was afraid of her own shadow.

They tried to convince him that the marriage was over, that she had moved on, that it would be in his best interest to get a divorce. They told him that she would never forgive him for leaving her like he did and not letting her know where he was all that time. He begged them to listen to his side of the story.

He confessed that he had met another woman at the Plaza and had left Amanda for her, planned to go to Texas and start a new life with her. But then everything changed: he'd ended up in Arizona instead, with amnesia. Told them that he'd become a successful remodeling contractor, and also built new houses and log cabins with a partner.

His memory had just returned and he wanted Amanda to come back to Arizona with him. What he didn't tell them was that when his memory first came back, he had telephoned the woman in Texas. She had married someone else in the meantime and didn't want to have anything to do with Arlie. He was devastated. That's when he decided to go back to Amanda.

Paula felt sure about Amanda, felt she was strong enough to face Arlie once and for all and send him off with a kick in the seat of the pants. If Amanda didn't do it, Paula surely would. So they contacted Amanda and sent her a roundtrip ticket to come home and deal with Arlie.

At first Amanda said no, but then she decided that it needed to be settled once and for all, and she needed a divorce so she could get on with her life.

Now she was to meet him face to face; he was coming to meet them at the house in one hour.

"Baby, are you okay?" Paula asked. "You're not going to let him change your mind and bully you, are you?"

"He ain't gonna bully me. He can't. As far as I'm concerned, he already made his choice when he ran off to begin with. He's out of my life forever!" Amanda declared. "It takes a truckload of nerve for that jerk to waltz back into my life after he took off for another woman and then expect me to come running back to him and pick up where we left off. I looked up Miami, Arizona, on the internet. There ain't no way. Not after all I've seen and done and plan to do. I'm free of him. I just need the paper to prove it."

Drake came into the kitchen. "He's here. He just pulled up the driveway."

They all took deep breaths. Drake went to the door to let him in. "She's in the kitchen, Arlie."

When Arlie saw Amanda he was surprised at how pretty she was. He didn't remember her being that pretty and said so as he reached for her.

Amanda folded her arms and leaned against the countertop. "Stop where you are, Arlie. I've got some things to say to you. You know, you can't blame your amnesia for not remembering that I was your wife when you first took off; a wife that you promised to take care of till death do we part. Remember them words, Arlie?"

"I know, babe," he said, still reaching for her. "I know I did you wrong."

"Don't come any closer to me or I'll have Drake throw you out of here after I kick you in the nuts, you son of a bitch!"

"Why you talking to me like that, Amanda? I thought you came home to see me." Arlie looked confused.

Amanda frowned. "I did come here to see you. I came here to look you square in the eyes and tell you what I think of you. And that's not much. You're a lowlife, Arlie. You don't deserve me. I'm getting a divorce. That's what I'm here for. Then I'm going back to Belgium. I have a great life there."

"You can't do that."

Paula stepped between them. "Arlie, why would you want Amanda when she doesn't love you anymore? And you obviously don't love her or you wouldn't have gone off to be with that sleazy skank in Texas. Isn't that right? So why not just sign the papers and get it over with. Then you can go your own way and do whatever and live with whoever you want to. Amanda is way beyond you now. She's going to have her own business, Arlie. She's been supporting herself this whole time. She's even gone to school and learned a trade. So just let it be, darlin'."

He looked at Amanda, then back at Paula and Drake. "Drake, is this right? Do you think this is right?"

"Yes, I do, Arlie. You messed up big time. She ain't coming back to you. I can assure you of that. So you might as well accept it. It's over."

Arlie looked down at the floor for a moment, his hands on his hips. When he looked up he surprised them all with eyes full of tears.

"I'm sorry, babe. I'm really sorry I did that to you." He turned and headed for the door. "Just send me the papers, I'll sign. I'm staying at the Holiday Inn. Oh, here's my card. It has my address and my cell phone number on it. My new name is John Cramer, by the way."

He tossed the card on the table and left.

Amanda filed the divorce papers the next day, and then called Richard in Cupertino.

Chapter 35

It was mid afternoon when Richard picked up Amanda at Paula and Drake's. They drove to Visalia, an hour north of Bakersfield, for dinner at the Vintage Press Restaurant.

"I am so happy you're here, sweetheart." He took her hand in his and kissed it while driving.

Richard's touch was sensual. Amanda felt good. She was glad to see him and he looked more delectable than ever. She didn't think she would react as she had toward him. Maybe it was because she knew she would be free from Arlie in six months, and that she was an independent business woman now. The slate was clean. She wasn't just some dumb, ignorant blond, with no ambition or means to support herself.

"I am so glad that things are finally beginning to work for me," she said as she squeezed his hand.

"Of course you are, and I'm proud of you, Amanda. I wish you would reconsider and come home for good. We can get married and you can open a boutique in Cupertino. We could be together and travel whenever we wanted, even go to Belgium

159

any time you wanted. We could go all over Europe and Britain, visit your friend Rachel. I'd love to meet her, she sounds intriguing. We could invite her to the ranch. It would be a good life, Amanda. Please think about it."

"I will. And thank you for being so kind to me."

"I adore you, Amanda, and I love you with all my heart."

Amanda's eyes bore into his. It was at that very moment that she truly trusted and believed him. She felt he would always be there for her, and felt so much gratitude that she could almost say the words he wanted to hear, without any provocation. But she wasn't through with Belgium. She might not ever be through with Belgium. It was home to her now.

She touched his face. "I do care for you, Richard. I do. But I must finish what I've started in Belgium. You can understand that, can't you?"

"I can understand that you're young and you want to sow your wild oats and do all you want to do before getting married and settling down again. Yes, I can understand that. But then, I want to be there with you while you do all that. I've already done everything I want to do, now all I want is to be with you. But, I can wait. I promise I'll wait for you, my darling. Oh, I almost forgot. How could I?" He laughed as he reached into his inside jacket pocket. He pulled out her engagement ring, loose in his hand. "I know you want me hang on to this, but will you wear it at least while you're here? Please?" He slipped it on her finger.

Chapter 36

Amanda was eager to return to Bruges. While in the States, she spent as much time as she could with Richard without taking precious moments away from Paula and the baby. She knew it was going to be hard to leave them again, but she was determined to get back and work night and day to meet the deadline she and Rachel had set. For the first time in her life she felt in control, felt her life had meaning, felt worthy.

The day came to leave and this time Richard took her to the airport to bid her farewell. He had slipped an envelope of money and a note in her shoulder bag without her knowing. She would never ask for help, he knew that, and although her friend Rachel had come to the rescue, this way he felt he could still be as important in her life, too.

"Please call me if you need anything, anything at all, Amanda. You must believe that I love you and want you to be happy. You do, don't you?" He was holding on to her, not wanting to let go as she was about to board the plane.

"Yes, I believe, you, Richard. And I hope you understand that I have to do what I'm doing."

"I know you do, darling. You just take care and don't forget me. I'll be there for the opening of your shop, you can count on that. I wouldn't miss it for the world."

He felt as if his heart was being yanked from his chest and Amanda was slipping through his fingers. He could do nothing about it.

They kissed one more time.

Amanda pulled away gently. "Bye, Richard. I'll call you when I get there." She began walking away.

He stood watching her till she was out of sight, his heart aching.

Amanda was borderline teary for the first hour of the flight. She wondered if she was doing the right thing. Maybe it would be better if she stayed and married Richard. She could have a shop in Cupertino. She could make lace and design clothing there. Why did she have to do it in Belgium? Why?

She leaned against the window and closed her eyes. The strain of the past few days had finally taken its toll and she felt worn out. She fell sleep.

Antoine met her at the airport in Brussels, which was a surprise. She'd given him her arrival time and flight number, but she didn't think he would be there. She thought he would be working that morning. Nevertheless, she was happy to see him. She didn't feel a sexual attraction to him anymore; but he was a good friend, more like a brother to her. She valued his friendship and loved his girls.

Antoine pulled onto the main road to Bruges. He glanced at Amanda and grinned. "I've got some news for you, Mandy. I'm thinking about going back to university to become a history professor." His eyes were bright and excited.

"I didn't know you wanted to be a teacher? When did you decide this?"

"Before I married and had children, I was in university when my father died and I had to stop and go to work fulltime to help my mother. Then of course, I met Nadia and had the children. But now, I believe I can do it again, if I stay focused. There is an assistance program here at the university in Brussels, and they provide work, too. All I have to do is move to Brussels and enroll in the program."

"Your mother will come with you to take care of the girls?"

"Yes, of course. We've been looking for a place already."

Amanda reached over and hugged him. "This is good news."

"I've already given notice at the restaurant and to the landlord. I'll miss you, Mandy." His smile was gone as he glanced at her and then back to the street before him. "But I hope you will visit us, and we can take the girls on outings. They love you, Mandy."

He wished it was different. He fell for Amanda the first day they met, but he was wise enough to know from past experience he couldn't make someone love him. He had to get on with his life, same as she. When he realized she didn't feel as he did, he made his decision. He admired her and her strength and tenacity. Now he wanted to go for what he wanted most, and that was to finish school and become a history professor. He had his girls to think of and his own career. He didn't want to be a waiter for the rest of his life.

"I believe you're doing the right thing, Antoine. For you and for the girls." Amanda heard the words that tumbled from her mouth. She wondered at what point she had gained such sureness and wisdom. It wasn't so very long ago when her self-confidence had been non-existent, when she had felt as if she was worthless … couldn't do or say anything right, was shy and afraid of people, afraid of everything.

They rounded the corner to their street and Antoine pulled up in front of the stone apartment building. Workers were on scaffolding all the way up to the fourth floor.

"What are they doing?"

"The owner is renovating. New everything … plumbing, electrical wiring, painting. I'm probably getting out just in time before he raises the rent."

They both laughed as they opened their car doors. Antoine carried Amanda's luggage to the entrance.

"I can take it from here; you go ahead and park the car. And thank you so much, Antoine. Let's talk later after I unpack and get settled. I want to hear all about your plans."

Chapter 37

Winter was upon them and the cold weather had arrived in Bruges. Although it wasn't freezing, most days wouldn't get below 40° and November wasn't as cold as it would get, Amanda was already feeling the chill. She was told that the most rain fell in November. It was the wettest month of the year. Then the snow would come after that – December and January. January was the coldest.

Weather was never an issue with Amanda. She loved it in Bruges no matter what the weather produced. She was indoors most of the time anyway, making lace and attaching it to fabric. She'd bought top-of-the-line sewing machines and other equipment with the money Richard had slipped in her bag, and had quite a modern setup in her sewing room at the flat. She'd never been happier.

Antoine had already moved to Brussels and she'd already taken the train one Sunday to spend time with the girls and him.

She was stressed and pressed to have enough ready to open her shop in December. She and Rachel had decided it would be best if they rented a shop in Brussels and could open for business before Christmas, taking advantage of the holiday season. That is if they could get the licenses and all that was necessary to open on such short notice.

So Amanda found an existing shop that the designer was vacating on a busy lane leading to the Grand Place. The designer would sublet to Amanda till her lease was up, giving Amanda enough time to get the appropriate licenses after the first of the year. Amanda would sell on the existing designer's permit and would give her a cut. The shop would be empty the first week of December, so there wasn't much time left.

Rachel planned to be there a few days before, would rent a car and an apartment so they could move all the clothing from Bruges to Brussels. Antoine was going to help move the clothing.

The apartment over the shop wasn't available, so Rachel had made a few phone calls and found one further down over another. Neither one of them had seen it, but they decided it didn't matter. It would suffice till they found something else, if Amanda wasn't happy with it.

Richard was all set to be at the opening, as well as Drake and Paula and A.G. They all were coming.

Amanda went through a myriad of feelings; she was thrilled, but frightened, nervous, irritable, and worried. Could she do it? Could she be ready in time? What if her clothing didn't sell? What if no one liked what she created? What if she failed?

From morning till night she made jackets, skirts, blouses, dresses, pants, aprons, handkerchiefs, and scarves. Even a few kimonos like the ones she'd seen in other shops.

The store was tiny, fifteen-by-fifteen, so she was thankful for that. It wouldn't take much to make it look full. She'd found two standing full-length mirrors, gilded antiques, and the two dressing rooms would be created by hanging

166

curtains across the back corners of the room. The mirrors would stand outside the dressing rooms against the walls. Rachel was shipping framed antique prints of lace makers at work to adorn the walls above the racks of clothing. She'd found them on the Internet.

Amanda got up from her chair and stretched. She'd been making lace for four hours straight. It was time to take a walk and get a bite to eat. She missed Antoine being at the Craenenburg. It just wasn't the same without him, but that was the nearest café and she was starving. She didn't want to cook for herself.

She grabbed her purse and left the apartment and headed for the Markt.

Two hours later Amanda was still sitting at her regular table when she heard loud sirens. People were running outside and looking down the lane that ran alongside the Craenenburg. That was her street. She paid her tab and went outside to see what was happening.

As she rounded the corner of the Craenenburg, she was horrified to see trucks and ladders in front of her apartment building which was engulfed in smoke and flames.

"No! Oh God, no!" She ran down the lane but was stopped by the police who had set up a barricade preventing anyone from getting too close.

She screamed, "I have to get in there, please! I have to get everything out! Let me go! Don't you understand? It's all I have in the world!"

The policeman held her back. "You cannot go, Miss. The building is full of fire. There is nothing you can do. I am sorry, the building is destroyed."

Rebecca Randolph Buckley

PART FOUR

"Time removes pain and disappointment while you receive a renewed spirit and abundant blessings from the universe. Ask, believe, and it is yours."

Rebecca Buckley

Rebecca Randolph Buckley

Chapter 38

It was foggy at the Bakersfield airport. Amanda's heart flipped as she stepped from the airplane and saw Richard with Paula, Drake and A.G., waving and calling to her. Tears came to her eyes and she couldn't imagine ever leaving them again.

It had been determined that the cause of the fire had been faulty wiring by the electricians who had been doing the renovation. Nothing was salvageable from Amanda's apartment – not the machines, not the mirrors and other décor she'd collected for the shop, not the beautiful garments she'd made.

Now all she had was Richard. She was too tired to think of anything else. She loved him, she knew she did. She'd loved him all along; she just wasn't ready for a commitment so soon after being married to Arlie. She'd been caged by Arlie and she fought being caged by another.

Now all she craved was a protective and secure feeling with a person she knew would always be there for her. One who would never abandon her, one who would stand by her no matter what, one who would take care of her. She believed she would have that with Richard.

She had her chance in the world; she almost achieved her dream. She almost made it, but she failed. She figured that was more than most people achieved, and it didn't matter anymore.

As she stepped from the final rung of the descending steps of the plane, she ran right into the arms of Richard, who was striding quickly toward her on the tarmac. They held on to each other tightly. Yes, she felt safe in his strong arms and didn't want to ever leave them again. This was where she belonged … with Richard.

Paula tugged at Amanda, "Hey, I want to hug you, too, baby girl. You've got Richard for the rest of your life. My turn is now."

Amanda and Richard laughed as they stepped back from each other and Amanda wrapped her long arms around her sister.

"Oh, honey, you're a sight for sore eyes! You're gonna be all right now."

"I hope so. I hope so."

They held on to each other for several moments.

Finally, Amanda stepped back and said, "Now where's my baby A.G.?" She squatted down and held out her arms as Drake led the toddler to her. "There he is! Come here to your auntie Am, sweetie!" She swept him up and smothered him with kisses.

A.G. giggled as he called out "Auntie Am, Auntie Am, Auntie Am," to his daddy.

"He can talk? I can't believe it! He's too young to do that."

"We're been teaching him, hon," Drake said. "He's so smart, you just wait and see what all he can do and say. We're so happy to have you back home. And Richard has missed you, too. He's at our house more than he is at his own these days."

"That's right, Amanda," said Richard. "But now we can plan our wedding. I'm so eager to take you home with me. Here. Here's your ring. Let me put it on you right now."

He offered the ring to Amanda and she lifted the appropriate hand and finger to once again accept the commitment. It was on her finger to stay this time.

Tears filled her eyes as she gazed at the beautiful diamond while memories of Bruges, the cobbled streets, lacemaking, her shop, Antoine and the girls, the waterways, and the cafes flooded her mind. She felt a loneliness she couldn't explain. She wiped her eyes quickly, hoping no one would notice.

"My darling, you needn't cry, you're home safe and sound, now. Come here." Richard pulled her to him once again, lifted her chin with his thumb and kissed her on the lips, soft and long.

She didn't resist the kiss. Here it was. Here was her Prince Charming. Yes, Richard was the one. Here was where she belonged. She had to put Belgium behind her. That part of her life was over. She and Richard would have a wonderful life together. Everybody was happy.

Paula was more perky and excited than ever. "Let's go to the house and have us a big party!" she said as she scooped up baby A.G.

.

Chapter 39

Christmastime turned out to be bittersweet for Amanda. Her mind was filled with thoughts of Christmas in Brussels. Antoine had emailed and told her how festive the Grand Place was; how it was filled with decorations and Christmas lights, and how he hoped she was happy. He said the girls sent their love. He told her about school and that he would get his undergraduate degree in the spring.

It was good to hear from him, although it made her want to be there. She thought she had put all that behind her, but she just couldn't shake the thoughts of Belgium. She missed it. Now she was sorry she hadn't gone to Ghent and Antwerp and all the other outlying towns. She'd spent all her time in Bruges as it turned out, other than when she visited Rachel and then Antoine in Brussels. But all that didn't matter now, it was over. Maybe someday she and Richard could go back there for a visit. He said they would.

"Amanda, where are you?" Paula had just returned from town. "I need some help with the groceries."

"I'll be right there!" Amanda called out to her. Her bedroom and bath were off the family room. It was a huge guestroom with a panoramic view of the Kern River.

It took them nearly thirty minutes to unload the SUV and put away all the food and staples.

"I got us some sorbet, girl. Let's eat some right now, before A.G. wakes up." She set the container on the counter in front of Amanda.

Laughing, Amanda opened it and began scooping it into two dishes. "So when will Drake be home, did he say when you talked to him this morning?"

"Oh, in a couple days. You know how he is. He doesn't like to commit to a certain time and day. I think sometimes he likes to keep me guessin' so he can catch me doing something I shouldn't be doing." Paula sat at the kitchen bar and took a bite of the sorbet.

"Ha! And what would that be, pray tell?"

Paula shrugged. "Well, maybe I might get me a lover or something."

"You with a lover? I doubt that very much."

"Why would you doubt that?"

"Are you pulling my leg, Paula? You wouldn't do that. You love Drake." Lemon sorbet was Amanda's favorite and she was enjoying it, savoring the tartness.

"Well, that doesn't mean you can't have a little something on the side, does it?"

"Oh, Paula, stop it! I know you don't mean it."

Paula giggled. "No you don't. I just might want somebody younger. A toy boy, like on that cougar reality TV show." With a napkin she dabbed the sorbet that had dripped on her chin.

Amanda laughed. "Now that is the most ridiculous thing I've ever heard you say."

175

"Well, I might one of these days. You never know. Drake might get too old for me."

"Let's not talk about old. I mean, Richard is twenty-two years older than me. If anyone gets a toy boy, it should be me."

They both broke out laughing and couldn't stop.

"Have you and Richard done the deed, yet?"

"Paula! No, we haven't done the deed. And we're not going to till we're married."

"You're kidding me. You aren't going to get fitted for the saddle before you take it home?"

"For heaven's sake, no!"

"My, my, my … aren't we the old-fashioned one. It's not like you haven't done it before, Amanda. Why can't you do it with Richard?"

Amanda rose from the bar stool and rinsed her dish under the faucet. She'd been asking herself that same question. She didn't know why she couldn't make love with Richard. He wanted to, they talked about it, but she couldn't. "I'd rather not talk about it right now, if you don't mind." She thought of Adrian's lovemaking and how it had awakened something in her. She wasn't dreading it anymore.

"I bet I know what's wrong. You're scared. You ain't had nobody but Arlie, and I bet he wasn't the best in the sack. Hon, don't judge everybody else by Arlie. He seems like he'd be the most boring lay ever."

"Paula!"

"I mean it. I bet he was, wasn't he? Tell me, I'll tell you about Drake."

"I don't want to hear about Drake and you making love, Paula. How could you even think about telling me. That's too personal. All I know is that I didn't like it with Arlie. Let's change the subject. So when should we wrap the Christmas presents?"

Paula grinned. "Tonight after A.G. goes to sleep. We can hide them all in the sewing room. It's too bad Richard can't be here for Christmas."

"He had to go to Montana, something about cows."

Chapter 40

Paul knocked on Rachel's cottage door. He hadn't seen or heard from her in a week and he was worried. It was a stormy day in Newlyn on the afternoon of New Year's Eve.

"Rachel, it's Paul."

She opened the door and stood there in her robe, no makeup, her hair unkempt like it hadn't been combed for several days. "I'm not feeling well, Paul."

He caught her as her eyes rolled back into her head and she fainted. "Oh no! Rachel, darling?"

He didn't mean to say 'darling,' it just rolled off his tongue, although he knew it was okay to call other women 'darling.' He knew Belinda wouldn't mind him saying that to Rachel. So why was he so self-conscious about it? Nevertheless, he was glad Rachel hadn't heard it.

After he placed her on the sofa, he ran to the bathroom and moistened a towel to put on her forehead. He was patting her cheeks with it when she opened her eyes.

"What happened?" she said as she sat up, removing the towel from her face.

"You answered the door and passed out."

"Yikes! I'm so sorry. I'm just a little weak, have the flu."

He frowned. "Are you sure it's the flu, Rachel? You've been having the flu a lot in the past few weeks. Maybe you should get a thorough checkup."

"No, it's just that my system has had a shock and I'm still getting over it, Paul. That's all it is. You have enough to worry about. Don't worry about me."

"I can't help it; I couldn't take it if both my girls—" He stared tearfully into Rachel's face for a moment and then covered his own face with his hands and wept.

"Oh, my darling, Paul." She stood and bent over him from behind as he sat on the footstool, wrapping her arms around him, resting her chin on his head. "You have way too much to bear. Don't worry about me. I'll be fine. You just concentrate on Belinda, and you have to believe she's going to recover. You know that, don't you?"

He took hold of Rachel's arms and pulled her around in front of him. He stood up and held her tightly to him. "Rachel … Rachel … Rachel … "

They held on to each other, feeling each other's pain for what seemed like minutes, but was really only seconds. Finally Rachel loosened her grip and so did he. There was a moment of awkwardness, and then they were back to normal.

"I'll fix some tea. You just sit over there and relax. I want to tell you my new plans, okay?" She went into the kitchen.

Paul took a deep breath, sighed, and sat down on the sofa. "This is New Year's Eve, you know."

Rachel appeared in the kitchen doorway, holding the tea kettle. "And five years ago to the day, we met." She threw him a kiss.

179

He laughed as she returned to the tea-making, remembering their first New Year's and all that had followed since. How he and Belinda got together: his heart attack, her rape, the move to Cornwall …

"Here we go, tea for two." Rachel seemed to have regained her strength. She'd even brushed her hair and put on lipstick.

"So are you doing anything special tonight?" he asked her.

Rachel shook her head. "No. I hadn't planned on doing anything."

"Why don't I take you to the Ship Inn for dinner? Just the two of us."

"But what about Belinda?"

"She's really sick right now, Rachel. She told me to get out of the house and do something. Actually, she told me to come over here and take you to dinner. Her mother is with her. I hated to leave, but there's nothing I can do for her when she's like this. Those treatments are nearly killing her." He began to get emotional again.

"All right, I'll go to dinner with you. Just give me a few moments. Drink your tea, I'll get ready. Maybe it would be good for both of us to get out amongst the living." She realized what she'd said and immediately tried to take it back. "Oh, I didn't mean that like that … I'm so sorry, really—"

"I know you didn't. But you're right, it's time we thought of ourselves for at least one night." He grinned at Rachel and his silver-blue eyes lit up for the first time in a long time.

Chapter 41

Mousehole's Ship Inn was crammed with people. Rachel had dressed in black jeans and a black angora sweater with a low V-neck. She felt much better than she had in weeks.

They'd gone to see Belinda first, and Paul changed into slacks and a sweater himself. Belinda had been asleep, and not wanting to awaken her, Paul and Rachel spoke with her mother and left quietly. She had had a very rough day of pain from the treatments that were taking their toll on her back and legs, and the painkillers had finally taken effect and put her to sleep.

The Ship Inn was a local watering hole in Mousehole, and everyone for miles came around on important holidays - the eve before Christmas Eve and on New Year's Eve, especially.

"I love this place!" Paul said loudly over the noise, which consisted of music and the impromptu choir of imbibing celebratory voices. He escorted Rachel to the bar where they were surprised to find two stools unoccupied. The bartender said the couple had just left to go to Penzance, so they were lucky no one had taken them yet.

"I wonder if Tom and Peter are coming in." Rachel lifted the champagne that Paul had just poured for her. He'd ordered a bottle and it was in a cardboard ice bucket in front of them on the bar.

"I haven't seen them around lately. One of them usually drops by the studio, at least on the weekends. Maybe they went away for Christmas or decided to stay in London for New Year's. I would imagine their friends have fantastic parties in London."

"They probably throw the parties themselves. Can you imagine? Tom a decorator, Peter a painter. Their apartment in London must be over the top, if it's anything like what they've done to the cottage here." She sipped from the glass.

"Hey, wait a minute. We have to make a toast."

"Oops. Sorry." She laughed.

"Let me see ... how about to all those who are dearest to us."

"And may we have the happiness we deserve," Rachel added.

"Hear, hear."

They clanked glasses and looked into each other's eyes as they sipped.

Rachel looked away first. Paul's gaze still did something to her, after all this time. That had never changed. It was his gaze that had captured her attention in the first place.

"So how are the painting sales these days?" she asked.

Paul came out of a reverie and double-blinked his eyes, attempting to clear his mind. "Oh, well, sales are good. We hit records this season. Belinda's sculptures, too. Both of us did well. What about you, are you working on your novel?"

"Nope. I can't seem to get back into it yet. Oh it's done; I just need to do the final edit before sending it to my agent. But I'm useless right now."

"Maybe you should take a trip, get away from the reminders." He was reluctant to say it, but he felt he must.

She sipped her drink, not responding.

"Rachel, you have to move on. He's not coming back."

She remained silent without looking at him and continued sipping. Finally she gulped the remaining liquid and asked for another drink.

He poured, and then they both gazed at the people around them.

The Ship Inn pub had a low ceiling; it was dark with gigantic beams holding up the floors above them, heavy wooden tables with benches and chairs filled the dining rooms. The front of the building faced the harbor. A narrow lane passed between the building and the sea wall edge and only one vehicle could traverse at a time. A lot of backing up and waiting for the other to pass took place every day and night. The wise and experienced visitors parked on the outskirts of the village and walked in.

Mousehole was a tiny fishing hamlet set in the hillside along the sea. Its yellow-lichened granite cottages covered the hillsides in rows all the way down to its harbor. A tourist attraction, many artisans soon found their way to the quaint village to work and sell their wares, Belinda and Paul among them.

Rachel's cottage in Newlyn was two miles south overlooking Newlyn Harbor, and Paul's home was a half mile further south above the Penzance Road on the hillside facing Mount's Bay.

"What shall we have for dinner?" Paul asked her. "Any suggestions?"

Rachel looked up on the chalkboard above the bar and after a moment's thought she said, "Let's be simple and order fish & chips. I haven't had that in a long time."

"Works for me." He motioned to the bartender and ordered for both of them.

"So how is it working out with Belinda's mother here? She's got to be a godsend, right?"

"I don't know what I would do without her. A friend of hers is managing the B&B in London while she's here, and of course she goes back a couple days every two weeks to check on things and take a rest. So it seems to be working out all right for her, business-wise. When I go to London I stay at her place to see what's going on, too. Her friend doesn't know who I am, so that works to our advantage."

"So what are the doctors saying about Belinda?" Rachel sipped as she watched Paul's reaction.

He sat up straight, stretched his neck and placed his glass on the bar in front of him. It took a few moments before he answered. "They don't know at this point. It's a non-Hodgkin's. They're saying it's T-cell lymphoma. As long as it doesn't spread to the bone marrow, she'll be all right. That's what they're trying to prevent. Once it's in the bone marrow there's only a forty to fifty percent chance of survival. So that's where we are. It isn't in her bone marrow."

"Thank God! So that's good, isn't it? She's going to make it, Paul. I just know she is."

"We'll find out after the third round of chemo. But c'mon, let's not talk about it tonight. We both need some R&R from our miseries, don't you think? Let's think of all the good things in our lives. Here, give me a hug." He stood up and put his arms around her. "Now this feels good. I wish we could stay this way all night."

Rachel didn't comment. She was stunned that he'd said what he said as well as by what he was doing. She had to admit it felt good to have a man's arms around her again. Thoughts of Pete began to flood her mind … she had loved being held by

Pete, making love together. She wondered what it would be like to make love with Paul—but as soon as she thought it she flinched and pulled away. What was the matter with her? Paul was her best friend's husband! She shook her head and picked up her drink.

Paul frowned. "What's wrong? Did I say the wrong thing?"

"No, I was thinking the wrong thing!"

"Like what?" He sat on the stool and took a drink from his glass.

Rachel shook her head. "I don't want to talk about it, really."

"Well, I do wish we could be in each other's arms all night. I meant it, Rachel."

"Don't say that! Belinda's my best friend! Your wife!"

Paul straightened his shoulders and fidgeted in his seat. "Nothing wrong with thinking. I love Belinda, you know that. I adore her. But I've felt something for you since the first day we met. And I know you feel the same. I can see it in your eyes."

"We've talked about that before, Paul. It has something to do with our past lives. If you want to talk about past lives, fine, but let's enjoy the rest of the evening in the now and be true to Belinda and to the memory of Pete. All right? Excuse me; I'm going to the ladies' room."

Paul felt terrible for what he had just said and hoped it wasn't too late to get back on track. He didn't mean to upset Rachel even though he enjoyed holding her, he had to admit that. But he would never cheat on Belinda, never. Especially during her illness. He loved his boys, loved their life together, and he wouldn't do anything to jeopardize any of that.

He had Belinda to thank for saving him from his addictions – sex and cocaine, a deadly mixture. Both had been killing him, and when he had the heart attack she'd been right there for him when no one else was. But that wasn't enough; it took the tragic gang-rape that almost killed her to finally get them together. She was so fragile during that time, and all he wanted to do was to take care of her. And he did. And they fell in love.

"Hey, big guy … I'm sorry I jumped at you. Forgive me?" Rachel ran her hand along his shoulders as their eyes locked. "Nothing wrong with hugging. Here, one quick one before I sit down."

He swiveled around and pulled her toward him, squeezing her tightly. "I just need to hold someone, Rachel. I'm sorry I frightened you. I didn't mean anything by it. I miss Belinda."

"I know. I miss Pete. Okay, that's enough. Let's not overdo it."

They both laughed and lifted their glasses.

"Happy New Year, luv."

She clanked his glass and replied, "Happy New Year."

Chapter 42

In March Amanda and Richard drove to his ranch northwest of Santa Cruz along the Pacific coastline. He picked up Amanda in Bakersfield to take her to her new home, his ranch, for the April wedding. The drive from Highway One to the house nestled in the coastal range was two miles from the entrance gate. The name of the ranch, *Miller Valley Ranch*, was sculpted in metal over the entrance and very impressively done. Amanda was amazed at the artistic rendering and the electronically controlled rustic metal gates. As they drove through, Richard told her the gates and the archway had been sculpted by a local artisan.

When they pulled up in front of the sprawling adobe buildings, resembling a western resort rather than a single ranch house, a young woman near Amanda's age opened another ornate gate fronting the main courtyard. She stood waiting.

Richard called out to her as he stepped from the car. "Darys! Come greet Amanda."

Darys wasn't smiling. She was frowning.

"Who is she, Richard?" Amanda felt the cold stare from Darys long before she was close enough to see it.

"Darys is my daughter," he said as he popped the trunk and waved to some ranch hands that were standing by smoking cigarettes.

Amanda stopped dead in her tracks and gave Richard a questioning look. A feeling of doom shot through her. "You didn't tell me you had a daughter." She adjusted her purse strap over her shoulder and stood tall as Richard reached for her hand.

"Will you take Amanda's luggage upstairs to the blue guest wing, Jered?" He looked at Amanda. "Actually, I was afraid to tell you, darling. I hope you'll forgive me." He led her to his daughter and formally introduced them to each other.

Four weeks passed and Amanda was falling in love with ranch life almost as much as she was in love with Richard. His ranch stretched all the way to the Pacific Ocean. They would ride horses to the top of the coastal mountain range and gaze out over the sea. A few times they took wine, blankets, food, and would picnic on the grassy mounds with the terrific views: the coastal road curving up the mountain to the cliffs to their right, the road to the left ran along the sea's edge to Santa Cruz. Amanda had never seen such beauty.

Her memories of Belgium were dissipating, except when she would lie awake at night, unable to block them from her mind. She knew she would be all right with Richard; she just had to separate the thoughts of all she'd left behind from reality.

The reality was that she was with Richard now, and they were to be married in two weeks in the little chapel on the hill in Cupertino. Her sister was coming, her brother-in-law and little A.G., too.

Even Frenchie and her fiancé Lance were flying up. She told Amanda on the phone that she wouldn't miss her wedding for anything in the world.

Paula told Amanda that Frenchie felt responsible for her and Richard getting together, and she reveled in that fact. Frenchie said she felt as if Amanda was her own daughter, and had cried for joy when she found out about the impending wedding.

Everyone was happy for Amanda.

Amanda opened her eyes after lying awake for over an hour. She looked out the windows above the window seat and marveled at the streaks of light of the rising sun peeking over the mountains. The early morning shadows were intriguing to Amanda. She stared into them every morning, making out the shapes of the dwellings and objects slowly coming into focus.

She loved mornings. Richard would already be up and ready to have his morning coffee with her. They slept in separate bedrooms. She still hadn't given her body to him, but she knew it was going to happen very soon. Richard said he could wait until they were married. She felt guilty about making love to Antoine before Richard. She didn't know why it was such an issue with her, why she couldn't make love to Richard.

She glanced at the clock and moved gracefully through the spacious bedroom into the walk-in closet housing her meager wardrobe. Although Richard had offered to expand her wardrobe, she told him no, she had all she needed.

After donning a pair of jeans and a long sleeved navy blue pullover, Amanda went into the bathroom that was almost as big as her apartment in Bakersfield had been. She brushed her teeth and hair, washed her face and slipped her feet into sandals as she left the bedroom, eager to get to her husband-to-be.

Darys was coming down the hall toward her.

"Good morning, Darys."

"If you say so."

Amanda turned and watched Darys continue down the hallway. She hadn't had any luck in getting through to her. It was plain and simple: Darys didn't want Amanda in her father's life. She was rude to Amanda, and was doing all she could to sabotage her stay at the adobe, hoping Amanda would just give up and go away. Amanda hadn't told Richard the mean things Darys had said and done to her.

For instance, the day they went horseback riding together. Amanda invited Darys to go with her, hoping to bond with her somewhat. Darys had insisted they ride bareback, no saddles. Said she'd teach Amanda how to ride without a saddle. So Amanda went along with it.

They took off together across the pasture and up the small hills, heading up the mountain. At one point they stopped and Darys suggested they take a shortcut over the hill. It was a steep one with loose and damp dirt from a recent landslide after the rain. Darys took off up the hill with her horse lurching at every leap to grab hold with his front hooves and then following with his hind feet. It was a violent gallop uphill, in almost a bucking motion. She called down to Amanda to follow.

So Amanda, being a novice and not knowing how difficult it would be with a saddle much less without one, attempted to repeat the effort of Darys. Halfway up she'd started sliding back toward the hindquarters of the horse, holding on to his mane for dear life. She dropped the reins. With every lurch, the horse's upper backbone slammed into Amanda's chest. The pain was horrific and it was hard for her to breathe, but she held on to his neck and mane all the way to the top where she let go and immediately slid to the ground. She lay there in pain, unable to move.

Darys laughed.

"I think … you better … get some help. Pain … can't breathe …"

"Oh, you'll be all right. Just give it a minute. I'll meet you back at the house." She rode off, leaving Amanda on the ground.

After a few minutes, Amanda figured she couldn't just lie there forever. It was getting dark.

She screamed as she sat up, the pain piercing her chest. She leaned forward and got to her knees and then to her feet. She felt nauseated and dizzy as the pain enveloped her body. *That damn girl! I'll kill her!*

She stepped to the horse who luckily was still standing by. He hadn't followed Darys's horse back to the ranch. Now she had to get on him. Without a stirrup. She led him to a fallen tree and managed to climb up on him after several tries, still writhing with pain. It felt like someone had smashed her chest and it was caving in with every breath she took.

The horse was easy to control heading home, which was to her advantage, for if he would have galloped she knew she wouldn't have been able to hold on.

When she reached the stables, Jered and a few of the ranch hands were standing around waiting to have supper. Jered saw her pained expression and the mud on her clothing and ran to her.

"What happened, Miss?"

"… went riding with Darys … got hurt … she left me."

"Bill, get the boss, right now! Al, you call Doc." Jered helped her from the horse and was carrying her to the house, her head on his shoulder, when Richard appeared, running toward them with Bill behind.

"Oh, God! What happened, Jered? Darling, what is it?"

Jered kept walking to the house. "You might ask your daughter, Mr. Miller."

Amanda was unconscious.

Darys's version of the story was that she and Amanda had gone riding. When she wanted to go home, Amanda told her to go ahead, that she wanted to stay out longer. And that's all she knew.

Amanda didn't dispute the story, although Jered and the ranch hands knew she was protecting Darys, didn't want to make waves. They all knew how merciless Darys could be when crossed. They'd experienced it themselves. Her father would never believe she was capable of doing anything wrong.

Two days before the wedding, Amanda was sitting in the den in front of the fireplace, reading. Darys came in and sat across from her.

"You're after our money, aren't you?"

Amanda looked up in disbelief at Darys. "What?"

"You're after our money, but you won't get it. When he dies, I get it. So why don't you just move along?"

"Darys, I'm not after your money. I'm not after anything – the house, the money, it's yours. That's fine with me. I don't want it. Surely you don't feel that about me."

"You don't fool me. Everybody knows it. No one likes you. None of our friends want you here, and neither do I. He was going to marry Elaine before you came along. She should be his wife. She's his kind. He bought that ring for her you're wearing. She picked it out."

Amanda sat silently for a few moments, glancing at her ring and hearing Darys's words echoing in her mind. She closed her book, stood up, and said quietly, "I love your father and he loves me. I'm sorry about Elaine, and the ring."

She sadly left the den and went to her bedroom to get ready for the pre-wedding party Richard was giving that night for all his friends.

Although she still had twinges of pain in her broken sternum from the horse hammering his back bone into her chest, the pain medication and carefulness in which she carried herself was helping her mend.

Her thoughts switched to what it would be like to make love with Richard on their wedding night, just two nights away. Would the sternum pain interfere? Would she be able to be what Richard wanted? She wanted everything to be perfect. And she wondered what he would say if he knew she and Antoine had been intimate. She pushed that thought out of her mind almost as fast as it entered.

That night before the party, Richard told her the story of Darys's mother. She had never married Richard. They had had a torrid affair when they were young; she'd gotten pregnant, and after she had the baby had left it with him. She didn't want anything to do with a child. She took off and he had never heard from her again. He tried to find her when Darys became a teenager and was asking questions he couldn't answer.

He felt his daughter needed her mother, but she was not to be found. He felt guilty and protective of Darys, shielded her from real life, gave her all she wanted, spoiled her. When she was sixteen, she rebelled and ran off and married the wrong guy. Richard went after her and brought her back home. He paid off the groom, who gladly took the money and ran.

Since Darys was ten years old, Richard had dated Elaine Morris, who owned a gift shop in town. The only thing that bothered him about Elaine and had kept him from committing to her was that she had a terrific temper. And she was possessive. But he'd finally made the decision to ask her to marry him just before he met Amanda. He felt he was getting older and that it was time to settle down.

He had discussed it with Darys, who was one hundred percent in favor of it. Elaine and Darys were good friends, and Elaine had even told Darys which ring she'd like to have. She'd taken her to the local jewelry store and pointed it out to her. Darys told her dad and he bought it, planning to give it to Elaine.

But before that happened, he met Amanda on one of his trips to Bakersfield and everything changed.

Darys was unhappy.

Elaine was unhappy.

Richard knocked at Amanda's bedroom door. "Darling, are you ready?"

She opened the door, looking like a puff of pink cotton candy.

He gasped. "You are the most beautiful creature I've ever seen! Where did you get that dress?"

"I made it myself. Wait till you see my bridal gown," she teased.

The dress she was wearing could have been the wedding dress, except that it was pale pink. It had a pink lace, strapless, fitted bodice with pink tulle flowing in layers from the waistline to mid-calf in a full, puffy skirt. Matching lace-covered dancing slippers enhanced the creation.

"Your shoes, did you make those, too?" He was flabbergasted.

Amanda laughed. "Actually, I did make the lace that covers them. This is what I learned while I was in Bruges. I make lace, design and make dresses, and cover shoes."

"You are spectacular! And your hair, how did you do that? I've never seen it twisted up like that. It looks so elegant. Darling, I am proud to have you as my wife."

"Not a wife yet." She grinned up at him, sensually.

His mind flooded with thoughts of how much she had evolved, changed. It was just a little over a year ago when he'd first met the shy, young, timid girl from Arkansas who wouldn't even look into his eyes. She'd stolen his heart then and now she had captured his mind, body, and soul. How he loved and adored her!

"Shall we?" He held out his arm and they headed down the corridor toward the ballroom he'd built for special occasions such as this.

As they rounded the corner and entered the hall leading past the den, Darys and Elaine stepped in front of them.

"Good evening, ladies. What do you think of our princess Amanda here? Isn't she glorious?" Something warned him that all was not right. He drew Amanda to him, put his protective arm around her. "So why aren't you two in the ballroom?"

"You can't do this, Daddy. You can't marry this woman. She's after your money, can't you see that?" Darys pulled at Amanda's arm. "Get away from my daddy, you gold digger!"

"Darys! How dare you! What's the matter with you?" He stepped in front of Amanda, guarding her.

"She's right, Richie! You've been fooled!" Elaine warned. "That girl is too young for you and she's no good. She treats Darys horribly, and you don't know what's been happening! What's the matter with you? Your pecker taking control of your brain, as usual?"

Jered and Bill came running toward them after hearing the commotion. "What's wrong, Boss?"

"I think these ladies need to be escorted from the premises, Jered. Put them in the Jeep and drive them to Elaine's house. Right now."

Darys screamed, "I'm not leaving my own house! I won't go! She's evil! She planned this! Please, Daddy! Don't send me away; you're all I've got! Please ... please!"

Jered was practically dragging her out the side door as Bill escorted Elaine behind them.

Elaine stopped and glared back at Amanda. "You won't last, you bitch. We'll run you out of town, just you wait and see. Your life will be miserable."

Bill jerked her arm and they disappeared into the night.

Amanda shivered. "I can't go in there now."

"Yes, you can," Richard assured her. "You're going to be my wife, darling. Don't listen to those two. I'll deal with Darys. she'll get over it. She will."

Later, while everyone was sleeping in the early morning hours before daybreak, Amanda knocked on Paula and Drake's door at the motel in Cupertino where they were staying for the wedding and asked them to take her back home to Bakersfield. She told them what had happened and that she wanted to leave right then. They bundled up little A.G. and left for the San Joaquin Valley.

By noon, when Richard realized Amanda wasn't asleep in her room, the phone at Paula and Drake's started ringing off the hook. No one answered. The calls went to the answering machine.

"That's him again. I have to go back to Belgium, Paula. I can't stay here," Amanda sobbed. "I've got to go. He'll give up calling and will come down here after me. I can't go back to the ranch. I'm afraid of Darys and Elaine."

"Are you sure you want to do this, hon?"

"They'll hurt me. They'll find a way. You know they will. Darys has already tried."

"Okay, okay. Let's talk about this. Hold on." Paula stuck her head out of the bedroom and yelled, "Drake, come in here, right now! Hurry!"

Drake came running, thinking something terrible had happened. "What is it? What's the matter, babe?"

"Amanda wants to go back to Belgium, today."

Amanda wiped her eyes and took Drake's hand. "I have to go. I can stay with Antoine. He moved to Brussels from Bruges to be closer to school. I told you about him. I'm sure I can stay with him till I find my own place. I can do it, Drake. I can make a living with my lace and dresses. It's a designer's Mecca, especially new designers, beginners. I just need some financial help until I get on my feet. Can you help me out? I'll pay you back, I promise."

"Amanda, I have no doubt that you would, but don't you worry about paying any of it back to us. We have more than we need anyway. You're a gutsy girl, and I admire your strength and braveness. So figure out what you need, but we've got to get going. I'm sure Richard is on the road right this minute. We can figure out what you need on the way to the airport. We'll drive to L.A., you can fly out of LAX and we'll buy the ticket over the phone on the way. So grab what you absolutely need and let's get going."

"I'll sign a paper, Drake. We'll say that you and Paula are partners in—in Mandy Malone Designs. That's what I'm going to call my shop. Deal?"

"Okay, okay, deal! Now get movin'!" Drake hugged her and headed for the garage to get the SUV.

Paula grinned. "See why I married that lug, Amanda? I'll get little A.G.'s stuff, so you hurry up now. Okay?"

Amanda put her arms around her sister. "I love you, Paula."

"I love you too, honey babe. Like I always say, we Conroy sisters have got to stick together!"

Chapter 43

When Amanda arrived in Brussels, she went directly to the Metropole Hotel and got a room. She'd made the decision on the plane. Even though it was an expensive hotel, she didn't know of any others. It was familiar to her. She still had some of the money that Rachel and Richard had given her before. Besides, with Antoine's mother and two daughters with him, it would most likely be crowded. It shouldn't take her long to find an apartment. She figured she could always sell the engagement ring if she needed to, now that she knew it had been purchased for Elaine, it didn't mean a damn thing to her.

Amanda was feeling stronger and more determined than she ever had. She knew exactly what she was going to do. She would recruit lace-makers at the school in Bruges to make the lace for her garments that she would design. She would set up a sewing room above a shop and pay seamstresses to do the work. She would manage the shop and the sewing room.

If she was frugal, she could do it. Within two months, by the end of June, if she could find the people she wanted, she could be back in business. She also had to get all the necessary permits to have a business in Brussels. And she had to see if they could rush it all through for her … evidently it usually took four months to get all the paperwork cleared.

She needed Rachel.

"Rachel. Hi, it's Amanda." She sat at the window in her hotel room looking down on the busy boulevard.

"Amanda! Oh, I'm so glad you called. I talked to Paula last night and she told me what had happened. Girl, you are doing the right thing. So what's the plan? Where are you?"

"I'm at the Metropole, decided not to stay with Antoine, don't want to bother him. And tomorrow I'm going to find a shop with an apartment overhead. I'm sure if I look hard enough, I'll find one, even if I have to talk to the existing shop owners. I hear that sometimes they move out at a moment's notice. Lots of new designers just out of school set up shop then sell all the merchandise they have and close up. So that might be a way to go, too."

"You're absolutely right." Rachel walked to the edge of the cliff in her back garden overlooking the boats in Newlyn Harbour below. She'd been sitting on the iron settee that Pete had given her when she moved into the cottage. On her approval, he had arranged the purchase for her cottage while she had been in the States at her mother's funeral. She'd been thinking about Pete all morning and how he ought the cottage sight unseen because he knew what she wanted, and that she trusted his judgment.

"Rachel, I was thinking, maybe you could help me get the permits. I don't know a thing about that. I've decided to hire lace makers and seamstresses to help me put together a collection and I think I can be ready in two months so we can open in June. But they say the permits might take about four months to get. Do you have any ideas?"

"Just leave that to me. We can do anything we set our minds to, luv."

It immediately dawned on Amanda that she'd been selfish and had not asked Rachel about how she was doing. How insensitive it was, when here she was still grieving over the loss of Pete.

"I'm so sorry, Rachel. I should have asked you about you. Are you all right?"

"Oh, I'm doing okay. I'm even better now that you're back and we can get back to planning. I haven't felt like writing, can't get my mind off Pete. I finished the book before I left Brussels, though, but haven't done the final read-through and edit. And Belinda has been having a really rough time, is on another round of chemo. I don't know how that girl can stand it. So it's been pretty depressing around here."

"Well, as soon as I get the apartment and shop, why don't you come and help me get everything ready?"

"That's a terrific idea!" Rachel walked across the lawn to the French doors that led into her bedroom. "You know, I could come and help you find a place. Would you like me to do that?"

"Could you? That would be even better, two of us looking. Besides, I'd like the company. I really would. This has all been rather overwhelming, although I feel fantastic!"

"Okay, I'll make arrangements to come by the end of the week. You go ahead and line up the lace makers and seamstresses and whatever else you'll need. This is exciting! You're just what the doctor ordered."

"You're a dream come true, Rachel."

"See you soon."

The next few days were a whirlwind for Amanda. She took a train to Bruges to talk to the sisters at the Kantcentrum and was able to find some women to make lace for her. She would pick up the pieces, made to her specs, on Mondays and Thursdays.

Then she found seamstresses through the Brussels newspaper who advertised for work. She was set; all she needed now was the equipment and the space.

The night before Rachel was to arrive, Amanda decided to clear her head and relax without thinking of anything. She went downstairs to the Metropole Café and had a light supper and a glass of wine. As she was sitting there watching the people enjoy their Friday night after work, out of the corner of her eye a familiar shape was taking form.

It was Richard coming through the doorway heading straight for her.

Her heart skipped a few beats and then began to pick up speed. She was getting dizzy with surges of adrenaline. How did he know where she was?

"Hello, little lady." He scooted close to her in the leather booth in the corner of the café. "This is a cozy café, isn't it? Waiter?" He motioned to a nearby server. "I'll have the same as the lady, please. In fact, bring a bottle of it, will you?"

Amanda was speechless and her mouth was hanging open. She couldn't think of anything to say.

"So. You're looking lovely."

She finally gained her wits and whispered, "How did you know I was here?"

"It was easy to find out. I'm pretty clever that way."

She could tell he was angry, but in control of it. His words and mannerisms were tight and restrained.

"I'm sorry I left like I did, Richard. I should have discussed it with you."

"Yes. That would have been the right thing to do."

The waiter brought the bottle and poured two glasses.

"Let's make a toast, shall we?" He lifted his glass and waited for her to do so. His eyes were cold and steely. "To the truth, now and forevermore."

Amanda hesitated, and then took a sip. She was a little frightened—she'd never seen him this way.

"So when were you going to explain? You left me at the altar, Amanda. Why was that?"

"I ... well ... I—"

"Is there someone else?"

"Oh no! Not at all! Of course not."

"Then why?" His eyes were filling with tears. He closed them for a moment. "Never mind, don't answer that just yet. Let's just have a glass or two. I need to relax, and then we can talk. Is that all right with you?" He breathed deeply.

"Richard, I am so sorry. I really am. But I didn't know what else to do."

"Let's just not talk about it right now, okay?"

"All right. But will you forgive me?"

He moved closer to her and put his arm around her. "Darling, I could never be angry at you for very long. You must have had a good reason to run like you did. And I've been miserable ever since. Did it have anything to do with my daughter?"

She hesitated, "Yes, it did."

"I thought so. My foreman told me some of it, and Paula hinted at the rest."

"I thought we weren't going to talk about it right now." She attempted a smile.

"You're right. I'm just so happy to see you. I didn't know if I'd find you or not. I couldn't get it out of Paula, but Drake came through like a champ."

Amanda smirked. "That stinker."

They both laughed.

After dinner together, the tension had subsided and it was like it had been before the wedding fiasco. Amanda told Richard what had happened and he assured her that he would take care of it, would make sure nothing like that would occur again.

Amanda just listened to him at that point, wondering how she was going to tell him she wasn't going back to the States, ever. She was going to live in Belgium.

They each ordered a brandy with cheesecake and Richard grinned at Amanda as they waited for it.

"You know, you're even prettier than you were when you left. Belgium must be good for you."

"It is. I love it. I'm happiest here." Amanda almost told him more, but stopped herself.

"I have some business to take care of in Belgium, believe it or not, so I'm going to stay for a couple of weeks. Do you mind?" Richard asked her.

Amanda hesitated. "Uh, well, I'm going to be pretty busy, and my friend Rachel is arriving in the morning to spend some time with me—"

"That's all right, sweetheart, I won't interfere with your plans. I'll be busy most of the time anyway, during the day. Maybe we can meet for lunch occasionally, and of course dinner. I'd love to meet your new friend."

She knew she had to tell him soon, but not right then, at that particular moment. Later.

"I think you'll like Rachel." She smiled and lowered her eyes to her glass.

The waiter brought the dessert and the brandy and they ate and sipped until it all had disappeared.

Amanda smiled. "Would you like to take a walk to the Grand Place?" She touched his hand and gave it a squeeze. "Come on, let's walk."

"That's a great idea. I need to walk off all the calories I just gobbled up and drank." Richard wasn't accustomed to an aggressive Amanda. This was new to him. He liked it.

"I do, too. Let's go."

Richard stood up. "Let me tell the waiter to put the tab on my room."

Amanda looked up at him. "You're staying here?"

"Yes, I checked in earlier. Called your room, but you didn't answer. Then I saw you in here."

"Pretty slick, Mister," Amanda mumbled as she pushed her chair back and stood.

Chapter 44

Amanda was up at seven. The plan was to have breakfast with Richard in the breakfast room downstairs, and then he was going out to take care of his business. Rachel would be arriving around eleven. So Amanda had plenty to do. She was going to try and locate a supplier for commercial sewing machines. It shouldn't be difficult since Brussels was a fashion center for new designers and there were several designer schools around.

Richard was waiting for her in the foyer of the hotel. He had a commanding presence and looked even more handsome in a grey suit with an open-collared black shirt. His graying blond hair, tan skin and blue eyes topped off the perfect portrait before her. She couldn't believe he was there for her. How did she ever capture this man's heart?

"Ah, there you are. Are you hungry, darling?"

Amanda smiled. "As a matter of fact, I am. I don't know why, after all we had last night." She laughed. "The pastry on the square and the champagne afterwards. It's a wonder I was able to get out of bed this morning after all that."

"The walk offset it all," Richard said through a grin.

They went into the breakfast room, reserved for guests only, and had a light meal. The huge buffet spread was tempting, but they decided to keep it simple to save room for later.

"So when does Rachel arrive?" asked Richard.

"Eleven, but I have some things to do before she gets here, so I'll be busy."

"I'll be back around four or five; shall I meet the two of you in the café?"

"That will be perfect," Amanda answered.

They went their separate ways after breakfast. Amanda back to her room to make phone calls, Richard left the hotel in a cab.

Once in the cab, he used his universal phone to call an estate agent he'd found in the phone book earlier. He confirmed a nine o'clock appointment to look at country estates outside of Brussels and had hoped to find what he was looking for in one day. After a lengthy phone conversation with Paula, he knew exactly what he wanted, so it shouldn't be difficult.

By two in the afternoon he found it. It was perfect and was twenty miles from Brussels, east of Leuven. Although he would negotiate the asking price of seven million Euros, he was determined to buy the estate regardless. It was a nineteenth century castle in Belgium's most beautiful country setting.

By four o'clock they had come to an agreement and he had signed the deal; the transfer of funds would be made the following Monday.

Richard was back at the Metropole by five.

"There he is," Amanda whispered to Rachel. They were sitting at the sidewalk table of the Metropole Cafe when Richard got out of the cab.

"Wow, he's a looker," Rachel replied.

"That he is." Amanda blushed and stood up, waving, "Richard! Over here!"

He nodded and took a few long strides and joined them. "What a day it's been!" he said as he bent down and kissed Amanda. He straightened up and held out his hand toward Rachel. "And this must be the writer I've heard so much about."

"Rachel O'Neill," Rachel said and shook his hand.

"Richard Miller," he said, then signaled the waiter for drinks all around. "I'll have a Scotch, and give the ladies what they've been drinking, please."

"So what did you do today, Richard?" Amanda asked.

"Oh, just took care of some business. Nothing you would find exciting."

Rachel tilted her head. "What kind of business is it you would be having in Brussels, Mr. Miller? I understand you're in cattle ranching."

Richard nodded. "Right, I'm here to buy some Belgian Blues. They've been genetically bred and developed, so crossbreeding increases their commercial value. But then, you don't want to hear about cattle. Boring subject for you ladies. So how was your day? Did you do everything you wanted?" He picked up Amanda's hand and held it between both of his on the table.

Amanda glanced at Rachel who nodded slightly. "Yes, we did, as a matter of fact. Would you like to hear about it?"

Earlier the two of them had discussed whether or not she should tell Richard about her plans to open a shop and sewing room in Brussels. At first she'd wanted to keep it to herself until after he went home, but Rachel convinced her that she should level with him.

"Absolutely! So what is the big secret you've been keeping from me, darling?' Richard grinned as he continued to hold her hand.

She took her hand from his and passed him a file folder that was in front of her. "Take a look at this here."

He opened the file and began to leaf through the papers inside: a lease agreement to a shop and overhead apartment, a list of names and phone numbers of lace-makers and seamstresses, a drawing of a floor plan with notations, and a sketch of a business sign that said *Mandy Malone Designs*.

"Looks like you're getting ready to open a shop here in Brussels?" He feigned surprise, for Drake had already told him what was happening.

"I ain't going back to California with you, Richard. I'm staying here." She was happy that Rachel was sitting beside her; it gave her the strength to tell Richard the truth. "And, while I'm at it," she handed him the engagement ring, "I don't want a ring you bought for somebody else. It don't, I mean, it doesn't belong to me and never did. Take it."

Of course he already knew about the ring, Drake had told him everything, had left nothing out. He put it in his pocket without looking at it.

"I'm sorry I offended you, Amanda. It wasn't my intention. You're right; you should have your own ring."

"Didn't you hear me, Richard? I ain't going back with you to get married."

"I hear what you're saying, I do. But how about we change the subject for now. So tell me more about your shop? Do you need any help? Financial or otherwise? I'm a good carpenter; I can build shelves and racks, whatever you need. Tables? Put me to work while I'm here."

Rachel slapped the table. "You've got a job, Mister. A carpenter is exactly what we need. We haven't found one yet."

"Rachel's investing her money and is helping me with the planning part of it," Amanda explained.

"Well, with the two of you good-looking girls running it, the business can't help but be successful. So when do we start?"

Amanda frowned. "Don't you have to go back home and run the ranch?"

"Nope. Jered and Darys can run it. It'll do Darys good since it will all be hers some day. And Jered has been my foreman for years at the Cupertino ranch. So I got it covered. I'll just buy the Belgium Blues and ship them to my spreads in Wyoming and Montana. Don't have to be up there, either. I go up twice a year and check on them, though."

Raising her eyebrows, Rachel asked, "How many ranches do you have?"

"Oh, eighteen at last count. I just sold a couple of them in Idaho last month. Two of my biggest."

"I didn't know that, Richard!" Amanda's eyes widened. "I thought you just had the one in California."

"We never talked about it, darling. I'd planned to tell you after we were married."

Amanda leaned back into her chair and sighed. "No wonder Darys thought I was marrying you for your money. Lordy! You must have boxcars of it."

He and Rachel laughed.

"I love that Arkansas side of you, Amanda, when you let it out." Richard took her hand and kissed it.

"I've been trying to fix that Arkansas side of me." She hesitated. "But aren't you mad at me, Richard?"

"Should I be?"

"Well, I just told you I ain't going home with you, and I gave your ring back. Don't most men get mad when that happens?'

Rachel answered before Richard had a chance. "Not this man." She smiled at them both and lifted her wine glass to toast them. How she wished Pete was there.

Chapter 45

It was a Thursday morning three weeks before *Mandy Malone Designs* was to open. The sewing room had shelves of fabric and the racks were filling up with finished and unfinished garments. Six seamstresses were busy ten hours a day so they could be ready on June 15 to open their doors.

Richard had built the shelves and cupboards in the sewing room, as well as the cutting and sewing tables: three of each, so that while three women were sewing, three were cutting fabric.

The industrial sewing machines they'd found weren't new, but were in top notch condition. They'd been lucky and had the chance to buy them from one of the local fashion schools that had bought newer machines.

That morning Amanda and Richard had gone to Bruges to pick up lace from the lace-makers and were due to return soon. It was to be a quick turn-around trip, time was of the essence.

In her hotel room, Rachel was working on the final edit of her novel.

The room phone rang. It was Paul. Belinda had taken a turn for the worse. She was in intensive care at the hospital. He was unmistakably distraught so Rachel told him she'd take the first flight out.

Then she called Richard on his cell phone and told him that she had to make a quick trip home, that her friend was critical, and that she would be back before the opening.

Amanda and Richard both told her not to worry, that they could handle the rest for the opening, and that she should stay as long as she was needed.

Driving back from Bruges, Richard took a slight detour that took them north of Brussels and then east to Leuven.

"Where are we?" Amanda asked as they meandered through the town.

"Just wanted to come back another way. I hope you don't mind."

"I don't mind. This is a beautiful town, bigger than Bruges, though. Right? What's the name of it?"

"Leuven. Thought we would have lunch here. I hear the mussels and seafood are great," Richard said.

"I've never had mussels. What are they?"

"They're in the same family as clams and mollusks. We'll get one order of steamed mussels and you order something else you'd like and we'll share. That way, in case they aren't your cup of tea, you'll have something else to eat. How's that?"

"Perfect."

After lunch they continued a few miles further east before he was to swing back to Brussels. The weather was warm and the sky was clear so Richard put the top down on the rented BMW Z4.

"Isn't this the most beautiful countryside you've ever seen? I don't think I've ever seen anything like it before. I just love it." Amanda was grinning from ear to ear. She leaned over and planted a kiss on Richard's cheek.

"Look at that!" He pointed to a castle set back through some trees and pulled over to the side of the road in front of the lane leading up to it. "That is spectacular!"

"Oh my goodness! Is that a castle?"

Amanda's childlike excitement thrilled Richard.

"Looks like it." He said as he continued to enjoy her reaction.

"I've never been in a castle before," she said. "Do you think they have tours through it? I've heard some of them do."

"I don't know. Shall we drive up there and ask?"

Amanda thought for a moment. "Oh, we better not. I need to get back to the girls with the lace. They're waiting for it."

"We can always come back out here another day," Richard suggested. "It's only about seventeen miles from Brussels."

"That's not far at all, is it?"

"Not at all." He turned at the next road and headed back to Brussels, grinning all the way. He was happy.

Chapter 46

Mid-summers were sweltering in Cornwall, but the hospital was equipped with air conditioning. Rachel sat in the waiting room with the children while Belinda's mother and Paul were in the intensive care unit with Belinda.

The scare was over, however. After a severe life-threatening drop of her white blood cells due to the chemo treatments and an infection that had invaded her body, Belinda was now improving and the doctors were saying she would be moved out of ICU the next day. She'd been there for nearly two weeks.

Paul came through the door toward Rachel looking haggard and disheveled. He'd been at the hospital almost every day and night the entire time.

"Let's take the children home, Rachel. She's okay now, her mother is going to stay with her till I get back, then she'll come to the house. Will you stay with the children till her mother gets there?"

"Of course I will."

"Come on, big boy," Paul said as he picked up Jake and hugged him. "Let's go home."

Rachel carried Paul Junior and followed.

Later that evening when Rachel was back at her cottage, she sat on the veranda sipping tea, gazing out across the sea. The glimmer of the moon lit up a streak of water and filled the night air with enough light to see everything on the hillsides around her. She listened to the seagulls hunting for food and could smell the sea mixed with the scents of hyacinths and climbing roses growing all around her. She loved flowers and had planted an abundance of them in her garden and all around the cottage.

As she breathed deeply, her mind swirled with all the events of the past few months.

She wondered how Amanda was faring with Richard and the preparations for the shop's opening. She made a mental note to call her first thing in the morning. Only one more week until the grand opening and she was planning to be there.

Pete was on her mind. It had been nearly seven months since his death and she still thought of him every day and night. She wondered if one day she'd forget him. Thoughts of Ethan were diminishing; maybe it would be the same with Pete. It wasn't that she wanted to forget either of them; it was the sadness and heartbreak she wanted to erase.

Rachel wasn't the happy person she once was. How could she get that back? She'd been reading several books on overcoming sorrow and depression, and some days the methods seemed to work, while on others it didn't. She figured that the best way to handle it was to focus on what she loved doing the most and just do it. Writing and traveling, that was what she loved. And nesting. She loved her homes. If she traveled from home to home, writing as she went, maybe that would work.

She thought of the house in Brentwood, California that her father had left her. It was a slice of the '50s. And she adored her mother's log cabin in Montana – her American Indian legacy. She thought of her son, hadn't seen him in over a year when she'd last been in States.

And the house in Paris, in Montmartre, the one she and Janet had bought on the spur of the moment. She had loved being there with Janet and Shellie. Now Shellie lived in Switzerland with her husband and baby, but Janet was still in Paris.

At that moment she decided that after Amanda's shop was open and operating smoothly, she would go to the Montmartre house for at least a month. Yes, that's what she would do.

Belinda was out of the woods for now, so there was no reason to hurry back to Cornwall from Brussels. She also wanted to put some distance between herself and Paul. The past two weeks had been awkward and difficult for her, being in such close proximity to him.

Yes, after Brussels she'd spend the month of July in Paris. Maybe even longer.

Chapter 47

Brussels was having a record heat wave. Pedestrians were wearing straw hats and sunglasses, shorts and tank tops, sandals, and carrying water bottles as they shopped and walked on the streets of the city.

It was Saturday, a week before *Mandy Malone Designs* was to open, and Richard met Amanda for breakfast at The Roy before her day began at the sewing room. She'd moved out of the Metropole and into the sewing room above the shop, had sectioned off a living area and was very comfortable there.

Richard was waiting for her at The Roy. He'd been waiting an hour already, drinking coffee and making mental plans. He wanted to take Amanda to Antwerp to see its fashion sector, to see the fabric houses. That was the reason he gave to Amanda. She'd mentioned she needed more fabric.

He knew it was also the diamond center of Europe.

As they had their breakfast he told her about Antwerp, and even though she felt she should stay and watch over the girls, he persuaded her to take a day off. Convinced her she needed a change of scenery and needed to clear her mind. It was only thirty-two miles to Antwerp and the trip would be good for them both.

Again the drive through the countryside was gorgeous and green, even though it was heavily populated along the way in certain areas. At times it felt as if Antwerp might be a suburb of Brussels.

"We'll have lunch at the Grote Market. I hear it's not quite as large as the Grand Place, but the buildings are something to see … all the guild houses. Plenty of cafes and shops."

"I'm so glad we're taking this break. I needed it. Thank you for convincing me," Amanda said as she smiled at him.

Richard patted her hand. "It was obvious you needed a break. If you don't mind, I'd like to swing by the diamond district, too. We can do that first and get it out of the way. Seventy percent of the world's diamonds come from Antwerp and there are over fifteen hundred diamond companies and four gigantic houses where the diamonds are sold to the public. I've heard it's incredible. And since I've a bit of cash to invest, I'd like to invest in some uncut, rough diamonds. A friend of mine in Montana suggested it. He does it, says it's profitable."

"You buy rings or just the rocks?"

"Rocks."

"What will you do with them?" Amanda asked.

"Keep them in a safe place for a rainy day, I guess." He grinned, thinking of his ulterior motives. He was having more fun than he'd had in years.

"So you're in Brussels to buy cows and diamonds," she laughed. "Quite a combination."

"And to be with you, of course," Richard reminded her. "If it weren't for you I would have no reason to be here, actually. So I may as well make a business trip out of it so I can deduct it on my taxes. Makes sense, doesn't it?'

"I guess it does," Amanda said as she frowned and turned away, thinking how nothing was making much sense lately.

Amanda's attention was distracted by a field of flowers stretching up over the foothills. She pointed, "Oh my gosh! Look over there! The daisies, aren't they pretty? I love daisies."

They took a tour through Diamond Land, the largest diamond house in Antwerp. They saw the diamond polishers, setters, and goldsmiths at work. The guided tour took twenty minutes. They learned about cleaving, sawing, bruting, polishing and the international rules for grading diamonds - carat, color, cut and clarity.

"Oh my goodness, would you look at that ring!" Amanda's eyes were fastened on a 4-carat emerald-cut white diamond set in a halo of pale yellow diamonds. "That ring takes the cake, doesn't it?"

"It sure does," Richard agreed. "Want to see how it looks on your hand?"

Amanda looked up at him. "Is it all right, will they let me try it on for fun?"

Richard motioned to a sales person, "This one, please."

It fit Amanda's finger perfectly. She put it on the right hand, though, not the left.

"A perfect dinner ring." Richard was excited. He stood behind her as she was admiring it on her finger and motioned to the salesman that he wanted to buy it, and indicated he didn't want her to know.

Amanda took it off her finger and handed it back. "Oh my, there's another one. Look at that one over there. Not as pretty, but wow! These are something else, aren't they? How could a person make up her mind?"

Richard laughed. "I don't know. I guess you have to be able to afford more than one if you can't settle on one."

"But they've got to cost thousands. Who could afford it?"

"Darling, would you mind if I go talk to the man over there in his office? I've got an appointment with him about the uncut diamonds. It shouldn't take long. Will you be all right till I come back?"

Amanda nodded. "Sure I will. In fact you go on ahead; I'll just browse through the rooms." She turned to the salesman. "Where is the nearest restroom, please?"

Later, as they walked to a lovely café on the Grote Market, Richard could hardly contain himself. The ring was in his pocket. He ordered a bottle of champagne immediately, before they were seated outdoors. It was a clear day with a slight breeze to filter the heat of the sun's rays. Assorted flowers were in pots surrounding the patio area where they were sitting. A violinist had been strolling through the square and stopped a few feet from Richard and Amanda, playing softly, romantically.

After the champagne was poured, Richard lifted his glass to Amanda. She did the same.

"Richard, I am so happy you're here. I have to tell you that when I first saw you come through the door at the Metropole, I didn't know what to do or think."

"I know, darling. I know. So let's toast to us. To us being together for the rest of our lives."

Amanda frowned and set her glass on the table. "I can't do that. I'm not going back."

"Lift your glass, darling." Richard smiled and cocked his head. "And let me finish the toast, please."

She reluctantly lifted her glass, looking away from him.

"I love you with all my heart, Amanda. I have since the first day I saw you in KC's. Will you drink to that with me?"

She clinked his glass with hers. "Yes, I can drink to that." She looked across the table to him, "I know you love me. But—"

"And will you marry me, Miss Mandy Malone?" He held out the brilliant white and yellow diamond ring from Diamond Land. "Will you wear this beautiful ring as a commitment and promise of our love for each other?"

Amanda was stunned; her hand holding the glass froze in mid-air. Her eyes were popping out of her head and her mouth was hanging open. She couldn't breathe.

Richard lifted her left hand from the table and slipped the ring on her third finger. "It's your very own ring, my love. You chose it. It belongs to nobody else."

Amanda was numb with disbelief. She looked up at Richard. "But— Oh— Richard! I do adore you, I do— but I can't go back to live with you in California. I just can't. I have my own business here now—"

Richard placed his hand over hers. "Amanda, darling, I don't have to live in California. We can live here, together. I want to be here with you wherever you are. Please say yes."

It was beyond Amanda's comprehension of a dream come true. How could this be happening to her? This was fairy tale stuff, it wasn't real.

She gazed into his magnetic eyes and said "Yes, I will marry you."

Chapter 48

Four days before the opening of Mandy Malone's, the permits still hadn't been issued. Amanda was frantic; all the advertisement had gone out, the shop was ready, two of the seamstresses were lined up to help with the opening as sales clerks, it was all set. It took all of Richard's cleverness to calm Amanda. He promised her she would be able to open for business, not to worry.

He'd already found out he had to file for a *Certificate of Residency for the Marriage Purposes*, which he did. He made a few phone calls to business acquaintances in Brussels and a few political contacts at the EU which is based in Brussels. He was told to go to the American Consulate, that possibly that would be his solution.

So he made an appointment to meet with an old buddy of his; one he'd done business with in the States before the guy had been assigned to Belgium.

John Crane's assistant met Richard in reception and took him down a long corridor to Crane's office.

"Richard, what a surprise! How are you?" Crane asked as he held out his hand.

"I'm doing great! It's good to see you, again, John Boy."

"Well, I've packed on a few pounds since I saw you last," he said as he laughed.

Richard noticed that right off. And he also noticed the receding hairline where curly red hair used to reside. "Hey, we all get older and changes do take place."

"But you haven't changed a bit. You're still a handsome devil. So what brings you to Brussels? You buying some Blues?"

Richard nodded. "Yes I am. And I'm also here for pleasure. Am getting married."

"I'm all ears. Have a seat."

Richard sat in a chair in front of the desk, John Boy behind the desk.

"Well, I'm marrying an angel whose dream is to live in Belgium. A few months ago, she came over to learn how to make lace and took classes at the Kantcentrum in Bruges. Now she's designing clothing using the lace. She has hired seamstresses to sew her garments and uses the lace-makers in Bruges to make most of the lace, since she can't do it all herself."

"She sounds pretty industrious. Is she originally from Belgium?"

"No. She's American, isn't a permanent resident here yet, but she wants to be. In fact we'll be living here just outside of Brussels as soon as we get married. I just bought the Sargent estate near Leuven."

"The castle?" John Boy raised his eyebrows in disbelief.

"Yes. She doesn't know about it. I'm going to surprise her."

"So how can I help you?"

"Well, she applied for the business permits and there's a hang-up," Richard explained. "I just arrived a little over a month ago, by the way. So we need to speed up the permits so she can open on Saturday as planned. Everything else is ready. Can you help us get the permits?"

John Boy leaned back in his chair, thinking.

"And I just filed for a *Certificate of Residency for Marriage Purposes*. I'll be going back and forth to the U.S to check on the ranches, but Amanda plans to apply for permanent residency here. So, John Boy, what can we do?"

"I have a contact in the EU who might be able to help us." John Boy reached for a directory. "And he can also get the ball rolling on the residency situation. Hell, she's creating jobs for Belgian citizens and you're contributing to our export economy. How could they possibly refuse?"

The number he wanted wasn't in the directory, so he picked up the phone and buzzed his assistant. "Hillary, would you get Larry Grodin's private number for me? Yes, please." He stood up and asked Richard, "Would you like a cup of coffee while we wait?"

Chapter 49

It was Saturday, June 15, the hottest summer day on record for Brussels. But the extreme weather didn't prevent the shoppers from flooding the streets and lanes on this particular special day; *Mandy Malone Designs* was open for business.

Banners were crisscrossing her shop windows announcing the event, carefully placed so as not to hide the creations on the mannequins in the windows. The paneling on the stone front of the shop had been painted navy blue; the double doors' wooden trim around the etched glass panes was a deep crimson with brass fittings. Gold lettering on the glass spelled out:

Mandy Malone Designs
LADIES APPAREL
Hand Made Belgian Lace

Hours: 10 a.m. to 7 p.m.
For private showing see proprietor

The shop had been full of customers since the doors first opened at ten that morning. Rachel and Amanda were busy talking with potential buyers, helping them find the right fit, suggesting a garment that would be perfect in their coloring or shape. Two other salesgirls were busy—one monitoring the dressing rooms, one at the cash register. Although the shop was small and crowded, the traffic seemed to flow without feeling claustrophobic. The racks had been placed in a manner that allowed easy maneuvering around them. Horizontal clothing poles were also built into the walls at different heights with shelving above them.

Richard stood on the steps outside greeting people and displaying his natural charm. He handed out business cards and answered questions about the designer. Whenever he caught Amanda's attention, he winked or blew a kiss or waved.

Finally at mid-afternoon, when the pace had slowed down considerably and the two salesgirls had had their break, Richard stepped inside and asked Amanda and Rachel to lunch.

They gladly and wearily trudged to The Roy which was just down the lane on the square.

"My goodness, I am worn out!" Amanda plopped down at a table in the window.

"Me too." Rachel sat across from her.

Richard sat next to Amanda. "Well, you ladies have been at it for hours. It's no wonder you're exhausted. It's time for resting and refueling."

"I feel like goin' up to my room and crawlin' into bed when we get back," Amanda moaned.

Rachel laughed. "Looks like it's going to be an early night for me, too. I'm pretty tired myself." She took a sip of the water the waiter had just set on the table. "That's hard work, Mandy. I'm accustomed to sitting while I work."

"And I appreciate all that you're doing for me, Rachel. I really do," Amanda told her. "I don't know what I would have done without you and Richard." She reached over and gave both of them a squeeze of the hands.

Richard squeezed back. "Darling, I believe you could do anything you set your mind to. I don't have a single doubt about that."

Amanda shrugged. "Well, there have been some pretty rocky moments through it all. If it hadn't been for y'all … you were the one who made them give me the permits and built all the shelves and racks, Richard. And Rachel, if it hadn't been for you investing the money and encouraging me, helping me with the layout of the shop, well—" Tears filled her eyes.

"My pleasure, sweetie." Rachel whispered as she patted Amanda's hand. She took another sip of water. "And, Richard, those racks are fabulous. The way you cut out the ends that hold the brass poles and painted them navy blue to match the decor. What gave you that idea?"

"I saw it in a shop in the States."

Amanda gave a sly grin. "It wasn't Elaine's shop, by any chance, was it?"

Clearing his throat, Richard blushed, "Uh, well, yes it was, darling. I hope you don't mind."

"That was his old girlfriend. The one I told you about, Rachel."

"The one with the ring?" Rachel asked. "I would venture to say that you ended up with the most beautiful ring. Hers doesn't compare to the one you're wearing now."

"Speaking of rings, girls," Richard spoke up. "When are we going to tie the knot, darling? Now that the shop is open, shouldn't we set a date?"

Amanda's eyes widened. She looked at Rachel as if pleading for help. "I don't know. Uh, what do you think,

227

Rachel? I ain't ever planned a wedding by myself before. Richard was doing the planning in Cupertino. Arlie and me just went to the justice of the peace in Mountain Home, Arkansas, to get hitched."

Richard gently touched her elbow. "The law here says we have to have a civil ceremony. We can't have it in a church. That is, we can have a wedding in a church after the civil ceremony, if we want. But a church wedding alone isn't legal. It has to be at City Hall before a judge or whatever they call the guy that does it. So we just need witnesses at City Hall. Not much planning. And then we can have a big blowout somewhere else for everybody that wants to come celebrate with us – family and friends.

"You remember that castle I showed you, darling? The one out there past Lueven? I found out it can be rented for shindigs. Why don't I see about that for our reception?"

"Oh my goodness! I guess that would be all right. Sure!" Amanda looked at Rachel, becoming more excited about the subject. "Of course I want to make my own wedding gown."

Richard frowned, "But you already made one for the Cupertino wedding."

"I had Paula give that one to Goodwill in Bakersfield. So, I'll need a new one, and that's going to take some time. I have to plan that."

"Well, how long will it take?" Richard asked as he sipped coffee.

"I have to find the fabric and make the lace for it."

"Why not use some of the lace that your girls have already made. It'll take too long to make more, won't it?"

"All the lace and my wedding dress will be made by me, Richard," Amanda declared firmly.

He grinned and faced Rachel. "This certainly isn't the shy, meek little Arkansas princess I met a year ago in

Bakersfield. I think that castle will make a perfect reception party for Queen Amanda."

He and Rachel winked at each other, exchanging a secret-sharing look that Amanda missed.

Chapter 50

Amanda was standing behind the cash register after a customer had paid and left. "I'll miss Rachel," she said to Richard.

"She'll be back for the wedding, darling. That's less than two months away. C'mon, let's go to lunch."

They decided to go to the restaurant next door to The Roy for a change. It was less crowded and Amanda wanted to hurry and get back to the shop; a shipment of fabric was due to arrive.

Just as they got seated, Richard's cell phone rang. He looked at the screen and said, "It's Jered. I'll take this outside." He answered as he was walking out the door, "Jered. What's up?"

"Boss, I got some bad news. I don't know how to tell you this."

"Just spit it out. That's the best way." Richard walked into the square away from the ears of diners on the patio.

"It's Darys, Boss. She's had an accident."

"And?"

"She's in the hospital. You better come, Boss. It doesn't look good."

Richard put his hand to his forehead, breathing in short spurts. "What happened?"

"Spider threw her. She was up in the mountains and you know how wild she can get when she's riding horses. Well, she pushed him too hard and he threw her down an incline into a pile of boulders. It took us a day to find her after Spider came home. Her back is broken, Boss, and she's got some head injuries, along with a lot of other stuff. She's in a coma."

"I'll be out of here on the first plane. I'll call you when I get to the airport."

He hurried back into the café to tell Amanda.

Later that afternoon Amanda took a walk to the Gothic Beguinage Church of St. Jean Baptiste. It was just a short distance from the Metropole Hotel and its carved doors and façade was considered the most beautiful in Belgium. She'd been drawn to it several times before, mainly because she felt familiar with the name of John the Baptist, figured it might be similar to her grandmother's Baptist church in Arkansas.

When she was a child, Granma Conroy would take the two girls to Sunday school and church every Sunday. Amanda got away from the habit when she and Arlie got married and moved to Nevada, but lately she was being drawn back into it, bit by bit. It wasn't an every-week occurrence, just an occasional excursion.

The soaring vaults of the seventeenth century Flemish Baroque church captivated her as she sat quietly looking up at the expanse and beauty of them. The stained glass windows always gave her a sense of peace as she sat there and reflected.

Sometimes she even sent up a prayer, but normally she wasn't into praying. It made her feel uncomfortable. She didn't know why, but it did. She would pray occasionally in bed, but only in her mind, nothing spoken aloud. It used to amaze her how people could pray loud, long and hard like they were giving a speech, and so eloquently, when all she could do was stumble over words and say something that didn't make any sense and would embarrass her. So she had decided way back then that prayer wasn't for her, at least not the spoken kind.

She wondered if she would be able to teach her children how to pray since she couldn't do it. She felt that children should definitely learn the basics of religious beliefs; she would want them to go to Sunday school and church like she did when she was a child. Oh how she wished her grandma was still alive. Amanda would bring her to Belgium to take care of her children, if and when she ever had any.

Her thoughts then drifted to Richard and his daughter. She closed her eyes and prayed to herself that Darys would recover and be normal again. She'd never known or heard of anyone with a head injury. Richard had told her that it could leave a person disabled or even worse. No, she didn't want that for Darys. As much as Darys had hurt her, she wanted her to get well. It would kill Richard if she didn't.

Amanda stood up and began walking toward the exit, wondering if she should postpone the wedding, not knowing whether or not Richard would be back in time. It depended on what happened with Darys, of course. It wouldn't hurt her feelings if the wedding were put off. Not at all. It was actually a relief that it might not happen in August. It felt too soon for her.

She was feeling guilty for thinking that way. Richard was such a wonderful man and she was lucky to have him. She had to push those thoughts from her mind.

Chapter 51

Richard flew into San Francisco where Darys had been transferred. The doctors told him she was suffering from *Traumatic Brain Injury* (TBI) and it was now a wait-and-see situation. They had already performed surgery on a ruptured brain aneurysm, but they couldn't agree on a prognosis on her brain or back injuries.

A lower dorsal vertebra had been broken and she was paralyzed from the waist down. Her left collar bone and arm were also broken and there was a deep gouge on her left cheek where she had hit a sharp rock.

It didn't look good at all.

Richard was terrified. He needed to talk to Amanda, decided to call her from the cafeteria's patio where he'd gone to get a cup of coffee.

When he stepped out onto the patio, the trees were rustling in the breeze over the sparsely inhabited tables and benches looking out over the cityscape. He could see the white Coit Tower on Telegraph Hill in the distance and the Golden Gate Bridge crossing from the city to the waterfront community of Sausalito beyond. Alcatraz was still an imposing institution in the middle of the bay, even though it was nothing more than a tourist attraction now.

He walked to the rooftop patio's railing and looked down into the courtyard below. The doctors and nurses had their own cafeteria and patio a couple floors down from the visitors' space.

He dialed. "Amanda, it's me … yes, darling, I'm okay. I just needed to talk to you. She's not doing well … I don't know. Maybe we should postpone the wedding. I'm so sorry. If she does recover, she's going to need lots of care—" His words choked in his throat. "I'll call you later, darling, to let you know what's happening … I love you and I miss you horribly. Bye."

Outside the *Intensive Care Unit*, Jered was waiting for Richard. He gave him a bear hug the moment he got there. "How you holdin' up, Boss?"

Richard sighed deeply and shook his head. "I feel so helpless."

"Well, there's nothing we can do, the doctors say, until she wakes up," Jered said as he stepped back.

Richard saw the tears in Jered's red-rimmed eyes and that was the first time he'd noticed the haggard lines of worry on his face. He grasped Jered's shoulder and said, "Hey, she's going to be okay, she's a toughie, you know that." Although he was having trouble believing his own words, he wanted Jered to believe them. Sometimes he felt like a father to Jered and this was one of those times.

"I gotta tell you, Boss, I'm in love with your daughter. Have been for a long time, I guess. After you left I jumped all over her for treating Amanda like she did and for a few other things she was being stupid about, and first thing I know, she starts sidling up to me. Come to find out she loves me, too. We just admitted it to each other last week." He wiped his eyes and looked down at his boots. "I just want you to know, that if she pulls through this," he looked up into Richard's eyes, "I'm going to ask her to marry me."

Richard was speechless. This had come out of left field. It wasn't something he would have expected in a million years.

Jered was a few years older than Darys, was hired when he was a teenager to work with the horses. In fact, Richard had hired him as a favor to the high school principal who had been very fond and protective of him, saw something good in him, regardless of the fact he was such a troublemaker in school. Jered's parents had been killed in a car accident when he was ten and had been living with an uncle, who was in jail more than he was out. Jered had been more or less raising himself, so Richard took him in.

Jered took to the horse and cattle business with Richard as his tutor and worked his way up from stable boy to ranch hand to ranch foreman in ten years. He'd been the most honest, hard-working man Richard had ever seen.

Richard squeezed Jered's shoulder again. "Son, I'd be honored to have you as a son-in-law. I can't think of anybody else who could handle Darys. And if she loves you, then it's okay with me."

"I promise you, Boss, I'll always love her and take care of her, no matter what happens." Tears ran down Jered's cheeks.

Chapter 52

After Amanda's store opening, Rachel went back home to Cornwall instead of going directly to Paris as she'd planned, mainly to spend time with Belinda who was struggling to recover from the damaging chemo treatments. It was hard to tell which was worse, the disease or the chemo.

In the meantime Amanda had called and told her what had happened and about the postponement of the August wedding, said she didn't know when it would be, but would let her know as soon as it was rescheduled.

Then on the first day of September Rachel took a train to Paris. As soon as she arrived at the house in Montmartre, she opened all the windows and aired out all four floors of the remodeled and refitted eighteenth century house on the Place du Tertre.

Her friend Janet Corrigan had been caretaking the house, but lived with Bob Benton on his houseboat near the Eiffel. She and Bob were coming to the house that evening, though; they'd scheduled a full day of appointments with clients and said they'd meet Rachel for drinks and dinner as soon as they finished.

Janet and Rachel had met because of Shellie Singer - all three were Americans in Paris trying to decide what to do with the rest of their lives: Rachel the romance novelist, Shellie the jazz singer, Janet the real estate mogul. Janet had helped Shellie get to Paris to pursue her career and escape an abusive husband who was now history.

In fact, Rachel had met Shellie while doing research in Montmartre. She'd come to Paris once again seeking inspiration for one of her novels, and ended up sitting at a sidewalk table next to Shellie and Adrian, who happened to be on a first date. They began talking across tables to each other. Then Shellie recognized Rachel - she'd seen Rachel on the Oprah show segment about violence against women that gave her the strength to leave her own violent husband that week.

Later Rachel met Janet and Bob through Shellie. Bob owned the houseboat where Shellie had lived the first few months she was in Paris.

Since Rachel loved Paris and went there several times a year and Janet wanted to spend more time there, and because Shellie needed a place to live, they decided to buy the house in Montmartre. The deal was that Rachel and Janet would invest the money, remodel it, and Shellie could live in it full time, while they would be there part time.

However, life and its changes happened, and they all went their separate ways. But the house remained a haven for all three of them, to go to whenever they wanted.

Now it was Rachel's time. She loved Paris in the fall. The weather was crisp and clear. The flowers were blooming as if they didn't know the heat of the summer was over and that they should quickly retreat before the cold, bleak winter.

After Rachel unpacked, she went into the back garden and was thrilled to see all the vines and plants they'd planted that were climbing the walls and filling the flower beds and gigantic colorful, ceramic pots. She cut roses and gladiolas—late bloomers—cannas, and geraniums. Pink and coral bougainvilleas were terrific fillers in floral arrangements.

She carried the cut flowers into the kitchen and began filling vases: one for the dining table, one for the piano, one for the mantle, one for the sunroom, one for her bedroom, and one for Janet's in case she and Bob were staying the night. She figured they would be. Only Shellie's room didn't have flowers. She missed Shellie.

The candles in Lalique holders were lit on the dining table, soft instrumental music was playing in the background, and two trays of appetizers were on the bar pass-through from the kitchen. Rachel had opened the champagne and made sure there were bottles of wine, brandy, vodka, and gin in the bar cabinet. She was looking forward to seeing Janet and Bob; it had been months since she'd seen them. The last time she was there, they were in the States.

A knock was quickly followed by Janet's voice as she pushed open the door. "We're here! Rachel, where the hell are you?"

Rachel hurried from the sunroom where she had turned on one of the crystal lamps on the sideboard. "Here I am! Oh, I am so glad to see you guys!"

They hugged and said their hellos, and over drinks they caught up on the most recent happenings in their lives.

After bringing them up to date on Paul and Belinda and Cornwall, Rachel asked Janet, "Have you heard from Shellie and Adrian lately?"

"I've been up there several times," Janet replied. "You know how I feel like she's my own daughter. If ever I would have had a daughter, she'd be just like Shellie. They're having child number two now. Can you imagine? Two children when she didn't even want the first one," Janet said and went after more champagne. "Our little Shellie with two kids. Un-fuckin'-bee-lievable!"

Rachel laughed. She had always laughed at Janet's way with the vilest of words. No one could ever be offended by her; she was so funny when she said them.

Bob just grinned and shook his head. It had always amused him how Janet could be so crass and still be loveable and feminine.

"I sure do miss her," Rachel added. "Does she ever come here anymore?"

"Last time was before she was showing. The beginning of summer. Little Henry is a living doll, Rachel. Isn't he, Bobby?"

Bob nodded in agreement. "He's the spitting image of Adrian."

"I'm thinking about visiting them after the wedding," Rachel said. "Switzerland is right there, may as well take advantage."

"Oh, she'll love that, honey," Janet said as she reached over and squeezed Rachel's hand. "You've got to do that. She's having a girl this time. They already tested. And you'll never guess what they're naming the poor little thing." She glanced at Bob with a wide grin. "Tell her, Bobby."

"Jan Rachel van Allman."

Rachel gasped. "She isn't!"

"She is." Janet laughed as she got up for the champagne bottle.

"For heaven's sake!"

"That's what I said, Rachel, honey."

"A girl. Named after us. Wow!"

Janet continued laughing and sat back down on the sofa by Rachel as she poured. "So, honey, how are you doing? Is it getting any better … you know … I mean … Pete?"

Rachel sighed. "Some days I'm all right and then other days I'm not. When I see couples together, it just reminds me. And then I fall into a pit. But it's getting better, it is."

"Oh, honey," Janet hugged Rachel, almost spilling her glass of champagne. "I worry about you, you know. You're too young for all this shit to be happening to you. Isn't she, Bobbie? But I'm so glad you're here now. We're gonna have us some fun. Just like old times."

"Works for me!" Rachel stood up. "But first let's eat some of these hors d'oeuvres and then decide if we're going out to eat or not. All of a sudden I'm hungry."

Bob rose from the overstuffed chair. "We are definitely going out. I've made reservations in a super cafe." He reached for a morsel.

"And does he ever know his food, honey." Janet popped a bite-size appetizer into her mouth. "You can bet it will be fuckin' great … just like these appetizers. Lordy, did you make these all by yourself? When did you find the time? You just got here today."

"They're quick and easy. I'll give you the recipe."

"Don't bother to give me any recipes, hon. I don't do food, I eat it." She popped another into her mouth. "Mmmmm, this one is really good. Taste that one, Bobby Boy. So, tell me about your friend in Belgium. You said her name is Amanda?"

"Yes, Amanda and Richard."

"When did you say you're going back up there?"

"It was to be in August, but that's been changed. Now it'll be when Amanda lets me know the new wedding date. I plan to go about a week before to help her."

"Why don't we go to the café to talk about all this? Is that a possibility, ladies?"

"Bobbie Boy must be hungry," Janet teased.

"Bobbie Boy *is* hungry," he replied.

Chapter 53

"What should I do, Rachel?" Amanda sat at her desk sipping coffee with a deep frown on her face. This was the third time that week she'd phoned Rachel in Paris. "I feel like Darys fell off the horse on purpose so Richard would cancel the dang wedding. I sure wouldn't put it past her."

"But he's saying she's getting better, right?"

"Yes, that's what he's saying. But how can he leave her when she's in the rehab center? She can't even walk. I just don't know. Sometimes I think it's not meant to be, you know? I didn't think I loved him this much, but now I know I do. I really miss him, Rachel. I think of him all the time—" she choked up. "I'm sorry. I don't mean to cry."

"Mandy, it's okay to cry. It's how you feel. You can't help that."

"I know, but my mama always told me that weak people cry, strong ones don't."

"Not true, honey. I can attest to that. I'm a very strong woman, and I do my share of crying. So get that out of your head. It's good to show your emotions anyway. It's healthy."

"Well, I just don't like to cry."

Rachel laughed. "You're so funny. I really miss you. You know what I think would be good for you?"

"What?" She wiped her nose with a tissue.

"Come to Paris."

Amanda blinked in surprise. "Me, come to Paris? I ain't never been to Paris."

"All the more reason," Rachel shifted the phone to her other ear and began pacing. "Look, you can leave Iona in charge of the shop. She can handle it. She's the best girl you got and she'd love the responsibility. You need to be able to get away periodically anyway, so this will give her the experience. Come stay a week or two. She can call you if she has questions. Take the train so you can see some countryside along the way; it's about a two-hour trip. I'll email you a Metro map so you can get to Montmartre once you're here."

"You think I should?"

"Yes, I do. It'll get your mind off Richard and give you a chance to clear your head. Honey, you've been working hard for weeks. You're on burnout."

Amanda thought about it. "Well … I guess I could do that. I mean, I can do anything I want, right? I'm not married yet. I ain't got no boss. I'm my own boss, dammit! Okay, I'll do it. I'll call you later tonight, okay?"

"Terrific! You're making the right decision, Amanda."

"Oh my goodness, I'm going to Paris! Paula will never believe this. She won't." Amanda's spirit soared.

Chapter 54

When the train from Brussels arrived at Paris Nord, Amanda couldn't believe it had only taken a little over an hour and a half to get there. Paris was only ninety minutes from where she lived. How could that be? She couldn't wait to tell Paula.

From Paris Nord she took the Metro to the base of the funicular in Montmartre and then followed Rachel's easy directions.

She was loving Paris already. It wasn't like Brussels at all. It was something special she couldn't put her finger on. The atmosphere, maybe? The people? The buildings? The buildings in Paris didn't seem as dark as the ones in Brussels. Maybe it was the difference in stone. And the iron gates, fence railings, and the artistic iron filigree on the windows and balconies. The balconies themselves. The trees and flowers. So different, so beautiful. She fell in love with Paris.

After she got off the funicular and was walking the rest of the way up the hill to the Place du Tertre, she was thinking how glad she was that she'd packed light. One cloth bag was all she brought. A sachel, actually, made from Belgian tapestry.

When she came to the famous Place du Tertre in Montmartre which was high on the only hill overlooking Paris, she stared at the beautiful square that was completely covered with tables and bright umbrellas. Artists were doing portraits and others were selling landscapes of Paris and floral paintings. The perimeter of the Place was lined with all sorts of quaint French cafés – each spilling out onto the square. She immediately saw Rachel's building with the red door and the brass number eleven on it.

It was a tall, narrow building that extended back quite a ways on the property. She looked up and saw that each floor had a large bay window that opened onto the square. Several types of climbing vines were covering nearly the entire exterior of the stone house and blue painted window boxes filled with geraniums and daffodils added a homey quality that took Amanda's breath away.

The smell of bread from the café next door to Number Eleven made her mouth water as she walked past it. Patrons were at the small round tables outside drinking wine and eating bread and cheese. She remembered she hadn't eaten in all the rush.

The doorbell had a chiming sound.

Chapter 55

It was late in the evening and Rachel and Amanda were sitting in front of the café next door. Earlier they'd been to the Eiffel Tower and the Musee de Louvre and they were both happy just to be sitting outside and imbibing and having conversations about life.

"Well, honey—" Rachel started, and then stopped herself. "Darn! You know I've picked up this habit of saying *honey* and I don't know where I got it."

They giggled.

"I don't usually say that, at least I don't think I do. Do I?"

"There's nothing wrong with saying it, Rachel. It's a nice word. It's kind and sweet, you know?" Amanda's smile was sincere.

Rachel looked at Amanda and couldn't for the life of her think of anyone else who was as pure and good as this girl. She definitely had something very special going on.

"My mama used to call me that all the time. You want some more?" She reached for the bottle of wine.

246

"Yes, I think I will have one more."

"Me, too." She poured for both of them. "Now what were you going to say?"

"Well, about your feelings for Richard … you said you don't know how you feel now that he's gone."

"I don't. I miss him and I think I love him, but, you know, I sort of like not having to answer to anybody but myself. I was thinking about that on the train coming here. That's all going to stop when we get married. It did with Arlie. Actually, it never even got started before Arlie, so I can't compare that with what it would be like with Richard, can I?"

"In my opinion, for what it's worth, I don't feel he will do what Arlie did to you, Amanda."

"You don't?"

Rachel shook her head. "No. For two reasons. One, you're a different person than you used to be. You're a business woman, a designer. You're independent. Two, Richard isn't that kind of man, isn't controlling. At least, I don't see it. Seems to me he wants you to see the world, to experience it. He's thinking of you, not himself. He wants you to have everything you've never had. He won't be holding you back. All you have to do is tell him what you want. After you're married and you want to come to Paris by yourself, just tell him. I don't think you have a worry in the world with Richard."

They both sat quietly for a few moments, sipping their drinks, watching the people milling about. A violinist strolled by with a guitarist. They stopped and serenaded a couple at the café across from them.

Rachel turned toward Amanda. "You know, I've had the chance, twice, to be with someone who loved me. Two times. And I believe I loved them, in my own strange, reluctant way. And I held off because of my career, for one, and two, not wanting to answer to anybody, just like you, and now they're

247

both gone. Poof! You know, you don't have all that many chances at true love in one lifetime. I wish I would have—" She covered her mouth and turned away to hide the emotion that was building.

"Oh, Rachel, I'm so sorry." Amanda reached out for her. "I don't mean to be reminding you of your heartbreak. Will you please forgive me? I won't talk about my pity-poor-me situation anymore. We need to have us some music, that's what we need. I'll get that violin man over here. "

Rachel held up a hand. "Hold on. I just want to say this while I'm thinking about it. And, sweetheart, don't stop telling me about your feelings, don't ever hold back. You have to talk to someone. I only mentioned my situation to maybe show you how we can sometimes let a good thing slip through our fingers, and then we lose them forever."

Remembering all the time she had wasted not telling Pete how she felt about him because she was afraid it would frighten him away, Rachel thought back over their brief life together. Usually they were off in different directions with their work, sometimes apart from each other for months at a time. Why didn't she go with him to Brazil when he asked her? Why hadn't she been more available to him? She could have written her novels anywhere. She could have gone with him. Regrets.

And Ethan. Why couldn't she be what he'd wanted her to be? All he wanted was a helpmate, a lover, a wife. But no, she had to have her freedom. She wished she could have been different. If only she could be a submissive housewife and cook and clean and greet the hubby at the door stark naked and make love to him at his beck and call. That's all a man wanted.

Amanda reached over and touched Rachel's arm. "Are you all right, Rachel?"

"Wha—? Oh. I'm sorry. I was off somewhere. Did you say something?"

"I just said that I appreciate having you as my friend. I ain't never had no friends besides my sister Paula, my whole life."

Rachel leaned across the table and clasped Amanda's hands. "Friends are hard to come by, honey. Most people will only have as many as they can count on one hand. So you're doing pretty well these days, if you ask me. And tomorrow I'm going to introduce you to Janet. She's dying to meet you."

Amanda smiled. "I'm looking forward to that. So, let's have one more glass of wine. We only have to crawl over to your door to get home. I think we can get there without anything too terrible happening to us. What do you think?"

"I think that's a damn good idea!" Rachel laughed.

Amanda poured, they clinked their glasses and said "To friends!" in unison, just as the violinist and his sidekick arrived at their table.

Chapter 56

The first week in Paris passed quickly for Amanda, and after the first day into the second week, she was beginning to get antsy, felt like she should get back to Brussels and to the shop. So she decided to leave on the tenth day of her stay, rather than the two weeks as planned.

Richard had telephoned twice, was surprised she was in Paris. She hadn't called him before she left Brussels. The updates of Darys' condition were encouraging. They'd brought in a specialist from New Jersey that had great success in rehabbing patients with the same paralysis. He'd already begun the process. His previous patient was walking again after only nine months.

Amanda and Rachel were watching television when Richard called the third time. During the conversation he asked Amanda if she might consider coming to Cupertino for a few days when she left Paris.

She told him she didn't think it was the right thing for her to do, not only because of the feelings between herself and Darys, but because she needed to get back to Brussels and create a new seasonal line. She told him she'd been in some of the Paris designer boutiques and had toured a designer school and learned enough to fill a book just by observing. Now she was eager to get back and go to work.

He said he wouldn't pressure her. All he wanted was to be with her and if it was to be in Belgium, then that's where it'd be. He said he'd be back as soon as he could leave Darys.

"So how is his daughter?" Rachel asked after Amanda closed the phone and sat silently for a few moments.

"She'll recover. Has a specialist working with her now." Amanda sighed and looked over at Rachel. "I need to get over not liking her. I keep telling myself that she hates me because she thinks she is losing her daddy. And I guess she's right. He's moving to Belgium to be with me. So I guess I am taking him away from her, but I don't mean to. She didn't object to Elaine marrying him, though."

"Sweetie, she already knew Elaine. They had been friends her whole life. She probably already looked up to her as a mother since she never knew her own mother. She didn't feel like she was losing him to a stranger."

Amanda shrugged. "That could be. I don't know."

"And you're nearer her age, so I would venture to say she's jealous of you. Anyway, all that will take care of itself in time. Don't worry about it. You aren't the one at fault here. Just keep going in your direction and Richard will catch up if he loves you."

They heard a pound on the door as Janet pushed it open and burst through. "Bet you didn't think you'd see me tonight!"

She was a whirlwind of curvaceous energy no matter what mood she was in. Her Marilyn Monroe hair was mussed and falling around her face. "Whatcha guys doin'? She plopped down on the sofa next to Rachel.

They were always glad to see her; she had the ability to lift a person's spirits even higher.

"Just watching a movie," Rachel answered. "Where's Bob?"

Janet growled. "I'm so damn mad at Bob, I could spit nails. I'm moving back in. My stuff's in the car."

"What?" Rachel sat up from her reclined position. "What happened?"

Amanda couldn't believe her ears. If ever there was a perfect couple, in her opinion Bob and Janet were it.

"He's so gawd-dammed stubborn and fuckin' set in his ways and it seems like the longer I'm with the prick, the worse he gets. It's to the point that whatever I say, he says the opposite and he thinks he's always fuckin' right. We can't even work together anymore. We argue all the time. I'm so damned sick of it, I could puke!" She went to the liquor cabinet and got a bottle of gin. "And furthermore, I'm getting drunk tonight."

Rachel and Amanda sucked in their breaths and exchanged raised-eyebrow glances.

"O-kay … then … we'll have one with you, won't we, Amanda?" Rachel went to the kitchen after the glasses and ice.

"Are you leaving him for good?" Amanda still couldn't believe it.

"I don't know. But one damn thing for sure, I'm going to put some distance between us and see what the hell happens. I admit, I love the cock-sucker, but this just isn't working the way it is. That's all there is to it. When did you say you're going home, Amanda?"

"Day after tomorrow."

"I'm going with you. I've never been to Brussels, and I'd love to see your shop and buy some new clothes. Will any of them fit me?"

"Sure!" Amanda was ecstatic that Janet would even consider wearing her creations.

"Okay. I'm going to Brussels, it's a done deal." Janet downed two shots of gin on the rocks without stopping and then poured another double.

Chapter 57

Rachel went home to Cornwall for Thanksgiving. Her son and stepmother were flying in from the States to spend it with her. It'd been three years since they'd all been together and that was when they spent Christmas in Newlyn with her. Rachel was thrilled and excited. She invited Belinda and Paul and their children for dinner, too.

Janet was still in Brussels. She found a small apartment and said she was staying there through the holidays. Said if Bob wanted to see her, he'd have to come to Brussels. It was a comical stand-off between the two of them.

Of course Amanda loved the company; Janet was lively and always full of fun ideas on what to do on weekends. They'd been all over Belgium during the month she had been there, and the plan was to have Thanksgiving dinner at a medieval inn in the countryside that Janet had found on one of her outings.

On Thanksgiving day, while Amanda and Janet were in southern Belgium, Richard sent an email to Amanda:

I'll be there the week before Christmas, darling. I cannot bear to be away from you any longer. So I'll wind up things here and be back on December the 20th. Darys is improving quickly and you're not going to believe this, but she's marrying Jered as soon as she's walking. She's a changed person, Amanda, and she doesn't need me here with all the nurses and doctors and the house staff.

I love you, darling. You are my life now, and I don't want to wait any longer to have you as my wife. Time is precious. Please call me and let me know what you think of a Christmas wedding. A Christmas Eve ceremony? I love you.

When Amanda got the message she took a deep breath and her eyes began to fill with tears. Yes, she wanted to marry Richard. Yes, yes, yes. Being with Janet and Rachel over the past few weeks had been eye-opening for her. Now she understood the importance of a loving relationship. She listened to their stories and experiences and could see that Richard was her knight in shining armor. There was no doubt about it.

She learned from Janet and Rachel that a woman doesn't have to lose her individuality when she marries, and that it is entirely up to her to hold onto it and cultivate it. A woman is in control of what she thinks, feels and does. No man can take that from her. She learned that if a man attempts to take it away, it is in the woman's power to resist. It is her call. This was all new to her.

Chapter 58

It was a cold day on Christmas Eve in Belgium, but as the wedding party sped past Lueven towards Kortenaken and the pinkish stone castle where the rest of the guests were waiting, the coldness wasn't felt at all.

John Boy Crane, from the American Embassy, was driving the bride and groom in his BMW, Paula and Drake with A.G. were being driven by a friend of John's, Rachel and Janet were in a rental car.

Even in winter, the snow-patched lush green hills were predominant east of Brussels. Old farms, woods, fields and meadows filled the scenic view as they sailed along the road.

"Are you happy, Amanda?" Richard asked.

"Oh yes!" She leaned and kissed him sweetly on the cheek. "Are you?"

"You know I am. I'm the happiest man alive."

"Why did you marry me, Richard? Other than the fact that you love me." She laughed. "Tell me why you chose me. I still don't understand that. You could have had anybody you wanted, so why me?"

Richard considered his answer. "When I saw you that day in KC's, you were different. You were genuine and honest– didn't put on any airs– you spoke your mind. You have a natural beauty, not painted on. And you were modest. All the things I love in a woman.

"Then when I got to know you, I was drawn to your obsession and determination to learn, to travel, the excitement in your voice and your eyes captured me when you talked about life and your goals. The fact that you wouldn't jump into bed with me was a plus. That had never happened to me before. I knew you were something special from the beginning, my darling. And you are. I've never met or loved anybody like you."

He kissed her gently and drew her close, never wanting to let go. Tonight they would finally make love. He wondered if he would be a disappointment to her.

Amanda lifted her face to his as if she could read his mind. She whispered, "We should sneak away from the reception early so we can go up to our room for our wedding night." She was thinking of the Chantilly lace nightgown Rachel had given her for the occasion as she teased his lips with her tongue and then snuggled under his chin, nestling her head on his chest.

A surge of desire raced through his body. He nuzzled her silky hair that framed the soft wedding veil, tresses that smelled of honeysuckle, her favorite scent. He knew he had to think of something else to suppress the sexual desire that was consuming him at that very moment with her body so close to his.

He thought about how he had tried to buy expensive perfume for her instead of the Avon Honeysuckle cologne she loved. She wouldn't budge on that point. Said none of it smelled as good as her favorite. Finally he had given up and had a case of it shipped to Brussels for her. He grinned at her simple tastes.

It was his turn to ask the question. "Tell me why you married me, darling."

Without hesitation she replied, "Because you asked me."

Laughing, he leaned back and looked at her with narrowed eyes. "I know that isn't true. I asked you more than once as I recall."

She tweaked his nose playfully and giggled.

"John Boy, did you know that this little vixen left me at the altar back in the States? She actually ran out on me. Can you imagine anyone doing that to me?"

John was grinning from ear to ear, watching them through the rearview mirror. "You're lucky she went through with it this time," he teased.

When Amanda entered the castle with Richard and the wedding party, she couldn't believe the royal and majestic entrance hall with marble columns and murals, the huge curving staircase. Her mouth gaped at the grandeur. This was more beautiful than any magazine photo she'd seen of the castles in Europe. The atmosphere and setting were grandiose, too. Gigantic white, pink and yellow floral arrangements were in abundance. Food of all sorts was displayed on four long buffet tables. A stringed ensemble and pianist were playing in the background. Richard had convinced Amanda to let him handle the planning of the reception.

Amanda had busied herself with the making of a magnificent bridal gown – a floor-length, clingy, pale yellow, silk creation … covered with white lace, and dotted with seed pearls. Her veil was borrowed, had been Paula's. Her bridal bouquet was of blue, white and yellow marguerite daisies set in a lace holder with yellow ribbons streaming. A vision to behold as the guests verbally responded with expletives of complimentary approval.

Two bartenders were serving from portable bars. The guests who had been invited to the reception had been waiting impatiently for the wedding party. They consisted of other friends from the consulate, sewing-room girls, salesgirls, business associates and special customers of *Mandy Malone's*, ladies and nuns from the Kantcentrum, Antoine and his family, the van Nevels, Richard's Belgian and American cattle rancher friends and business associates and their wives, favorite waiters from the Metropole Café and The Roy, and the castle catering staff. KC's Frenchie and her fiancé were there, too.

After the initial greetings, Richard whisked Amanda away and gave her a quick tour of the formal dining room off the reception room with the exquisite marble fireplace. The fully-equipped kitchen had a romantic fireplace and breakfast nook decorated with white, yellow and blue rose-bud wallpaper. The view from the nook windows was of the back garden, with a pond and marble statues around a gigantic fountain. Also on the ground floor was an informal lounge with another marble fireplace, a family sitting room, another room with a bar and yet another fireplace.

Amanda was awestruck. "I can't imagine anybody living in all these rooms. And you say there are three more floors? How do they keep it all so clean?"

Paula suddenly appeared after having given herself a tour. "Well, honey, they have a jillion maids here. I'm sure the owners of this here castle would never have to lift a finger to clean it if they didn't want to. Isn't that right, Richard?"

Amanda didn't see the quick wink Paula gave the groom.

He took a deep breath. "You are so right, Paula. Now let's go back into the reception room and make a toast before we cut the cake. Shall we?"

Richard clanked a spoon on his glass to get the attention of all the guests. All eyes were upon him. He put his arm around

Amanda and drew her close. "My newfound friends and newfound family, I want to take this opportunity to welcome you here this evening, to witness my pledge to my beautiful and talented bride."

Amanda lifted her chin and kissed his cheek.

"Thank you, darling." He gazed into her sparkling eyes and wondered how he had ever lived without her. "I have something I want to say to Amanda in front of you all, as a part of the wedding toast." He turned and faced Amanda, lifting her left hand and kissing the rings on her commitment finger.

"My love, it didn't take me long to find the perfect wedding gift for a perfect woman." He turned to the crowd and took another deep breath. "Some of you know how excited I am about what I'm going to say. I need a quick drink." He took a sip of the champagne, "I hope it isn't bad luck to sip before the toast."

Everyone laughed.

"I'll do it, too, then it'll be okay." Amanda took a sip.

Richard chuckled. "See why I love her so much?"

The applause rang through the halls.

"Amanda, my darling, I wanted to give you something that would undeniably make you the happiest woman on this earth. And I know you deserve even more than I can possibly give to you."

Amanda tilted her head in curiosity as she waited to hear what her charming new husband was trying to say.

"Darling, look around you. Tonight we won't be going back to the Metropole Hotel. We will be spending our wedding night in our own home … here, in Camellia Gardens. This house is yours, my darling. My wedding gift to you because I adore you so much."

Amanda was confused; she couldn't grasp what he'd just said. Had he said this was where they were going to live? Had he said this home was theirs? Had he bought it, or was he renting it? What did he mean?

Paula read Amanda like a book. She went to her. "Honey, this here is your very own house. Richard bought it for you, baby. For you. You're going to live here, forever. And we can come visit and have our own bunch of rooms, can you imagine that? Richard already showed them to us. We're staying here with you till after New Year's. Can you believe you have a house that's bigger than ours?" Paula turned and looked at Drake. "Now you gotta build us a bigger house, Drake. I can't have my baby sister live in one bigger than mine. That ain't right."

Drake laughed. "There ain't no way I am gonna build you a house bigger than this one, so you can just get that idea out of your little pea-pickin' head."

The guests began laughing and applauding.

Amanda put her arms around Richard's neck and whispered in his ear, "I love you, Richard. I promise you, I love you more than anything or anyone in the world. Thank you—" She began to cry.

"Darling, no time for crying, we have to make the toast now. Everybody's waiting to drink their champagne."

John Crane stepped up. "Let me do it, Richard." He lifted his glass. "First of all, I just want to say that Adam and Eve had an ideal marriage. He didn't have to hear about all the men she could have married, and she didn't have to hear about how well his mother cooked." He waited for the laughter to die down. "Seriously, I am proud to be standing here to toast two of the most beautiful people I know, two people who deserve each other and deserve many years of enduring love together … and may all their joys be little ones."

Amanda's eyes widened as she looked up at Richard.

"Little ones?" he choked.

The elation continued to fill the halls as the night's merriment, music and dancing lasted until after midnight. The last of the guests had either left to go to their own homes or had settled into their rooms that Richard had offered them.

Amanda and Richard went upstairs to their bedroom suite and both had bathed in their individual bathrooms and had returned to each other in silk robes. Richard's was blue and yellow paisley and held together by a sash. Amanda's was pale yellow with lace across the yoke and around her wrists as well as along the hem. Both were mesmerized by the beauty before them.

Amanda felt Richard was the handsomest and sexiest man she'd ever known and still couldn't understand why he had married her.

Richard felt he was having a hallucinatory moment because of the incredible vision standing before him.

"My darling ..." He reached out his arms as he moved toward her.

She blushed, not knowing what was coming next. She wanted him, but she didn't want to hurry into it. She didn't know what kind of a lover he was. She hoped he wasn't like Arlie ... a *slam, bam, thank you, ma'am* kind of guy. Surely love-making could be romantic and beautiful like in the romance novels and movies. She'd almost forgotten the brief interlude she'd had with Antoine.

But once she was in Richard's arms, the moment felt natural, and the most wonderful thing happened – their lips met in sync, both desires were equal, both wanted the tender, sweet kiss that crescendoed to a deep, desirous longing.

Richard was the first to pull apart and suggest they go slow, have a brandy before they went any further.

Amanda was grateful. Her passion had been stirred like never before. She didn't understand it, but she wanted to savor it. It did feel as if she was in a romance novel, after all. Here she was, married to her Prince Charming and living in an outrageous castle in Belgium. How had this happened to her? She wished her mother and grandmother were still alive.

After Richard poured brandy from the nearby elaborately carved boudoir bar, they sat before the fire in the cozy alcove on an oversized powder blue brocade sofa.

He gently tapped her glass with his and kissed her.

After a sip, Richard placed his hand on Amanda's knee that was covered by the low-cut nightgown under her matching robe. "What do you think about having children, darling? We haven't discussed it, and I hadn't thought about it till John Boy told his little joke."

"I hadn't thought about it, either. I don't know if I want to have kids just yet, Richard. Is that all right with you?"

"Would you ever want to have children?"

"Well, I think so, don't you? It would be nice for us to have a girl and a boy, someday, don't you think? I mean, we should have at least one, a boy to carry on your name. Yes, I'd like that, if you would. Would you?"

Richard grinned from ear to ear, "I'm so happy you said that, darling. Yes, yes, yes." He leaned again and kissed her lightly on the lips. "I've always wanted a boy."

"How about after *Mandy Malone's* is up and running real good, and is successful, we think more about that?" Amanda suggested. The thought was starting to appeal to her, especially when she saw his face light up and saw how happy he was. That's what she wanted, to make him happy. And she decided at that very moment that she would do everything in her power to always give him happiness.

"It's getting a bit warm in here, isn't it? she asked. "Must be the fire. Do you mind if I take off this housecoat? Rachel gave this to me as a wedding present, isn't it pretty?"

"Almost as pretty as you are."

Amanda blushed. "Well, it's just too much to be wearing while we're sitting in front of a blazing fire." She stood up and removed the peignoir as she watched his face.

The lace nightgown was see-through enough to show the faint outline of her full breasts and areolas and the shadow of her navel and femininity.

Richard gasped and his eyes revealed the deep desire that had been and still was consuming him by the minute.

For a moment she continued to watch his face, and then she slowly moved the thin straps of the gown off her shoulders. The garment fell to the floor around her feet. She'd read in a magazine how to undress sexily.

"Oh my darling!" He moved to her and held her tightly against him, taking in the sweet aroma of her glistening hair of gold.

She was ecstatic when she felt his rock-hard manliness through his silky robe pushing at her pubescence. She'd been afraid he might be too old, might be impotent. She'd read about older men and their sexual problems, what a woman had to do to arouse them—if they could indeed be aroused, and she didn't think she would want any part of that. No chance of that with Richard. Maybe he took Viagra.

With Arlie she never had to do anything special, either. He just jumped on top of her and went at it and in a few seconds that was that. She found out in a magazine that she'd never had an orgasm before Antoine. She didn't even know what an orgasm was and had to look it up.

Richard lifted her in his arms and carried her to the huge four-poster, canopied bed that was fit for a queen. He laid her on the fluffy, cream-colored coverlet and placed the blue velvet and satin pillows under her head and shoulders to make her comfortable.

"I'll be right back," he whispered. As he headed for his bathroom he let his robe fall to the floor, exposing his gorgeous backside.

Amanda caught her breath at the sight of his smooth, naked body - broad shoulders that tapered to a trim waist above firm, rounded buttocks and long, muscular legs. She wanted him inside her right that minute.

"Darling," he said as he returned to the bed carrying a small packet, "if we don't want to have children yet, we have to use protection. You know that, don't you?"

After the shock of seeing his frontal nudity, Amanda blushed and answered, "No we don't. I went to the doctor and got me some birth control pills while you were in California. We're good to go whenever you want." She giggled.

He tossed the prophylactic packet up into the air and dove for her. They both laughed and giggled as they rolled around on the gigantic bed with their legs and arms entwined, excited with the intimacy and feel of their naked bodies pressed against each other.

After a few moments of teasing and kissing, a single gaze into each other's eyes halted the playfulness and the mood became one of intense seriousness and passion.

Richard hoarsely whispered, "I want you, Amanda." He continued to frantically kiss her forehead, eyes, nose, lips, chin, neck, and breasts. "I adore you … I need you …"

Desire nearly burst through Amanda's skin as his lips and hands caressed the rest of her passionate body.

"Oh, Richard … now … please … now … "

Chapter 59

It was Christmas morning and the guests were in the dining room enjoying a breakfast fit for a king. The massive, elegantly carved dining table was covered with an intricate lace tablecloth and the stay-over party was all seated at one end, minus Amanda and Richard. The rich aroma of the food and coffee was creating sounds of "oooohs and "ahhhhs" emanating from the breakfast group.

"I ain't never seen such thin pancakes before. Have you, Frenchie?"

The tall, thin, female Belgian chef, chuckled. "Those are crepes, madam." She was standing by to make sure everyone was happy, and overseeing the service to the six of them.

Frenchie grinned, "Yes, these are wonderful crepes. What is your name?" She directed the question to the chef.

"Martha, madam."

"Well, Martha, I make crepes at home for Sunday brunch. But these are extraordinary." She took a second bite. Ummm, very good. Try one, Lance."

Rachel took a bite and nodded to Martha. "They are delicious! Best I've ever had. Put some of the apricot jam on them, Paula. There's orange marmalade too."

"I like to roll up the sausage in it. See, like pigs in a blanket." Janet took a forkful and closed her eyes in pleasure.

Drake had put a big slice of sausage into his mouth and was savoring it with his eyes closed as well. "Oh my God, this is the best sausage I've ever had. You might want to find out how to make this, Frenchie, for KC's. It beats ours to hell and back. Taste it, Paula."

Paula frowned, "I will, but first I want to finish this here crepe."

"I walked out in the gardens earlier this morning." Rachel sipped her coffee as she spoke. "Now I see why the estate is called Camellia Gardens. There are hundreds of Camellia plants and trees out there – all colors. Did you see them? I had no idea Camellias bloom in winter. Just beautiful!"

Frenchie dabbed the corners of her mouth with a lace napkin. "It is lovely. I'm so happy we were invited to come."

Drake wiped his mouth with his napkin and answered, "Us too. This is surreal, isn't it?" He sipped his coffee. "And Richard was telling me that the garden stretches back for acres. There are paths and benches and atriums out there, too. And a bunch of ponds and statues. We'll have to go check it out after breakfast, Paula."

The bride and groom floated into the room, giving the impression that they were one person, with wide grins and exuberance in their synchronized steps. "Good morning," they both greeted in unison, and then kissed and laughed at each other's timing.

Richard led Amanda to one of the two chairs at the head of the table near the rest of the group. "Are we too late to join you for breakfast?"

"We just got started," Paula replied. "This is some pretty fantastic food, Richard. Have you had crepes before, Amanda? And the sausages, you got to try the sausages."

"Yes, I have. They serve them at the Metropole and at The Roy. Aren't they good?"

Frenchie looked up from her plate. "So good that I'm going to add them and the sausages to the menu at the restaurant when I get back. Martha, I need you to show me how to make them."

Martha nodded and left to alert the staff that Amanda and Richard were ready for their service. She returned almost instantly with the servers and food for the newly married couple. But first she placed a small green and red striped box with a gold ribbon on a plate in front of Amanda. "This is for you, Madam."

"What? What is it?" She looked at everyone around the table and then at Richard. "Richard, did you do this?"

"Well, it is Christmas, you know." He leaned over and kissed her lips.

"Open it, Amanda," Paula said with a mouthful of crepe and jam.

Amanda untied the ribbon and lifted the lid from the box. She pushed the tissue paper aside and stared into it without saying a word.

"So what is it? C'mon, show us!" Paula was as eager as a child on Christmas morning.

"Here, let me help you." Richard stood behind her and waited, his hands resting on her shoulders.

Amanda whispered, "It's the most beautiful gold locket I've ever seen." She pulled it from the box, its glittering gold chain spilling from her hand. A floral design was etched on the front. "Oh, it's a camellia, isn't it?'

"Yes, it is. It's an antique. Open it, darling."

She slipped her fingernail into the crevice and it opened, revealing two photos imbedded in the tiny frames, one of her and one of Richard. "This is so beautiful. Thank you so much, Richard." She stood and hugged him. "I love you." Then she looked around at her guests. "I just want you all to know, I am so very happy." Tears of joy were forming in her eyes.

Richard whispered in her ear, "We can give it to our daughter on her wedding day."

"I heard that! Does that mean y'all are pregnant?" Paula's excited expression was as bold as her voice.

Amanda laughed as she sat down. "Heaven's no. We're not pregnant. Of course not. We just got married yesterday."

"Well, that doesn't mean you can't be pregnant."

"Oh yes, it does," Richard said with gleaming eyes and a broad smile as he fastened the locket at the back of Amanda's neck. "It certainly does."

Rachel saw the blush begin to creep up into Amanda's cheeks and changed the subject by asking what the plan was for the week and added that she had some final editing to do, but would get with them as often as she could, and of course would spend New Year's Eve with them. They'd all decided to go to the Grand Place for New Year's Eve.

Janet added that she was going to go to Switzerland for a quick visit with Shellie and Adrian, and that she was thinking of going home to Paris for New Year's. She was missing Bob.

Paula said she wanted to at least spend one day during the week in Antwerp so that Drake could buy her a new diamond. (Drake grimaced). She said she also wanted to go to Bruges and see where Amanda learned how to make lace.

Frenchie squeezed Lance's hand and chimed in with gratitude. She said she was thrilled to be there with them all and was having the time of her life and that this was the first holiday season she'd been away from KC's and she was loving it. Said they were going to Paris for a couple of days to see relatives, but they would be back for New Year's Eve.

After breakfast they all moved into the garden room to have mimosas.

When they finally settled into the plush floral sofas and chairs and were served their champagne and orange juice, Amanda said, "By the way … Richard and I have a little something for each of you for Christmas. Can we do it now, hon?" She was excited and elated.

"Richard grinned. "All right. I'll get them." He left the room.

"We said no Christmas gifts!" Paula exclaimed.

"I know, but because I knew you all would give us such beautiful wedding gifts, I just had to do this. It's just something little, something to help you remember the happiest day of my life and happy that you were here to share it with me."

"And the happiest day of *my* life," Richard added as he returned carrying a red gift bag. "Would you like to do the honors, darling?"

Amanda shook her head. "No, you can do it."

He read the tags on the little boxes and cheerfully handed a gift to each person.

"Where's A.G.?" Frenchie asked. She'd just realized he was missing.

"Oh, he's off playing in that fancy playroom with Martha's grandchildren, Amanda explained. "He's happy. That was so nice to have all those presents for the kids to open when they got up this morning, Richard."

Richard nodded. "We didn't want A.G. to miss out on Christmas, so we invited the other children to make it even more fun for him. Martha did all the planning for the kids' breakfast and their little Christmas party," he said as he kissed the top of Amanda's head. "Of course, Amanda bought all the presents and wrapped them. I brought out all the gifts from Brussels yesterday while she was busy getting ready, so she wouldn't know about it. She thought we were going to be at the hotel today for the Christmas party."

Amanda grinned at him. "Yes, you really got me on this one. So go ahead, everybody, it's your turn now. Open your presents."

They untied the ribbons on their boxes. The women found gold bracelets with *Christmas in Brussels* and the date inscribed on the inside surface, while Drake and Lance had been given gold cufflinks and matching tie clips, with the same inscription on the back of the clip.

It was a happy Christmas morning at the Miller's Camellia Gardens estate.

Chapter 60

It seemed like fireworks and firecrackers were being set off at every intersection in Brussels. Police on foot, in cars with their sirens blaring, along with celebrating young pedestrians, were adding to the noise and excitement of New Year's Eve.

Richard was driving through the streets to find a parking place that would put them as close to the Grand Place as they could get.

"There's one," Paula pointed from the back seat.

Drake grabbed her finger. "He knows what he's doing, Paula, so don't be trying to drive from the backseat."

Rachel laughed. All week the two of them had kept her in stitches. They were born entertainers, she had told them.

Baby A.G. was at home with the house staff, and was most likely asleep already in his makeshift nursery. Amanda and Paula had created a space in an alcove in Paula and Drake's bedroom suite, fit for a baby prince. Amanda had decided that that part of the house would be their own personal quarters every time they came to visit, and was hoping it would be at least twice a year.

"Here we go." Richard pulled in right after another car pulled out.

"This is perfect," said Amanda. "Only two blocks from the square. We are dang lucky. I hope Frenchie and Lance found the place okay."

They grabbed their coats from the trunk of the car, donned their hats and gloves, and meandered up the lane, looking in shop windows as they sauntered along. Most of the shops were still open for business, especially the chocolate boutiques and food stores. Two lace shops and a tapestry studio were filled with patrons, and the tourist souvenir shops' doors were wide open. All the cafes and taverns were crowded with late-night patrons.

Near the giant tree left over from Christmas in the square, artists had set up partitions and were selling their oils and watercolors. A small band was playing music and a few people were dancing. Other than that, people were just milling about, going in and out of the cafes surrounding the Grand Place.

Frenchie and Lance were already sitting in a large circular booth at The Roy, where they were to meet. Rachel scooted in next to them, Amanda and Paula sat at opposite ends, their two husbands sitting beside their ladies.

The waiter brought two bottles of the finest champagne and poured for the seven celebrants.

"A toast!" Richard lifted his glass. "First, may all your wishes come true, my lovely Amanda, and know that I love you with all my heart. Second, to your loving family and bewitching friends, may you all feel and find the same love in your lives as Amanda and I share."

"That's the most beautiful toast I've ever heard, Richard," Paula said. "Isn't it, Drake? We'll drink to that, won't we?"

Drake lifted his glass. "You bet your bottom dollar, we will. And I want to add something to it. Here's to my wife, Paula, who brought our little A.G. into the world, and to the love that I have for both of them. May you all be as happy as I am right at this moment."

"Oh Drake, honey, that was a good one." Paula leaned and gave Drake a hug and a kiss. "You did good, baby. You did good."

"To all of us: may this be the best New Year's Eve celebration ever!" Rachel added as she lifted her glass.

"A votre sante!" Frenchie added as she joined by lifting her glass.

They all gaily clinked the glasses over the table and then continued to work on the second bottle as the midnight hour drew near.

"You know, the fireworks are at the Mont des Arts instead of the Grand Place," Amanda commented. "I hope y'all don't mind that we decided to come here instead. I just love this place, and it's more romantic to us here at The Roy; not so many people to deal with."

Rachel took a deep breath. "Well, honey, like I've told you already, I've been on a quest these past few years because I promised my father on his deathbed … don't mean to be morbid here … but I promised him that I would live out his dream of going to major New Year's Eve celebrations around the world. But it's not only his dream; it's become my dream now. So if you don't mind, I may go over to the fireworks at midnight. I've done the Eiffel in Paris, Trafalgar Square in London—"

"Then by all means you should go to the Mont des Arts, Rachel. We can meet back here or at the Metropole." Richard patted her hand that was resting on the table. "But not in the café, the lounge has a combo tonight."

Amanda placed her hand on Rachel's arm. "And you're not being morbid, that's a nice thing to do for your daddy. Nothing wrong with that. If my mama would have asked me to promise something while she was on her deathbed, I certainly would have done it. Of course she didn't know nothin' about cities around the world. She never even went to Little Rock. When did your daddy die, Rachel?"

"It's been a few years now," Rachel replied looking down at her glass to hide the emotion that was suddenly surfacing.

"An exciting quest indeed, Rachel," Richard said in hopes of lifting her spirits. "We could all walk with you to the Mont Des Arts, if you want. It's just a little east of here. Not far."

"No, no, no. You don't need to do that." She blinked back the tears and gulped champagne. "Please, do as you planned. The crowd will be ridiculous. If this one is like the usual ones I've seen, it'd be crazy for all of us to try and squeeze through. Really. I'll go for the midnight countdown and come right back. Just want to do it for my daddy … and for me … " Her voice trailed off as she quickly lifted her glass again and drained it.

Richard spoke up. "Well, then, that's settled. We'll either wait for you here inside or out in the square, or at the Metropole."

Rachel nodded. "At the Metropole, will be fine. Excuse me, I should get going," she said as she put her purse over her shoulder.

Amanda leaned over and whispered to Rachel, "Are you all right?"

Rachel hugged her and whispered back, "I'm just feeling lonely. I'll be okay, sweetie."

The slight uphill walk to Mont Des Arts was intriguing with its rows of cafes and upscale shops along the way. Rachel hadn't visited that part of Brussels before. It was absolutely wonderful, escalating in affluence and prestige, she noticed. She would definitely tell Amanda about it. It might be a good idea to open a Mandy Malone Designs in that part of town, too.

She already knew about the square, though, had read up on it when she'd decided to go there for the midnight festivities. Originally it had been created for the 1910 World's Fair. A park and monuments were added, as well as an expansive staircase leading from the Royal Square above to the Mont Des Arts below. Cascading fountains flanked the stone stairway, making it even more impressive. Royal museums of all sorts surrounded it, mingled with more cafes and shops. A show of utter magnificence. The Palais Royal was on the Place Royale, where the king presided as Head of State.

Rachel didn't plan on viewing any of the historical buildings, however. She just wanted to be near and feel the presence and emotion of the masses as they stood at the Mont Des Arts greeting the coming of the new year in Brussels.

As the countdown began and the fireworks spewed high into the sky, her thoughts were of Pete. Tears flowed as she whispered, "I will miss you forever." Then loving thoughts of others who had gone on to the next life flashed through her mind – Ethan, her mother, her father.

She closed her eyes and smiled at the image of Paul's face and the memorable kiss on that first New Year's Eve in London's Trafalgar Square. She shook her head to shift to thoughts of Belinda's love for Paul.

A man had bumped her off balance, but caught her before she fell. "Excuse me!"

"That's okay, really. I'm all right." Rachel stepped back and sat on one of the stone planter boxes, trying to stabilize.

"Are you sure you're all right?" he asked.

She didn't look up at him. "Yes, yes. I'm fine. Thank you," she murmured, obviously dismissing him.

He moved away a short distance, but he glanced back to the sad, beautiful woman shedding tears on the planter box.

Rachel was wondering what Amanda was feeling right at that moment, and she envied the beautiful life that lay ahead of the bride and groom, envied the love they shared. Then the inevitable image of her father appeared in her mind.

As fast as she could wipe them away, tears continued to spill down her cheeks. She wondered if her daddy was looking down on her, could see that she was in Brussels on another New Year's Eve. He would love to be there sitting beside her. She knew he would.

The voices screaming '... *THREE ... TWO ... ONE!'* shook her from her reverie as they echoed loudly over the thousands of people congregated in the square. It was midnight.

The man who had bumped her stepped closer to her.

"Madam?"

She stared at the gloved hand held out to her. Then she looked up into the face of a silver-haired gentleman whose dazzling eyes and smile were as grand as the rest of him.

"Yes?" she replied weakly, still sitting, dumbfounded.

"Would you be so kind as to allow me to rescue a damsel in distress, in exchange for a New Year's kiss? One should not waste precious moments that are so few. Wouldn't you agree?"

Rachel's heart skipped a beat. She couldn't believe the boldness of the man, but then she remembered a New Year's Eve not so long ago when another man had been just as bold. And so had she.

She smiled, wiped the tears from her eyes with one hand, took his hand with the other, and rose from the planter.

He slipped his arm around her waist gently, pulled her closer, and bent down to touch her moist lips with his.

Rachel was surprised at how good the kiss felt to her. She was surprised that she'd allowed him to do it. She was surprised that the sadness that had overwhelmed her just a few moments before had totally disappeared. Her heart was racing.

He released her, grinned, stepped back and bowed slightly. "Let me introduce myself, I'm Maxim Balanchine. And you are … ?"

"Rachel O'Neill."

"Ah, an Irish lass, yes?"

Rachel nodded. "Yes, and you're Belgian? Is that the accent I hear?"

"I'm Russian, actually, but I have had a home here for twenty-five years. So I would say it's a combined accent. Are you living here?"

"Just visiting. I came for a wedding."

"So where is your home?" he asked her.

"In England, but I'm originally from the U.S."

"That is good. England is very close." His grin grew. "May I buy you a drink somewhere, so that we may continue to talk?"

"I'm meeting my friends at the Metropole," she explained. "You may come along, if you wish. I'm sure they wouldn't mind."

"I would like that. Thank you."

Chapter 61

The streets were overflowing with pedestrians: cheerful elderly couples arm-in-arm, energetic students on a mission carrying and setting off stashes of fireworks wherever they could, young lovers billing and cooing, police cars wailing and foot policemen trying to catch the independent pyrotechies. The sidewalk cafes were filled with patrons observing and enjoying the late night jovial events.

Maxim and Rachel made their way along the winding lanes to the Metropole Hotel.

"Do you ever go back to Russia?" she asked him.

"I go home every year for three months at a time, sometimes twice a year. Depends on how much I am needed there."

Rachel smiled. "I may be going to Moscow next winter for the holiday season, am a writer and my next novel is set in Russia. It's amazing that we've met like this. Quite a coincidence, isn't it?"

"That depends," Maxim said. "do you think it is coincidence or fate?"

"That's a good question, and regardless, I should glean your mind about Russia while I have the chance," she said as she looked at him with curiosity and an even more brilliant smile than before.

He smiled back. "That I would welcome. My mind sometimes needs a good gleaning."

They both laughed and continued to walk in silence, dodging oncoming foot traffic while catching their breaths from the excitement they both were feeling.

As they rounded the next corner, the street ahead was blocked off by police cars, lights and sirens screaming.

"Let's go this way," Maxim said as he put his arm around Rachel's shoulders, guiding her in a different direction.

She thrilled at his touch that gave her a terrific sense of safety. Suddenly she felt protected and relieved, something very new to her. For a moment it was as if all her fears and heartbreak had disappeared … *poof!* … into thin air. And at that moment she felt completely happy and content, not a care in the world. Her thoughts were only of the man next to her who had tucked her safely into the warmth of his body.

As they traversed the detour, Rachel told Maxim about her father's last wishes about her celebrating New Year's Eve in cities around the world. She told him about her closest friends, her cottage in Cornwall and the house in Paris.

Maxim told her he was a widower and told about his partnership with his brother in Moscow. They were in the jewelry business, amber and diamonds, mostly.

They turned at the next corner and the canopies of the Metropole loomed just a few steps ahead of them.

"We're meeting in the lounge," Rachel said as they passed in front of the Metropole sidewalk café and turned toward the front doors of the hotel. "It's to the right, down the corridor from the café."

"Yes, I know. I have been here many times." Maxim held the door for her.

A combo was playing American standards and jazz. Normally a solo jazz pianist was there. It puzzled Rachel that no matter where she went in Britain and Europe, the music in the cafes was American – either Frank Sinatra ballads or hits by other popular American singers. Tonight was no exception.

"There they are, up in the corner to the right of the piano." She walked ahead of Maxim, grinning widely and raising her eyebrows at her friends, signaling, as if she had a secret to tell them and couldn't wait to do so.

"It's about time! We were beginning to worry about you," Richard said as he took a few steps toward her and gave her a hug.

Amanda stood and joined them. "Did you get lost, Rachel?"

"No, not at all. I want to introduce you to someone. This is Maxim Balanchine. We met at the square." Rachel's eyes had a glow that none of them had seen before. "And Maxim, this is Amanda, she's the designer *Mandy Malone* … and Richard Miller, a cattle rancher. They are the newlyweds."

Maxim shook hands with both of them. "Congratulations, Amanda, Richard."

"Paula is Amanda's sister visiting from the states, and her husband, Drake …"

Maxim moved toward them, holding out his hand, "Hello, so nice to meet you. Happy New Year!" They responded in the same manner.

"And this is Frenchie, our restaurateur friend from the States. Owns a fabulous steakhouse I hear. And her fiancé Lance."

"Hello, Frenchie, Lance."

"It's so nice to meet a Belgian gentleman," Frenchie said.

"Oh, he's actually Russian," Rachel explained. "But has lived here for years. He was out on the town alone, so I thought I'd invite him to join us. Can't let a perfectly good New Year's Eve go to waste without being with friends, now can we?" Rachel took his hand and led him to the empty leather loveseat in the cozily seated grouping.

Richard had already ordered trays of appetizers that were on the cocktail table before them. "Please help yourselves to the food. I think I over-ordered, so we're happy to have two more mouths to feed. What would you like to drink, Maxim?"

"I'll have champagne with the lady, if you don't mind. You are having champagne, Rachel?"

"Absolutely! Always champagne on New Year's Eve." She chuckled. "And any other time."

They all laughed.

"So tell me, why is a handsome man like you alone on a night like this?" Frenchie asked in a flirty, tipsy manner.

Paula gave her an amused startled look. It wasn't like Frenchie to flirt in front of Lance.

Richard chuckled as he leaned back and put his arm around Amanda. It wasn't very often one would see Frenchie inebriated. But it was okay, it was New Year's Eve.

Maxim smiled. "Thank you, madam, for the compliment. As for being alone tonight, that isn't the case." He looked at Rachel. "You see, I am with this lovely woman who shares my sentiment of a magical evening. It seems we both have similar promises to keep – she to her beloved father, I to my deceased wife."

Renewed excitement rose all around. *The man is single!*

Amanda quickly added, "Well, we're tickled pink as we can be that you're here with us, Maxim. If you don't mind me saying so, Rachel, this is meant to be. I ain't never seen you this happy. Oh dear. There I went and did it again. Rachel's been

282

helping me talk better English. Sometimes I remember, sometimes I don't."

Richard laughed. "Darling, you don't have to worry about how you talk. I love you no matter what or how you say it." He gently squeezed her shoulder, pulled her closer to him and planted a sweet kiss on her lips.

"He is right, Amanda," Maxim said. "You are charming and delightful."

"You should listen to these two handsome men," Rachel said as she avoided Maxim's pale blue eyes that were looking at her almost every second.

He reached for her hand, which forced her to look at him, and he lifted it to his lips while speaking softly, "I am so happy I met you tonight. It was a prayer answered."

Rachel gazed into his eyes and whispered as softly, "I believe *two* prayers were answered."

NEXT

"Midnight in Moscow"

The fourth novel in the continuing saga of Rachel O'Neill as she travels from city to city on New Year's Eves, becoming entangled in the lives of the people she encounters. In *Midnight in Moscow* she meets Della Doheny, Anastasia and her brother Valentin Andreyev (Maxim Balanchine's siblings).

Excerpt

Over the next few days, Della settled into the simple little house in the simple little Russian village. She didn't want to go to Moscow at all; she didn't want to go back to the States either. The village women were kind and she had begun to feel comfortable walking through the settlement each day, stopping to talk with those who spoke in broken English. She made a few friends and learned a few Russian words she found on an Internet site that gave the audio pronunciation of Russian phrases - which came in handy.

She emailed her assistant Miley back in New York on Valentin's computer, to let her know what she was doing, her change in plans. No WiFi connection for her laptop computer.

Miley was thrilled and wanted to know all about Valentin. Of course Della had nothing to tell her other than what little she knew, having only just met the man.

She told Miley that he was in the amber business, traveled all over Russia, but mostly to the major Amber mine in Kaliningrad, and occasionally the diamond mines in Siberia. Anastasia told Della he went to Kaliningrad more than any other place, though, but his office was in Moscow with his brother Maxim. And that was it, that's all Della knew about him. Except that he was a big man, and strong, and reminded her of her father.

Miley assured her that everything would be all right in New York, she'd handle everything and Della needn't worry, told her to stay as long as she wanted.

It was a perfect morning for Della to cut fresh flowers and place a bouquet on the center of the dining table and one on the table in front of the leather sofa. She opened all the windows in the house to let the cool breezes flow through.

Then she took her cup of coffee to the porch and sat in a painted Adirondack-type wooden chair. She could tell it had been hand-hewn.

It was a sunny summer day, but the breeze was cool and nippy. Valentin was due to return home that afternoon after being away for three weeks. She hoped he wouldn't mind her being there all this time, he said he didn't. He had phoned her almost daily to make sure she was all right, that she had everything she needed, and he hadn't sounded as if he didn't want her there. But she'd told him two days before, the last she'd talked to him, she was leaving, she had to go. But here she was, still in his house.

She felt like a bride waiting for a groom to come home from work. She had been pretending and enjoying every minute of the imaginary relationship with anticipation. In fact she laughed out loud at herself and the ridiculous fairy tale she was weaving, but it wasn't harming anyone, she was just playing a solitary game. She certainly was glad none of her friends could see her; they would think she had totally lost her mind.

Here she was . . . one of the most up and coming brilliant independent publishers in New York City. She'd begun with ten book titles and had built the business into a three-imprint company publishing hard covers as well as trade and mass paper and eBooks—over 500 titles now, and still counting. She went from a two-employee company working out of her apartment to three floors in a skyscraper in the middle of Manhattan - one floor was her apartment. No one would believe where she was at that very moment in Russia, and how she was living. She could hardly believe it herself. It was a fluke. How could she know that befriending a Russian woman, Anastasia, on a train would land her in Valentin's (Anastasia's brother) house for a holiday while he was out of town?

Valentin arrived at noon. He drove up the drive and stopped the car.

Della stood up and waved at him from the porch. His look of surprise puzzled her, for she wasn't sure if it was a pleasantly surprised look or a *what-the-hell-is-she-doing-here* look.

He left the car door open and hurried to the stoop where she was standing. He stared at her for a moment and then suddenly scooped her up in his arms and hugged her tightly.

"What a surprise that you are still here," he said as he set her down. "I am happy to see you."

She pulled her shirt down and nervously straightened her collar. "I'm happy to see you, too. You don't mind, do you? I hoped you wouldn't mind."

"Of course I do not mind. Excuse me; I must bring my things into the house." He hurried back toward the car.

3

Della immediately tried to calm herself and willed the flush from her face and the speedy flapping of her heart to subside.

She held open the door for him as he walked through with packages and luggage, as usual hanging and dangling from him.

He took the bags to his bedroom that was off the kitchen and great room, and then returned with a huge grin. "I have something for you." He handed her a flat, blue velvet box.

She stared at it, speechless and not moving.

"Please, I give it to you. You take."

She reluctantly reached for it, and then opened the snap that held the lid down. It was a beautiful box trimmed in gold, a lovely gift in itself.

"Oh my God!" Inside was a stunning amber necklace. "This is spectacular! It's prettier than anything I saw in all the jewelry stores in St. Petersburg. It's Hermitage quality. I can't take this from you. It's too valuable! You must sell it to your customers. Don't give it to me."

"I give it to you. It is yours. Please."

Della couldn't believe it. "Oh my God, I love amber. In fact I have a small collection of it. But this is the grandest of all. Oh my God! Thank you so much."

She stepped in front of a small mirror hanging on the wall, lifted the multi-strand filigree necklace with its large oval pendant from the case.

Valentin took the case from her and placed it on the table.

She opened the clasp.

He took the necklace from her to place it around her neck.

She lifted her hair and he fastened the neck adornment.

Then he rested his huge hands on her shoulders, still standing behind her.

4

Her heart stopped at his touch. She felt dizzy.

He bent down and kissed where her shoulder met her neck.

Goosebumps covered her entire body. She turned and looked up at him.

Their eyes and lips met at the same time. It was the softest, most thrilling kiss that Della had experienced in her entire life.

He didn't push further, didn't do the tongue trick.

Thank god! She hated that.

He just gently caressed her lips with his and then slowly leaned back to look at her as if for the first time.

"You are beautiful in amber," he whispered. "It is same color as your hair and spots."

"My freckles," she said as she giggled.

She turned and again looked into the gilded-framed mirror. "Look at that, it does match my hair, doesn't it?"

Moving close behind her, he wrapped his arms around her waist, clasping his hands against her body. "How long will you stay with me? I do not want you to go."

Photo by Dennis Dillow

Rebecca Randolph Buckley resides in Arizona with her three cats … Princie, Oreo, and Albee. She spends her spare time gardening, reading, collecting and watching classic movies – mostly romantic. She travels around the world not only for pleasure, but to find settings and character inspiration for her novels and short stories.

www.rebeccabuckley.com
rebeccajbuckley@aol.com